The Moscow Sleepers

Stella Rimington

BLOOMSBURY PUBLISHING
LONDON · OXFORD · NEW YORK · NEW DELHI · SYDNEY

BLOOMSBURY PUBLISHING
Bloomsbury Publishing Plc
50 Bedford Square, London, WC1B 3DP, UK

BLOOMSBURY, BLOOMSBURY PUBLISHING and the Diana logo are trademarks
of Bloomsbury Publishing Plc

First published in Great Britain 2018
This edition published 2019

Copyright © Stella Rimington, 2018

A catalogue record for this book is available from the British Library

Library of Congress Cataloguing-in-Publication data has been applied for

ISBN: HB: 978-1-4088-5974-2; TPB: 978-1-4088-5975-9;
PB: 978-1-4088-5977-3; EBOOK: 978-1-4088-5976-6

2 4 6 8 10 9 7 5 3 1

Typeset by Integra Software Services Pvt. Ltd.
Printed and bound in Great Britain by CPI Group (UK) Ltd, Croydon CR0 4YY

To find out more about our authors and books visit www.bloomsbury.com and
sign up for our newsletter

S ENIOR NURSE SARAH BURNS was sitting at the nurses' station checking the day's records. She would be going off duty in half an hour, handing over to Emily, who was in charge of the night shift. The patients had all been washed and fed – those who were still capable of eating.

People came here to die. And die is what they all did. Nobody left here cured. Some took longer to die than others but they all died sooner or later. Nurse Sarah didn't mind this. She liked the peace. There were no emergencies, no dramas. True, she had to deal with grieving relatives, but when it came, death was expected so the grief was muted.

Evening visiting didn't start for another half hour and the families and friends who'd come would be Emily's responsibility. Most came regularly, some twice a day. There was only one patient who had no visitors. Sarah Burns had been a nurse in the hospice for almost ten years and thought she'd seen it all, but Lars Petersen was unique in her experience. Each morning when Sarah arrived for the day shift she half expected to find the bed in Room 112 empty, linen stripped. But Petersen clung on stubbornly, though that wasn't what puzzled her: she had seen countless patients die and in every conceivable way. But all of them had had somebody there in their last days – a relative or a friend. *Someone*.

Not Lars Petersen. No family, no friends, no colleagues from the university where, according to his hospital entry form, he had been an associate professor. This total absence of visitors made it even stranger that Sarah had been asked to keep a special eye on him – to report to the man called Boyd if he said anything about himself or if he had any visitors. But he hadn't. There had been nothing at all to report.

Sarah started thinking about supper. It was going to be a hot evening; she didn't fancy cooking in such sweltering heat, so she thought she'd have her husband prime the grill on the deck instead. She'd put her feet up on a lounger then let him bring her a burger and a large glass of chilled wine.

As she planned her evening meal she heard the swing doors of the ward bang open. Surprised, she looked up at the monitor on the wall; her view of the doors from the nurses' station was obscured by a bend in the corridor. She saw the image of a man with dark hair striding towards her, heard his heels clicking sharply on the tiled floor. As she stared at the screen, he rounded the corner and came up to the desk. He was tall, slightly balding, dressed rather formally in a grey tweed jacket that looked far too warm for the weather, with a button-down shirt and a striped tie.

'Can I help you?' Sarah asked, about to explain that he'd have half an hour to wait before visiting hours began. But there was something in the man's eyes that made her pause.

'I am hoping to see a patient here.' The voice was slightly accented – it seemed Scandinavian, which was confirmed when he said, 'Lars Petersen.'

She could barely contain her surprise. 'Can I ask who you are?'

'My name is Ohlson. I hope I am not too late. I have driven straight down from Montreal.'

'No, you're not too late. Visiting hours don't start till six.' She felt a little churlish; the man had travelled a couple of hours to get here. She asked more gently, 'Are you family?'

He smiled. 'As close to family as he has. His parents died long ago, back in Sweden. He was their only child. If there are cousins, he never spoke of them.'

'So you're a friend?'

The man nodded. 'His oldest. We went to nursery school together in Sweden.'

'Then you know that Mr Petersen is very ill?'

'Yes. I didn't know *how* ill, until I tried to contact him and couldn't. I spoke to his department head at the university and he told me he was here. That's why I came down.'

'All right. Would you please put your details in the book, then come with me?' Emerging from behind the desk, Sarah led the visitor along the corridor to the end of the hall. Tapping lightly on the door of Room 112, she went in.

It was a corner room, with a view of the birch and maple trees that bordered the hospital grounds. Petersen was lying motionless in bed but he stirred as Sarah came in and his eyes opened slightly. When he saw Ohlson they opened wider; Sarah couldn't tell if he recognised him or if he was just surprised to see a visitor.

'Someone here to see you,' she announced cheerfully.

3

Petersen watched as Ohlson pulled up a chair and sat down beside the bed. 'Hello, Lars,' he said and laid a hand on the bed. After a moment, Petersen's right hand moved down the bed and touched Ohlson's.

Sarah hovered for a moment, until Ohlson looked up at her. She could tell he wanted her to leave, and there really wasn't any reason for her to stay. 'I'll leave you in peace,' she said. 'I'll be at the desk. Don't be too long, please,' she added, then looked down at Petersen. 'Ring the bell if you need me.'

She left the room and closed the door behind her. But she stayed just outside, making a show of consulting the small notebook she carried with her, while straining to hear the conversation going on inside the room. Through the door she could hear Ohlson's voice, speaking in a low murmur. She couldn't make out anything of what he was saying or even what language he was speaking – she guessed it would be Swedish. The pattern of his voice suggested he was asking questions – lots of questions. From the pauses, she thought Petersen was replying but his voice was barely audible. After a minute she went back to the nurses' station.

Emily was there, scanning the patients' chart book. She looked up as Sarah approached. 'Lucky you. It's meant to stay like this all evening.' She nodded through the windows at the bright afternoon.

'You'll never believe it,' said Sarah. 'One-one-two's got a visitor. He's with him now.'

Emily, who had also been briefed on the special interest in Petersen, said, 'You'd better let them know.'

'Just going to,' replied Sarah, and she went into the little office behind the desk and closed the door. She looked at her notebook again, this time for real, and dialled a local number.

When someone answered, she said, 'Special Agent Boyd, please.' She waited until she was put through, then said, 'It's Sarah Burns from the Kovacs Hospice. You asked me to phone you if our patient had any visitors. Well, he's got one now. Sitting next to his bed and asking lots of questions.'

A s HE SAT IN his car in the visitors' car park, appearing to read the *Burlington Free Press*, Special Agent Boyd was watching the cars arriving. Visiting time was about to begin, and groups of people with carrier bags and bunches of flowers were gathering at the door of the hospital, making it difficult for him to see if anyone came out. The nurse had given him a good description of the man, and Boyd was fairly sure he knew which one was his car. The car park had been almost empty when he'd arrived and it had been easy to find the only vehicle with Canadian number plates – the visitor had told the nurse he'd driven down from Montreal so it must be his. Boyd had parked in a spot where he could see both the door of the hospital and the car. Now that the car park was beginning to fill up he felt less conspicuous.

Boyd was used to surveillance work but his usual targets were drug-runners and other crooks. He had no counter-intelligence experience, but he'd been told that the man in the hospital might be a spy. That would mean that the man who had come to visit him – this Ohlson character – might be a spy too, and that would mean he'd be a lot more professional than the average criminal. Boyd was just a bit nervous; he didn't want to screw this one up.

What looked like a family group – three people with a couple of children – was just going into the hospital when a man emerged. It must be Ohlson; he fitted the nurse's description. The man paused just outside the doorway, lighting a cigarette. Boyd recognised the move; he was looking for surveillance, although he seemed more interested in people on foot than the parked cars. Boyd slid down in his seat; he had a couple of discreet mirrors inside the car for just this sort of situation.

Having apparently decided the coast was clear, Ohlson walked directly towards the blue Volkswagen Passat with the Canadian number plates. Boyd photographed him as he did so. The car started up and drove straight towards the nearest exit, turning on to the highway. He was sorely tempted to follow but restrained himself. Single car surveillance was almost impossible without either losing the target or being spotted, and this guy was a pro. Boyd knew he'd be out on his ear if he let himself be spotted by Ohlson, which would be a lousy end to his career after seventeen years with the Bureau, half of them in his native Vermont.

He was the senior resident agent in Burlington, Vermont, which was not a Field Office since Burlington was deemed too small to support one. So Boyd had to report to the SAC, Special Agent in Charge in Albany, New York, across the waters of Lake Champlain. This rankled with him, as it would with most Vermonters, who resented the dominance of their bigger and more populous neighbour.

But it was not through the Albany Office that the Petersen job had come in. It was a SAC in FBI Headquarters in Washington DC who had contacted him a month or so ago. He had been frustratingly vague about just what Petersen, the Swedish lecturer at the University

7

of Vermont, was suspected of. But it was Top Secret so Boyd guessed it was espionage. All Boyd was to do was to look out for any visitors he had and get their details, but he was not to do anything to alert them to his presence. Then he was to contact Washington immediately. Not Albany, but FBI Headquarters in Washington. That was all he had to do. No more than that.

As the Passat disappeared into the distance, he shrugged, accepting he would probably never find out what was going on, and drove back to his office to pass his observations, photographs and the address that Ohlson had written in the visitors' book on to Washington.

IN LONDON THE RAIN was steady and unceasing, as it had been for much of the preceding week, and it remained unseasonably cold. Peggy Kinsolving picked up her telescopic umbrella as it came through the outside scanner and opened it carefully so as not to shower herself and the security guard with raindrops. Then, head down, she ran up the steps of the US Embassy in Grosvenor Square.

As she sat in the lobby waiting to be collected, she wondered whether visiting the Embassy would be less or more hassle when it moved to its new premises in Wandsworth on the south bank of the Thames. More, she thought gloomily. She'd seen computerised images of what it would look like – a huge rectangular glass box on a circular island. She imagined the discomfort of getting there on a day like this and shuddered. It would be OK for MI6 she mused; they were practically next door.

In her present job in MI5's counter-espionage branch, Peggy was the main liaison on espionage with the CIA Station in the Embassy in Grosvenor Square. At least once a month she met the Station Head, Miles Brookhaven, to exchange information on current trends and cases. Peggy looked forward to these meetings, not least because she got on well with Miles. He'd been Head of Station for just about six months and was unusually young for the post. He was regarded by Peggy and her colleagues as a breath of fresh air after his predecessor Andy Bokus.

Bokus had always made it very clear that he disliked London and the Brits. In particular, he disliked his opposite number in MI6, Geoffrey Fane. The feeling was mutual and each man had set about further annoying the other by becoming almost a caricature of himself. Bokus had adopted an exaggeratedly boorish manner, playing up his humble immigrant background, while Geoffrey Fane, appearing as an archetypal English gentleman in his old school tie, three-piece suits and polished brogues, had patronised the American. It was a game observers suspected they both enjoyed, but it had made collaboration difficult, and Peggy and her boss Liz Carlyle were relieved when Bokus left and was replaced by Miles.

In contrast to Bokus, Miles was an Anglophile, having spent a year as a boy at Westminster School. He had been posted to London several years previously as a junior officer at the CIA Station. He was rumoured to have done stellar work in the Middle East, in the course of which he had been badly injured; it was assumed that the plum London posting was something of a reward.

Up in his office on the third floor, Miles was gazing out of the window as Peggy and the secretary who had gone down to collect her arrived in the CIA suite of offices.

'Come in, Peggy. Call this a summer?'

'Well, you look pretty summery,' Peggy replied. Miles was casually dressed in a khaki cotton suit, striped Brooks Brothers tie and cherry-coloured penny loafers. His hair had been cut, making him look even more boyish than usual.

'I've been spending a few days with my mother. She goes to Chautauqua every year. It's an old cultural centre up near Buffalo. The weather up there can get pretty warm in summer. I just got back this morning.'

'You should have postponed this meeting,' said Peggy. 'You must be tired and I haven't got anything urgent to report.'

'But I have something for you,' he replied. 'It seems to be connected to that case we shared earlier in the year. Those two Russian Illegals; it was a pity you sent them quietly back to Russia. I would have liked to see them prosecuted, though I'm sure it's not diplomatic to say so.'

'I agree,' said Peggy. 'Though I probably shouldn't say so either. But the FCO didn't want to worsen relations with the Russians. I don't suppose we would have learned much more than we know already, even if we had put them on trial.'

Miles said, 'I'd like to ask Al Costino to join us. You know him, don't you?'

'Of course,' Peggy replied. Costino was the Senior FBI Agent at the Embassy and a regular contact of MI5 on counter-intelligence and terrorism matters.

'He can tell you what his head office has just learned.' Miles reached for the phone on the table and punched in an extension number. 'Hi, Al,' he said. 'We're ready for you.'

Unlike Miles, Al Costino was dressed conservatively in a dark flannel suit, white shirt and the blandest brown tie. He had short dark hair and a broad pair of shoulders that testified to a lot of hours spent in a gym. From his features – he had a square slab of a face with a dimpled chin and, even this early in the day, a five o'clock shadow – you would have placed him on the other side of the law, a 'heavy' from central casting. But his face changed as he grinned at Peggy, holding out an enormous paw of a hand.

'Good to see you, Peggy.'

Sitting down heavily on a two-seater sofa, Costino looked towards Peggy. 'I bring news from Bureau HQ and it's hot off the press. So hot in fact,' he said to Miles, 'that Langley hasn't even been told yet. It's about this man we've been watching in Vermont.'

Miles turned to Peggy. 'Do you remember that when our Russian source Mischa told us about the two Illegals who had been sent here to UK, he also said that there was another one in the States? But that this other one wasn't in play because he was seriously ill and about to be admitted to a hospice?'

Peggy nodded.

'That's right,' said Costino. 'Our guys in Foreign Counter-Intelligence eventually identified him – to their satisfaction anyway.' He paused.

'And?' said Peggy.

'And, he died two days ago.'

Peggy groaned. So this was the news, but it wasn't very helpful. The hospitalised man in America had been the one remaining lead to the network of Russian Illegals they'd been told about. They'd also been told of another Illegal operating in France, but the French intelligence agencies had so far not made any headway identifying that one.

Al was still talking. 'We kept a quiet eye on the dying man. His name was Petersen, documented as a Swede, lecturer at the University of Vermont. The hospice made it clear he wouldn't be coming out, and we didn't think he'd tell us anything if we made contact with him. So we just watched, waiting to see if anyone showed an interest or turned up to visit him. Nobody did, which was odd in itself. Until two days ago. Then, out of the blue a Swede named Ohlson turned up, just before Petersen died, claiming to be a childhood friend.'

He paused. Peggy held her breath, waiting.

Al scratched under his chin. 'He said he'd driven down from Canada and he was in a car with Canadian number plates. All we've learned so far from the Canadians is that he hired the car the day before he turned up at the hospital. He showed a Swedish passport and gave the address of a hotel in Montreal. He's not there any longer and the Canadians are trying to trace him. We've sent a guy up there to work the case. Someone with a lot of counter-intelligence experience. He'll be very discreet.'

Peggy said, 'If Petersen was the Illegal, what was he doing in Vermont? Is there anything special there to interest the Russians?'

'Couldn't it be the same thing as the two you caught here?' mused Al.

Peggy shook her head. 'I shouldn't think so. The pair we caught here probably had a general brief to begin with – to stir up trouble in whatever way they could, back protest movements, foment disruption and anti-government feeling. Standard disruption stuff.'

'But rural Vermont?' asked Miles. 'That's not where you'd plant an Illegal with such a general brief.'

Peggy nodded. 'No. That kind of stuff could only be effectively done in the capital or in a major city like New York.'

Al looked at them both. 'And why is this new guy in Montreal? Is he a replacement for Petersen? What happens in Montreal that also happens in Vermont? And would be of value to the Russians?'

It was Peggy's turn to shrug. 'Your guess is as good as mine. Better in fact,' she added with a grin. 'I've never been to Vermont or Montreal.'

'Perhaps he's not based there,' suggested Miles. 'Maybe he just used it as a base to visit Petersen.'

'Took him long enough,' said Costino. 'That guy was dying for weeks.'

The three of them sat in silence for a moment. Finally, Al Costino spoke. 'Well, folks, thanks for your time. I guess I've given you something to think about. Questions but no answers.' Turning to Peggy he said, 'My HQ asked me to say that they'd be grateful for your cooperation on this one. As the Service with the most recent experience of this sort of activity, we'd really appreciate your input. And could you also brief your colleagues in MI6 in case they have any sources who might be able to give a steer on what is going on? And we'll keep you informed, of course, if we learn anything more.'

With that, he unfolded his long legs, heaved himself up from the sofa and with handshakes all round left the room. After he'd gone Peggy and Miles sat down again and looked at each other. They knew they were both thinking the same thing.

'Mischa?' said Peggy.

'Exactly,' replied Miles.

'Is he contactable?'

'I believe our Station in Kiev still has an emergency method of communication. But they'll have to agree to do it. He's their source and they are responsible for his security. I'll contact them and see what they say.'

'Meanwhile I'll brief Liz and Six about the mysterious Mr Petersen and his visitor from Montreal,' said Peggy. Gathering up her now dry umbrella, she set off into the rain with a spring in her step.

4

IT WAS ONE THIRTY and Liz Carlyle was walking to work. Her enjoyment of the walk was not dampened in the least by the rain. No more gloomy Northern Line tube journeys for her, she reflected, just a stroll through Pimlico and along the river. A few months ago, at the end of a very stressful period both at work and in her private life, she had sat down and thought about what changes might make her happier. She had often thought how much better it would be if she lived nearer to Thames House, where she worked in MI5's head office. So she had taken the plunge, stepped into the local estate agent and put her flat on the market.

It had turned out that her particular part of Kentish Town was a lot more desirable than she realised, and the asking price the estate agent suggested had amazed her. But before long she had a firm offer. She'd hesitated for two days before accepting it, thinking of how thrilled she had been to be able to buy her flat in the first place and of all the happy times she had spent there. But finally she had shrugged her shoulders, told herself it was time to move on and accepted the offer. Within a few weeks she had found and fallen in love with a top-floor flat overlooking the gardens of St George's Square in Pimlico. What really sold it to her was the small roof terrace, which had a tremendous view over the rooftops of Westminster Cathedral in the distance.

She had moved in a week ago and had woken every morning looking forward to the mile or so walk to work. The fact that it had rained almost every day had not depressed her in the least. Today she had taken the morning off to take delivery of a large, comfortable sofa and was feeling particularly pleased with her choice and how well it fitted in to the sitting room.

Up in her small office in Thames House she hung her dripping raincoat on the back of the door and sat down at her desk. As she did so she reflected how lucky she was to have an office, however small, in these days of open-plan floors and hot-desking. When the building had been repartitioned to form large open floors to accommodate the increase in manpower – first after 9/11, then again in the wake of the 7/7 bombing of the London Underground – something had gone slightly awry and some odd corners had been left out of the open plan. Some were big enough to form small meeting rooms, though Liz's space wasn't big enough for anything except a small office with just enough room for a desk and two chairs. But it did have a window and the window looked over the Thames. There wasn't much to see at present, since the steady rain distorted the view until it flickered like a television on the blink. But Liz liked her own space and even when the weather was bad she liked the outlook too.

As she sat down at her desk Liz wondered how Peggy was getting on at Grosvenor. She had delegated the liaison role with the Americans because she was busy running her counter-espionage team and also because she thought it was time to give Peggy some extra responsibility. Peggy had originally joined MI6 as a researcher, having become bored by her first job after leaving university in a small private library in the north of England.

She and Liz had first met when Peggy was seconded to MI5 to work with Liz on a particularly delicate case involving both their Services. Liz had been impressed with Peggy's talent for research and her tenacity and Peggy had admired Liz's drive and operational skills. When the case was concluded, Peggy had decided that the domestic service would better suit her abilities than MI6 and, encouraged by Liz, had transferred to MI5. Since then she had worked closely with Liz, moving with her from the Counter-Terrorism Branch to Counter-Espionage.

During that time Peggy had developed from a rather shy, scholarly young woman who hid behind her hair and her glasses. She had turned out to have considerable operational skills, particularly in extracting information from unsuspecting people. To Liz's, and her own, surprise, she had become highly talented at role-playing and had successfully transformed herself into, among other things, a social worker, a census official and a debt collector. Liz felt a little like a proud mother hen as she watched and encouraged her junior's development.

Recently, Peggy had suffered something of a blow, however, when Tim, her partner of several years and a lecturer in seventeenth-century English Literature, had go himself into trouble – by behaving like the spineless erratic geek Liz had always suspected he was. His behaviour had come as a shock to Peggy, who had seen only the gentle, scholarly side of Tim. The revelation of this other side had upset Peggy greatly and their relationship had broken up.

It was partly to take Peggy's mind off all this that Liz had asked her to be the main contact point with Miles Brookhaven at the CIA Station in the US Embassy. But there was another reason too. When Miles had been posted to London several years earlier, he had asked Liz out, sent her flowers and behaved like a lovestruck teenager. Though Liz had been amused by Miles, she had found his romantic attentions entirely unwelcome; when she heard that Miles was returning as Head of Station she had tried to avoid a repeat of his failed courtship by appointing Peggy as liaison.

In fact, she needn't have worried. The Miles who arrived in London this time round was a much more mature character. Liz found they could now meet as friends and colleagues without any embarrassment. Miles was still unmarried, however, and was undoubtedly attractive – something Liz noticed Peggy had recognised as well. Half of Liz hoped that Peggy would get over her breakup with Tim and start a relationship with Miles; the other half worried that an American CIA officer, however Anglophile, might not be the right choice for Peggy.

Liz was mulling over this when Peggy herself appeared in the doorway of her office. Her coat was soaking wet but her face was glowing.

'Heavens, Peggy, you look chirpy for such a rotten day. How did you get on at Grosvenor?'

'It was fascinating,' said Peggy. 'Do you mind if I just dump my coat for a minute? I need to check my emails, then I'll come back and tell you.'

In a few minutes she was back. 'Have a chair,' said Liz. 'And fill me in. I hope it's good news.'

'Well, I don't know about good. But it's certainly interesting.' She told Liz what Al Costino had reported about the Swedish lecturer in Vermont and his mysterious visitor from Canada.

'They seem pretty certain that the Petersen man who died was the Illegal that Mischa said was in America. Now the Bureau is pulling out all the stops to find out about his visitor. He called himself Ohlson.'

'Another Swede.'

'Yes. He claimed to be a childhood friend of Petersen. Anyway, Al Costino said his HQ in Washington asked if we and Six had any source that could help. Miles and I both thought of Mischa.'

'Mischa?' asked Liz thoughtfully. Her mind went back to the church in Tallinn last autumn. Mischa was a Russian army officer, a specialist in sophisticated weaponry who had taken a degree at Birmingham University. He had been in Ukraine with the Russian forces when a Malaysian passenger aircraft had been brought down by a Russian surface-to-air missile. Disgusted by this, and by the denials of any involvement immediately issued by the Kremlin, Mischa had made contact with the CIA's Kiev Station through an American journalist who had been at the crash site. Mischa had rapidly become a paid source of the Kiev Station, providing information on Russian military activity in Ukraine. Then, out of the blue, he had asked to meet a more senior officer of the CIA, and Miles Brookhaven had gone to Ukraine from London to see him.

It was Mischa who had provided the first information about the Russian Illegals operations in Europe and the US. His source was his brother, a middle-ranking officer in the Russian intelligence service, FSB, who was working on the Illegals programme in Moscow and liked to boast about it when he was drunk. Mischa's information, though tantalising, had not been sufficiently detailed to act on, and it was not until months later when he had resurfaced in Tallinn, asking to meet a contact from the British Special Services, that Liz had met him. She had gone out to Tallinn under the cover of a recently bereaved schoolteacher who had joined an academic-led tour group.

He'd provided her with enough information for MI5 to locate and the police subsequently to arrest two Russian Illegals working in Britain. After the excitement of the operation to round up the Illegals working in Britain was over, Liz had occasionally wondered whether there had been any repercussions for Mischa or his brother. There must have been an investigation in Moscow to try to find out how the Illegals had been discovered. She was curious whether Mischa's brother had come under suspicion and if so whether the suspicion had spread to Mischa himself. Nothing further had been heard from Mischa, and no information had come from the MI6 Station in Moscow – not that she had heard anyway – though she knew they had made some effort to find out who Mischa's brother was, as he sounded like a possible recruit.

'Do the Americans have a way of contacting Mischa?' she asked Peggy.

'Miles is going to find out. He thinks the Kiev Station may have an emergency arrangement.'

'It'd better be a secure one,' replied Liz. 'I would imagine the FSB grew very suspicious once we wrapped up two of their Illegals.'

'Shall I set up a meeting with Six? They don't know anything about the American Illegal yet and I said we'd inform them and ask if they have any useful sources.'

'Yes, do,' replied Liz. 'And then we can see what they think about contacting Mischa.'

5

'CONTACT MISCHA?' EXCLAIMED Geoffrey Fane after Peggy had reported on the meeting with Miles and his FBI colleague at the American Embassy. 'What on earth are the Americans thinking of? There'll be a full-scale FSB enquiry going on in Moscow as we speak into how we got on to their people here. If the Americans want to land their man in prison, and his brother too, that's the way to do it.'

They were sitting in Fane's office on an upper floor of Vauxhall Cross, MI6's London Headquarters. Liz always enjoyed a visit to Fane's office, unchanged in all the years she had known him. Through all the structural changes in the Vauxhall Cross building in recent years to accommodate the explosion in manpower, Geoffrey Fane had somehow miraculously managed to hang on to this large room with its tall windows and river view.

He had also managed to acquire a large nineteenth-century wooden desk, a couple of button-back chairs and a leather Chesterfield sofa thrown out from the Foreign Office in some refurbishment programme years before. To these he had added an antique coffee table left to him by his grandmother and the Persian rugs, picked up for a song by clever bargaining, so he claimed, on his various posts in the Middle East. To Liz they epitomised Geoffrey Fane: elegant, discreetly flamboyant and out of date.

'I think everyone agrees that it's very risky,' said Peggy mildly, 'but it seems they have no other assets in a position to throw light on what's going on in Vermont. They did want to know if you had any sources who could help.'

Fane looked at the fourth person in the room, his colleague Bruno Mackay, who merely shook his head. The behaviour of the two men struck Liz as distinctly odd. She had known Bruno Mackay for years; when they were both much younger he had been a thorn in her side. She had found him irritatingly self-satisfied, with his Savile Row suits, unruly straw-coloured hair and skin tanned from postings in exotic countries. But age and experience had rubbed the raw edges off both of them. Liz herself had recently suffered a personal tragedy, while it was rumoured that on a recent posting in Libya something very unpleasant had happened to Bruno. Whether it was as a result of their experiences or merely because they had grown older and kinder, both seemed to find it easier now to work together.

But today Liz had a strong feeling that something was hanging in the air; something was not being said and she wanted to know what it was. She waited, saying nothing herself.

Peggy broke the silence. 'Miles thinks their Kiev Station has an emergency contact arrangement set up with Mischa and he's getting clearance from Langley to activate it.'

'Oh. I see,' said Fane. 'So Langley haven't given clearance yet? I can tell you, they're not going to, either.'

It was obvious to Liz that Geoffrey Fane had something going on with the Americans that she didn't know about. She wondered whether Miles Brookhaven knew what it was, although it sounded unlikely. Peggy, seemingly oblivious to the undercurrent in the room, said, 'The FBI are desperate to know what can link Petersen in Vermont with Ohlson and Canada.'

'I can see their point,' said Fane, 'but it's not going to happen.'

Peggy looked about to argue, but catching Liz's warning eye said nothing.

Liz reached for her bag and stood up. 'Thanks for your time, gentlemen. We've done what we were asked to do and brought you up to date, and we've passed on the Bureau's request for help. So we'll leave you to it.'

Fane and Bruno both stood up too. Peggy, scrabbling to get her papers together and retrieve her bag from the floor, was the last to rise.

'I'll see you out,' said Bruno, holding the door open. He came out into the corridor with them and said quietly to Liz, 'Have you got a minute? There's something I'd like to discuss.'

'Sure,' said Liz, curious. When the lift arrived, Bruno got in with them and pressed the button for the second floor.

'Do you want me to wait downstairs?' Peggy asked when the lift stopped.

'No, you come too, please,' said Bruno. 'It won't take long.'

He led them into a small windowless meeting room across from the lift. 'Do sit down,' said Bruno. He took a seat at the end of the room's table. 'Sorry to be so mysterious, but there's something I need to tell you. I thought Geoffrey was going to, but you know what he's like: he can't bear to give away any information when he doesn't have to. He'd have told you eventually, but I think you need to know now, because it affects how we handle this new business with the Bureau.'

Bruno paused as if hesitant to come clean. Liz waited patiently and finally Bruno went on again. 'I'm being posted to Moscow. I'll be there under cover, not diplomatic. The cover is being worked on now so I can't tell you any more than that. But I've got one task and that is to get alongside Mischa's brother. Our Station has been working with the Americans out there and they have identified the brother, Boris, and know quite a lot about him and his lifestyle. We've given him the codename "Starling". I'm to try to recruit him and keep him in place.'

He exhaled nosily, seemingly revealed to have spilled the beans. 'You can see why Geoffrey is nervous about initiating any contact with Mischa. If it went wrong, it would compromise this operation – and Starling is a much bigger prize than his brother. He's at the heart of the FSB.'

'Well,' said Liz, reeling slightly from this disclosure, 'it goes without saying, if there's anything we can do to help…'

'At the moment you can just look surprised when Geoffrey tells you. Which he will. When he's ready.'

'Who else knows?' asked Peggy. 'Does Miles?'

'I don't think he does. I'm not sure about Langley. I assume the Director of Counter Intelligence and his most senior staff do. Even Geoffrey wouldn't dare keep this from them. And of course their Head of Station in Moscow and the head people in the Ops Directorate. There'll be an indoctrination list soon but so far you are the first people to know in your outfit.' He looked at Liz. 'Given your dealings with Mischa, you clearly need to be in the picture.'

'I appreciate your telling us.' But she was uneasy about keeping a secret about a secret, and was puzzled that Bruno Mackay was going behind Fane's back. She added, 'Let's hope Geoffrey decides to tell us officially before too long.'

As they walked back to Thames House across Vauxhall Bridge Liz said to Peggy, 'Something must have happened to Bruno. He used to be so difficult, but just now he couldn't have been nicer. It's hard to believe he's the same man.'

'Perhaps he's in love,' said Peggy, and laughed.

'Maybe,' said Liz, unconvinced. 'If he is, long may it last.'

6

THE LITTLE PLANE LANDED with a teeth-jarring bump and bounced along the runway. Special Agent Harry Fitzpatrick opened his eyes. He hated flying in small planes. They seemed to swirl about like kites, swooping and soaring with every thermal or breeze. He could cope with big planes; they seemed robust enough to survive turbulence, but propeller planes with just sixteen seats such as these were to his mind obviously unsafe. As soon as the plane had juddered to a halt he unclipped his seatbelt and stood up, anxious to be out of the flimsy little cabin as soon as possible.

As he climbed down the steps he saw a large, dark-haired man in a navy-blue suit and dark glasses standing on the tarmac. This must be Boyd, the local Agent who had alerted him to activity in what Fitzpatrick thought to be a dead duck case. When the first lead had come in from the British that there was a Russian Illegal in the States who had been hospitalised with a serious illness, it seemed important to quickly identify the man in case he recovered and became active again.

It had taken a good few months to locate the man and he had sometimes wondered whether he was justified in using the resources on a case that looked as though it would go nowhere. Eventually, after extensive searches involving dates and nationality, age and type of illness he had decided that the Swede Petersen was the best fit, however unlikely it seemed. By the time he had got on to him, however, Petersen had been moved from the large hospital where he had been having treatment to a small hospice.

Since then Petersen hadn't moved from his bed, and apparently no one had been in touch with him; it looked as if when he died, the case, if it ever was a case, would die too. But a couple of days ago Boyd's report had come in, and now it seemed possible that there was just the smallest of threads to unravel. And to Harry Fitzpatrick that was irresistible.

As Boyd drove them both to the hospice where Petersen had died he outlined the arrangements he had made for Fitzpatrick's visit. After the hospice they would go to the rented house where Petersen had lived for the last five years and then on to the university to interview the head of department where Petersen had worked. 'I got a key to the house from the realtor who manages the rental,' Boyd said, 'but I haven't been in. Thought you'd want to see it as he left it.'

'Good thinking,' said Harry. 'Has the realtor been in?'

'No. I told him not to.'

At the hospice, Nurse Sarah Burns showed them Room 112 where Petersen had spent the last four months.

'We haven't moved anything, except to strip the bed,' she said, looking at Boyd.

'Has anyone else been in here except you and your colleagues?' asked Fitzpatrick. She shook her head. 'So this is all the stuff he had in here?'

'Yes,' she said, looking over at the things on the top of the dressing table. A few books, a wallet, small change and some car keys. 'His clothes are in the closet.'

Fitzpatrick stood with his hands in his pockets, looking around him. 'Those are his keys?' he asked eventually, pointing to the dressing table.

'Yes. Car keys and house keys.'

'I can see the car keys. But where are the house keys?'

Sarah walked across the room to look. 'That's odd,' she said. 'They were always there – with the car keys. Where have they gone?' She paused, frowned. 'I wonder if Mr Ohlson took them.'

'That's possible,' agreed Fitzpatrick. 'Could you ask the nurse who was here when Mr Ohlson left whether he mentioned the keys? And did Mr Ohlson say how he learned Mr Petersen was dying?'

'No. I assumed he'd heard from someone else – I didn't have the impression he'd heard from Petersen himself.'

'But this "someone else" didn't visit Petersen?'

'No. He didn't have any other visitors. When he first came in someone from the university was with him but they never came back. No one else came. I'm sure of that because we insist anyone visiting signs the book.'

'How long was Ohlson with the patient?'

'I think it was no more than half an hour. He was still here when I went off duty but Emily – that's the night nurse – said he'd left shortly after she came on. I thought it seemed a long way to come for such a short visit, especially as he knew he'd probably never see Mr Petersen alive again.'

'Are you sure he knew how ill Petersen was?'

'Yes. I pretty much told him that he was dying.'

Fitzpatrick nodded. 'Did anything else seem unusual about this visitor?'

The nurse thought it over for a moment. 'Not really. He was Swedish, but then so was Petersen.' She paused, and Fitzpatrick could see that she wanted to be careful in what she said next. 'I guess if anything did strike me, it was the sense that they were talking confidentially.'

'Why did you think that?'

Nurse Burns looked a little embarrassed. She said reluctantly, 'I stood outside the door to the room for a minute after I left Ohlson in there. I was trying to hear what they were talking about,' adding defensively, 'I thought the Bureau might want to know.'

'Absolutely,' said Fitzpatrick reassuringly. 'And what did you hear?'

She laughed awkwardly. 'Nothing really. I suppose I was silly to think I would as they must have been speaking in Swedish. There was just what sounded like a lot of questions from Ohlson and murmured replies from Mr Petersen. It was all very calm and quiet.'

After the visit to the hospice, Boyd drove Fitzpatrick to the brick ranch house on the outskirts of the city Petersen had rented for the last five years. The landlord lived in Florida and the letting was managed by a local agent. From what Boyd had gathered, little was known about Petersen. There was no one still working at the agency who'd been there when Petersen had first taken on the tenancy, but from the file it seemed he had done it without seeing the house. They did a lot of lettings for the university and that was not unusual. No one currently working in the office had ever met him and they had never had cause to go into the house since he took up residence. He paid the rent punctually from an account at his bank in Burlington.

Boyd parked in the drive. The front lawn had not been mown or the front borders weeded, but once inside, the house was tidy, almost clinically so.

'He lived alone, right?' asked Fitzpatrick, pulling on thin cotton gloves. 'So why's there no dust?'

Boyd nodded. 'Looks as though it's been professionally cleaned – and very recently. They didn't mention a cleaner at the agency.'

In the study there was a wall of books, mainly sets of contemporary fiction. 'I guess they're part of the fittings,' said Boyd.

A filing cabinet contained folders of academic papers – student recommendations, student grades, applications for grants. 'I can't see much of interest here,' said Fitzpatrick, 'but we'll have to get it taken back to HQ to check. No sign of any private papers – no will, not even any bills.'

'Maybe we'll find them at the university.'

Fitzpatrick scratched his head thoughtfully. 'What do you make of this Petersen, Tom?'

'How do you mean?'

'What sort of guy do you think he was?'

Boyd looked bemused by the question, but eventually he said, 'I guess if I had to use one word to describe this man it would be *boring*. There's nothing unusual about him at all.' He saw Fitzpatrick's expression and asked, 'What's the matter?'

'I don't think it's so much boring as unreal. I think someone has been in here very recently and removed any sign of a real person. This place is like a stage set after the play is over. Tidied up and dusted and all the props put safely away. I bet Mr Ohlson has been in to make sure no trace of Petersen was left. I guarantee that when we get the labs boys in here there won't be a single fingerprint they can lift. Not one.' He exhaled in frustration. 'You know, when I flew up today I had real doubts about whether we'd got the right man. Now I'm sure we have. But what the hell was he doing here?'

Aт тне Uɴɪversɪтy oᴏ Vermont, Boyd parked in a half-empty lot. They walked slowly through the afternoon heat towards a gothic sandstone building that loomed over the university green below it.

'The students are all away and a lot of the academic staff as well,' said Boyd. 'We're seeing the deputy head of Computer Sciences – that's the department Petersen worked in. Her name's Emerson.'

Angie Emerson looked about seventeen. She was small and slim and wore a faded red T-shirt, jeans, flip-flops and large horn-rimmed spectacles pushed on to the top of her head. Her hair was dyed a dayglo blonde and pinned up in a loose bun from which strands were escaping. As they came into her office she leaped up from her chair and held out a thin brown hand, smiling broadly and talking quickly.

'Do come in,' she said, pushing some journals on to the floor to clear a couple of chairs. 'It's not every day I get to meet the FBI. I understand you want to talk about Lars Petersen. I was so sorry to hear that he'd died; not that I knew him very well. I knew he was ill but I didn't know it was terminal.'

She paused briefly while Fitzpatrick and Boyd sat down, then continued: 'I'm sorry the chairman of the department isn't here. He's on vacation with his family – giving his kids a cultural tour of Europe.' She smiled. 'My partner and I haven't got kids, so I look after things here during the summer. We go away in winter – skiing, not culture, for us.'

'It's good of you to see us,' Fitzpatrick said, thinking he'd better try and get to the point or they'd be there all day. 'I'm eager to hear anything you can tell us about Petersen. We think he may not have been quite who he said he was.'

'Oh,' said Angie Emerson in surprise. She scratched her head with the end of her glasses. 'Who do you think he was then?'

For a moment Fitzpatrick wondered whether she was being sarcastic. He said mildly, 'We think he may have been working for a foreign intelligence service.'

Angie Emerson seemed genuinely taken aback. Fitzpatrick went on, 'I'd like you to tell me whatever you can about his work here. What was his academic specialty, for example? Did he have a social life? Who was close to him? And we'd like access to his office. My colleague Tom Boyd here will send someone to take away any papers he's left behind.'

'I'm not going to be an awful lot of help,' she said, 'but I'll tell you what I know. His own work was on statistical pattern recognition, algorithms and image analysis. It's not my area at all, but he was well regarded – I do know that. As for his private life, I don't know much about it. I can't think of anyone who would. You see, he kept himself to himself. He wasn't one to frequent the bars – not that I am either – and we don't do a lot of socialising in this department; we're quite geeky. If he had a partner I never met her – or him.'

She paused, thinking. Then she continued, 'One thing about him was that he seemed to be around all the time. If he had family back in Sweden he can't have seen much of them; he didn't go away for the summer vacation. I know that because he used to teach the students at the summer school. It's a big thing here – we run summer schools in lots of disciplines, arts and sciences. They're for high school kids – teenagers, mainly juniors and seniors, though in our department we often get them younger: fifteen or even fourteen sometimes. Kids with a real flair for computers develop it young. There's a class going on at the moment. I'll walk you along to Lars's office and we'll pass the lecture room.'

As they left her office, Emerson carried on: 'We're very proud of what we do. These are not kids from privileged backgrounds. We give bursaries for poor kids and for kids from developing countries and war zones, if we can reach them. It's amazing how talented some of them are, even though they've had very little formal teaching. And they're so keen.'

By now they had reached the lecture room door and she stopped to let Fitzpatrick look in through a large glass panel. He saw a room full of children, boys and girls of all races and nationalities it seemed, sitting at computer benches. At the front a young man was writing out lines of code on a white board.

'How long do they stay?' he asked.

'About a month usually,' she replied, opening the door of a small office. 'This was Lars's place.'

'Thank you for all your help,' said Fitzpatrick, stepping into the room with Boyd.

There was a note of dismissal in his voice, and Emerson took the hint. 'I'll leave you to it then,' she said, looking slightly disappointed. What had her late colleague been up to?

Fitzpatrick had intended to hire a car and drive up to Montreal to see how the Canadians were getting on with their inquiries into the mysterious Ohlson. However, when they returned to Boyd's office to arrange the car hire there was a message waiting for him. The Canadians had established that Ohlson had flown into Montreal from Helsinki on a Swedish passport the day before he turned up in Burlington. He had stayed the night at the Marriott hotel at Montreal International airport and had hired the blue Volkswagen Passat there the following day. The car was recorded crossing into the United States at 15.30. It returned across the border at 21.40 and was photographed parking at the Marriott at 23:37.

Ohlson returned the car to the rental agency at 10.30 the following morning, checked out of the hotel at midday and flew out of Montreal airport on a flight to Copenhagen that left at 15.35. Photographs, a copy of the passport, copy of the credit card used at the hotel and driving licence were all on their way to FBI HQ in Washington.

'Well,' said Fitzpatrick when he'd finished reading, 'it seems there's no point my going to Montreal. Ohlson's flown the coop.' He looked at Boyd and shook his head. 'This case is weird and getting weirder. One man's dead and his supposed "childhood friend" has disappeared. Call me old-fashioned, but it would be nice to meet someone involved with this in the flesh.'

8

Lɪᴢ ᴡᴀꜱ ʜᴀɴɢɪɴɢ ᴜᴘ her wet raincoat on the back of her office door when her young colleague from the mail room walked in.

'Lovely day again,' he remarked. 'There's two for you.' He dropped two brown envelopes on to her desk.

'Thanks, and it isn't,' she replied. She knew what would be in the envelopes. Ever since her visit to Tallinn to meet Mischa the year before, she had been receiving fliers from the hotel she had stayed at, advertising unmissable weekend breaks at knockdown prices. She had used a cover address to go with her cover identity – she had been Liz Ryder, a former schoolteacher whose mother had recently died after a long illness. She had not given the hotel an email address so they were sending all their publicity by mail to the address she had used, where it was forwarded to her at Thames House.

She opened the first envelope; sure enough it was an advertisement for a Christmas break – full Christmas dinner with party hats and crackers, champagne and wine with dinner included. A tour of Tallinn to see the illuminations, plus carol service by candlelight in one of Tallinn's famous churches. Liz shuddered at the idea and chucked the whole lot in the waste basket.

She slit open the next envelope expecting more of the same but this envelope felt different. Inside it was a picture postcard. The picture on the front of the card wasn't of Tallinn. It was of a building she had never seen; it looked like an enormous glasshouse – examining it closely she saw it *was* an enormous glasshouse. When she turned the card over and read the caption, it turned out to be the main tropical greenhouse of the Botanical Gardens of Berlin – or strictly speaking, the *Botanischer Garten*.

Intrigued, she read the message written on the card in dark ink with slashing strokes:

I thought this looked a bit like St Olaf's. M

St Olaf's had been the church in Tallinn where she had met Mischa. But why was he sending her this picture? It didn't look at all like St Olaf's church. What was he trying to tell her? Was he in Berlin? That's where it appeared to have been posted. And how had he got this address?

The last question was the easiest to answer – he could have quite easily found which tour group she was in, found which hotel they were staying in, and it wouldn't have been too difficult to blag some unsuspecting receptionist to give out the name and address.

But what did this message mean?

The only thing written on the card, other than her name and address, were some numbers at the top, which she had at first taken to be the date the card was written. She looked at them more closely and suddenly understood that they were indeed a date and a time. Four days from now – that was the date. And 09:45 was the time. He was asking for a meeting, and it must be in this building – the greenhouse. Still staring at the card, she noticed that a small squiggle underneath the M, which she had taken to be part of the signature, was in fact a tiny drawing of a cup and saucer. So the meeting must be in the café.

Liz sat up in her chair, her mind racing. Four days – that was enough time; Berlin was a two-hour flight away. But she would have to get her ducks in a row first. There was Geoffrey Fane to get round, and just as urgently, the Americans. According to Fane they would put the kibosh on any attempts to contact Mischa. But it was Mischa who was trying to contact her. Would that make them change their minds? She hoped so.

She picked up her phone and punched in a number. The phone at the other end was picked up immediately. 'Hello, Miles,' she said, trying not to sound too excited.

9

'T**HAT'S ONE HELL OF** a coincidence if you ask me.' The image of Andy Bokus loomed over the video feed from Langley, a look of outrage on his face, while Miles Brookhaven watched from a secure conference room in the CIA suite in the Embassy in London. Miles could just make out the bulky frame below the large head, currently clothed in a khaki-coloured summer suit, white shirt and royal blue tie.

When Bokus had been Station Head in London several years before and Miles had been a junior officer, the two had never got on. Now Miles had succeeded him and it rankled with Bokus. Bokus was a former American football player, the grandson of an immigrant, and a Midwesterner; Miles was East Coast, Ivy League and a classic 'preppy'. They were oil and water – socially, politically, personally. When Bokus disagreed with Miles, Miles knew that it was often out of instinctive antipathy rather than from any actual difference of opinion.

The best way to deal with Bokus's aggression, Miles had learned over the years, was to punch back hard. He said sharply now, 'What's your point?'

Miles could see Sandy Gunderson, the Director of Counter-Intelligence and Bokus's boss, sitting next to him. His face was a study in bland neutrality. Miles thought there was something bloodless about the man; he was entirely unlike his predecessor, the legendary Tyrus Oakes, who had been a much-admired character, a wry, diminutive Southerner with gentle manners that belied a will of steel and a penchant for writing copious notes during meetings on old-fashioned yellow legal pads. Gunderson, by contrast, kept his notes strictly in his head, and his desk and office were almost fanatically tidy, and as neutral as his expression now.

Across the Atlantic, Bokus sat back in his chair. 'I'm not making any point,' he snapped. 'Just questioning the timing of all this. We tell the Brits we don't want to contact Mischa since we're trying to get a fix on his brother, and then lo and behold, up pops Mischa himself, demanding a meeting. Not with us, but with the Brits, no less.'

Miles was shaking his head. 'If you're suggesting this is a put-up job, I can't agree. Until now, the Brits hadn't heard from Mischa any more than we had. I saw the postcard Mischa sent. It's legit.'

'A postcard from Berlin,' Bokus said scathingly. 'It wouldn't take Einstein to manufacture that.'

Gunderson's expression remained impenetrable. Miles said firmly, 'I've worked with the Brits before – almost as long as you, Andy. It's not the kind of stunt they'd pull. And Liz Carlyle is a straight-shooter. Even you have to admit that.'

Bokus looked ready to dispute this, but then thought better of it. He sat back, lips pursed like an unhappy bullfrog.

Gunderson spoke at last, his voice roughly half the decibel count of Bokus. 'You say that Mischa wrote to Miss Carlyle specifically?'

'That's right. She met with him in Tallinn, if you remember.'

'Does she have any idea what he wants?'

Miles said, 'No more than we do. But she's determined to go herself, and given that he wrote to her, I think she's right. You have to remember that Mischa has lived in Britain; he was at college here. He's met Liz Carlyle and he must trust her as he wants to meet her again. If we sent one of ours instead he might well abort the meeting. We'd probably lose him for good then.'

'You can't be sure of that.' It was Bokus again.

Miles nodded. 'You're right; I can't. But then we can't be completely sure of anything about this. It could be a set-up but I think it's very unlikely.'

Was there the hint of agreement on Gunderson's face? Miles hoped so, but it was impossible to tell, especially with the flickering feed of the video. Whatever Gunderson decided, both Miles and Bokus would have to accept it.

'Gentlemen, I can see you've got a difference of opinion.' He turned to Bokus. 'Andy, we have no reason to distrust the Brits. If they say this is a legitimate approach, I'm sure it is. Miles has seen the communication and knows the circumstances of its arrival. If Mischa wants a meeting he must have something to say; so we should listen. It may be directly relevant to his brother's position and if so we need to know what it is.' He turned back to the camera to look at Miles. 'Tell the Brits we have no objection to this meet. Offer them backup in Berlin if they want it, which I doubt, and make sure you get briefed by them pretty damn quick after Carlyle sees the guy. OK?'

'Yes. Many thanks,' said Miles as Gunderson stood up and moved out of camera range. As the video feed terminated and the picture faded, all Miles could see was the angry face of Andy Bokus.

10

IT HAD BEEN A dreadful week in Brussels, Dieter Nimitz thought, though flying home to Hamburg for the weekend wasn't necessarily an improvement. A senior officer in the office of the EU Commissioner for Refugees, he worked devising and trying to implement European-wide policy on migration and refugees, but despite his best efforts and those of his colleagues the situation was a shambles. Thousands of refugees were pouring into the south of Europe and the member countries of the EU could not agree on even the first step of what to do about it.

Matters weren't helped for Dieter by his boss, a Dutchman called Van der Vaart, who was both critical of his staff and unhelpful. Dieter mentally divided the Dutch into two categories: the benign, pipe-smoking type, with liberal opinions, and the less common Calvinist sort, dour and right-wing. Van der Vaart was decidedly of the latter, and it made him an intolerant taskmaster, always looking for someone to blame. Dieter, the most senior of the staff, bore the brunt of the Dutchman's criticisms, and he sometimes felt that but for his friendship with his British colleague Matilda, and the loyalty of the juniors he spent much of his time defending, his job would be intolerable.

Coming through Customs now, Dieter froze. Ahead of him, waiting behind the rail, was a middle-aged woman, with greying hair parted in the middle. For a split second he thought it was his wife, come unexpectedly to meet his flight. But as the woman turned and the light fell on her face, he saw that it wasn't Irma, and he relaxed.

Once it might well have been her: in the early days of their marriage, Irma would often drive the forty minutes to the airport to meet him as he flew in from Brussels. Ostensibly, she came out of love, so delighted to see her husband that she couldn't wait for him to make his way home. But he knew even then, in the early days of their marriage, that she was there to keep an eye on him – to make sure he didn't stray; that he hadn't struck up a conversation with some blonde on the short flight home from Brussels.

Her jealousy seemed odd, since he didn't believe she really felt strongly for him even then. Sometimes he wondered whether it was jealousy at all, or just some need to control him. Thank God she didn't know about Matilda. There was nothing more than friendship between them, and there never would be, but that didn't mean Matilda wasn't special to Dieter. He was at pains to keep the friendship secret from Irma, and since he only saw Matilda during his working week in Brussels, that wasn't difficult.

He took the train from the airport to Blankensee, the affluent suburb of Hamburg where he and Irma lived. Theirs was a pleasant villa, not one of the larger houses on the street, but ample for their needs; they had no children. It had a garden with rose bushes and an ancient elm that lost a branch or two in the storms each autumn. As he reached the house and climbed the steps to his front door, Dieter tried to remind himself how lucky he was. And how far he had come.

A month prior to this, the German Chancellor, Angela Merkel, had visited their offices. Van der Vaart had escorted her around, staying close to her side, reluctantly introducing her to his more senior staff with a proprietary air. When it was Dieter's turn he had addressed the Chancellor in German. She had asked where he was from and he'd explained that he had grown up in Bavaria, which wasn't true at all, but that he lived now in Hamburg. This made her smile as she explained that Hamburg was where she had been born – though she had moved as a little girl to East Germany.

Dieter thought of the ironies in their exchange. Merkel, born in Hamburg, had moved to Templin, sixty miles east of Berlin, and grown up in the German Democratic Republic. He had moved to Hamburg after a childhood that he claimed had been spent in a village in Bavaria, hundreds of miles south, but actually he had been born and raised in Templin. None of this did he ever admit to anybody.

Dieter Schmidt had known from his earliest years that his father worked for the government of the GDR. This meant the family was not poor – well, everyone was poor then in East Germany, but they were less poor than others. They lived in one of the Stalinist apartment blocks erected in their thousands in the 1950s. Theirs was a block for government officials but they had one more room than their neighbours. Dieter had attended a local primary school, then a *Gymnasium*, gradually learning from the mixture of apprehension and respect that his teachers showed towards him that his father worked not just for the government, but for its most feared part, the *Stasi* – East Germany's lethal combination of intelligence service and secret police.

He never quite knew if this was why he was selected, but at the age of seventeen, as he prepared for his university entrance exams, two men came to visit the household. One of them wore a Homburg hat – he always remembered that – while his companion spoke German badly with an accent he later realised was Russian. His brothers and sisters had been sent outside, and his mother had withdrawn to the kitchen as they asked: Did he like school? Who was his closest friend? Did he have a girlfriend? Did he play football?

The two men had seemed almost bored by their own queries, until suddenly they became less banal. Was he good at languages? He was, as a matter of fact; he was top of his class in both Russian and English. Would he be interested in living abroad? Definitely – who in the grimness of East Germany wouldn't be? And finally, could he keep a secret – a big secret? Wordlessly, he nodded.

The two men had gone away, without an explanation for their visit, and his parents, whatever they knew, told him nothing. He had almost forgotten about this strange interview when a few months later he was summoned to the Head's office and found the man in the Homburg sitting there. 'Sit down,' the man said curtly, and nodded to the Head, who left the room. As Dieter listened with mounting incredulity, the visitor sketched out what the future was about to consist of.

And now, as he went into his house in Blankensee, calling out hello to Irma, Dieter reflected how accurate his forecast had proved.

He had been sent to Moscow immediately after his exams. There he had been schooled to an extraordinary degree in the details of what was to become his new identity. He felt like a man given a new shirt with instructions to memorise each and every stitch it contained. His name was changed immediately to Dieter Nimitz; thirty years later it took an effort of will to remember that he had been born 'Schmidt'.

He had expected that he would be given intensive schooling in Russian, but in fact he was schooled intensively in Bavarian German, since, it was explained to him, that was what the young Dieter would have spoken at home. After six months, Dieter had been sent back to East Germany and, after a final emotional farewell with his family, he had left for West Germany. He had travelled with a teenage group sent West on a two-week exchange, but he was the one member of the group to stay behind. Ten days later he entered Hamburg University as a languages student, having apparently freshly graduated from a *Gymnasium* in Bavaria. He'd worked hard at university, graduating with distinction, and then, obeying instructions he received, he took a job with an import–export firm in Hamburg. There he acquired managerial skills and some business acumen. He stayed in that small family-owned firm for seven years, having no contact with his family in the East – and hearing nothing from his controllers. He had become convinced that they had forgotten about him, when suddenly he was told to apply to the European Commission in Brussels.

By then he had met and married Irma, a German schoolteacher whom he met through friends at a picnic on the banks of the Elbe. Irma was a formidable character, who knew what she wanted and usually got it. She made it clear she wanted Dieter, and he felt both amazed and helpless in the face of her determination; they were married within a year. His explanation for the absence of family on his side at the wedding ceremony was that he had been orphaned early in life and raised by a succession of foster parents.

Other than two sets of instructions as to his employment, Dieter heard nothing from the Russians. As far as he could tell, they had utterly and irrevocably changed his life for no apparent purpose. Yet he felt no anger or regret about this, even when the Berlin Wall fell, since he was confident that one day the Russians would need him for something – he didn't know what, but he was certain of this. He also did not imagine his life would have been any happier had he stayed in Templin, and there was no prospect of going back there now – he learned of the deaths of his parents when browsing the online edition of the Templin local paper, and about his brothers and sisters, he knew nothing, and assumed they knew nothing of him.

He never revealed the truth about his real past to his wife; she seemed completely content with the version he had told her when they first met. He did sometimes think it strange that she never asked about his family, but they never talked much about their respective childhoods, so he knew very little about hers, either. It just was not something they ever discussed.

But from time to time, and more frequently as he got older, he thought of the man in the Homburg hat and the months in Moscow. At those times he felt certain that since a foreign power had gone to enormous pains to make him into something he was not, he would one day learn that there was a purpose to it all.

11

D IETER LET HIMSELF INTO the house with his key. Pushing open the door, he stepped into the little entrance hall and called down the passage that led to the kitchen at the back of the house.

'Irma. It's me. I'm back.'

There was no reply, so he walked to the bottom of the stairs. 'Irma,' he called, more loudly this time. Again, silence. He was a little surprised, since she was almost always home by now. Even though she worked in her study most evenings, and on the weekends as well, Irma liked to be home when he returned from his week in Brussels.

She had done well in her career as a teacher, and was now Head of the Freitang school, a new *Gymnasium* for immigrant children – once they'd been mostly Afghans and Iraqis; now they'd been joined by Syrians fleeing that country's never-ending spiral of violence. The Freitang did not discriminate between its pupils on grounds of race or national origin or religion, but it was nonetheless selective – all its students were of above average intelligence, and many of them were clearly gifted. Though most of them had survived extremely traumatic circumstances, they learned astonishingly fast – nearly all were fluent in German within a year, and soon after that were tackling the most difficult parts of the *Gymnasium* curriculum. The school was especially strong in IT, something that amused Dieter, since Irma was a self-confessed technophobe.

Leaving his case by the stairs, he went into the kitchen. There was no sign of Irma, and no note. He opened the fridge door, wondering what supper would be. Two pork chops sat on a plate and there was a bottle of Riesling, which he didn't dare open, even though he would dearly like a drink. Irma rationed alcohol in the same way she rationed affection – as something enjoyed in strictly limited doses.

He went upstairs, dumped his bag on the bedroom floor and swapped his jacket for a jumper. At a bit of a loss what to do while he waited for Irma to come home, he went down the corridor and into the small room she used as a study. It looked out over their back garden and he peered through the window just in case she was out there, though he knew it was unlikely as it was he who was the gardener. There was no sign of her.

As he turned back to the door he noticed a piece of paper that had slipped down between the filing cabinet and Irma's desk. He bent down and retrieved it, scanning it idly as he did so. It was a letter, addressed to Irma as Head of Freitang school, from the Director of the Lehrner Institute. He knew of the Institute; it was a local orphanage. In recent years, like similar institutions across Germany, it had been almost overwhelmed by the number of unaccompanied children who had arrived with the refugees flooding into Germany under Chancellor Merkel's open-door policy. The Lehrner was unable to accommodate all of its quota of children, and had made a public appeal for private households to offer accommodation to some of the older children. The

Institute retained responsibility for the children's welfare but in many cases a close, almost fostering relationship developed between the children and their hosts. The brightest and most promising of the orphanage children were selected by the Freitang school for fast-track tuition, so Irma had many dealings with the orphanage as a result.

The opening sentence caught his eye, and piqued his curiosity. He read on:

Dear Frau Nimitz

I write further to our telephone conversation of last week about the enquiry from Herr and Frau Gravenstein. I accept of course your point that since the young man who has sparked these inquiries is legally an adult, you are no longer responsible for him or obliged to monitor his movements and activities. Notwithstanding this, I would be most grateful for any information you can provide. You will appreciate that the Gravensteins are worried because they have not heard from a young man they consider to be almost a surrogate son. I have tried to reassure them by relaying your message that he has resettled in North America of his own accord, and that it is entirely his decision whether to communicate with them or not. As you have pointed out it would not be appropriate for me to intervene in any way.

But on a strictly human level, I would appeal to you. If indeed the young man has chosen to seek his fortune in America, would it not be possible to supply the Gravensteins with at least a postal address, so that they could perhaps write to him? Then of course he could make his own decision about whether he wished to reply and continue to have contact with the family. Perhaps you would agree with me that it is not in the best interests of our child refugee programme that those who have generously offered and given their help should feel rejected and ignored.

I hope you will forgive this personal appeal, but truly, the pain this has caused the Gravensteins is quite affecting.

Yours as ever,
Marthe Ritzenbach
Director

Something niggled at Dieter as he finished reading. The letter was oddly phrased, more a personal appeal than a professional inquiry. Marthe Ritzenbach must be a very humane woman, he thought, to be so troubled by the family's disquiet about this young man they had housed. But why had Irma not been more forthcoming? Surely there would be no harm in letting the Gravensteins know more about the young man.

He remembered now that a group of immigrant students from Freitang had gone to America the summer before. Had one of them stayed on for some reason? Why? And why had it been allowed? It seemed very odd, and when he heard the door opening downstairs and realised Irma had come home, he thought he would ask her about the letter. But he immediately thought better of it, envisaging her outrage that he had been 'snooping', and quickly put the letter back where he had found it, caught between the desk and the filing cabinet. When Irma came upstairs he was back in their bedroom, changing his clothes before they went downstairs to make supper.

12

THE DELPHINE WAS A small hotel on a quiet side street off Wilhelmstrasse in the arty Kreuzberg part of town. It boasted three stars, which indicated that its rooms were clean if slightly threadbare, and each had its own 'en suite' bathroom – though in this case the term meant a tiny space just large enough to accommodate a shower, a wash basin and a lavatory on which it was impossible for anyone of average height to sit without banging their knees on the shower. Other than two small towels, some neatly wrapped little bars of soap and a small plastic kettle with tea bags, UHT milk and sugar in paper tubes, the room lacked any amenities.

The place seemed just about right for Liz Ryder, the cover Liz Carlyle was using for her visit to Berlin to meet Mischa, just as she had done on the trip to Tallinn. Her mother had recently died, so Liz Ryder was now free to spend some time travelling, seeing parts of Europe that she had not visited. She was the sort of woman who went on cultural tours and city breaks, and who would not have considered splashing out on luxury hotels. The Delphine would therefore do nicely, thought her alter ego Liz Carlyle.

At least the bed was comfortable; Liz kicked off her shoes and lay down on the bedspread. Should she be out getting to know Berlin, she wondered sleepily. I'm sure that's what Liz Ryder would be doing. 'A city renowned these days for its vibrant artistic life and trendsetting culture,' she murmured to herself, quoting the guidebook, but she was tired after the journey and the flight (which had been delayed) and soon fell asleep.

She was woken by her phone ringing. 'Hello,' she said cautiously.

'Is that Liz Ryder?'

'It is.'

'It's Sally – Sally Mortimer. Mr Arbuthnot told me you were visiting. Would you like to meet for a coffee or a drink?'

'That would be very nice,' said Liz, recognising the name of her contact from the MI6 Station at the Embassy.

'Great,' said Sally. 'There's a little wine bar just round the corner from your hotel, on the Stresemannstrasse. It's called Oskar's. Shall we meet there in an hour?'

'Perfect. See you there,' said Liz, smiling to herself at the name of Arbuthnot. No plain Mr Smith or Brown for Geoffrey Fane.

Liz took a shower in her tiny bathroom, reflecting on how invigorating it was to be out in the field again after so much time spent recently behind her desk. She still had moments of sadness and loneliness when she thought about Martin Seurat, her much-loved partner who had been tragically killed in Paris nearly two years ago, but for the most part she was quite happy being on her own. She wasn't sure how long she would feel that way though, and for the first time since Martin's death she had considered agreeing to what she supposed was a 'date' with a most unpolicemanlike Chief Constable. She'd met him in Manchester when they had worked together on a counter-terrorist operation where, she reflected, he had probably saved her life. Recently he had moved to Suffolk, and had left a message on her answer phone suggesting they meet up sometime. She realised guiltily that had been over a month ago and she hadn't called him back.

As she dried herself on the inadequate towels she remembered that she had neglected to tell her very-much-alive mother that she was going away. Still, if all went to plan, Liz would be back in her Pimlico flat the following evening. She would ring her mother then.

Forty-five minutes later, Liz left the hotel with the stirrings of the excitement she always felt when she was working undercover on an operation. She knew it would only take her a few minutes to get to Oskar's so she walked slowly. It was early evening but some of the shops were still open, with a few late customers around. Liz window-shopped apparently aimlessly, though a close observer would have noted how she lingered at the fronts with large curved windows, and a professional observer might have concluded that she was using the windows to keep an eye on what was going on behind her. She seemed to conclude that nothing was amiss, for she turned with no hesitation into Strese-mannstrasse. There she walked past Oskar's without so much as a glance, but when she reached the corner she crossed the road and doubled back and went straight into the wine bar.

Oskar's wasn't crowded, as by now it was getting late for after-work drinks yet early for dinner. Liz recognised Sally Mortimer right away from the photo she'd seen. She walked over to the corner where the young woman was sitting, reading a newspaper with a glass of white wine on the small round table in front of her.

'Welcome to Berlin,' said Sally warmly, as Liz sat down.

'Thanks,' said Liz. 'It's nice to see you again.' A young waiter wearing a bright red bow tie came up, an apron round his waist. Liz ordered a glass of the house white, then looked at Sally, whom she had actually never met before. She was several years younger than Liz – roughly Peggy's age, Liz guessed. She had straight blonde hair that just reached her shoulders. In her smart black leather jacket, blouse and black trousers, she could have been any of the young women who worked in the offices and banks around the area. She was attractive but undramatically so, with blue eyes and a small nose that turned slightly upwards at its tip. No doubt she spoke fluent German or she wouldn't be one of the MI6 Station in Berlin.

'How long have you been here?' asked Liz, speaking freely now no one was within earshot.

'Six months.'

'Where were you before this?'

'Oh, just London,' said Sally.

The waiter came with Liz's wine, and she took a sip while they both waited for him to retreat again. Sally said, 'This is my first foreign posting. I've only been in the Service three years. I joined straight from university.'

Liz nodded. Modest, she thought, and honest. She remembered the young Bruno Mackay whom she'd first met when they had both been in their different Services for only a few years. In those days he had dressed to look like James Bond at the Ambassador's cocktail party, and he would have had you believe that he knew everything there was to know.

The conversation drifted on for a while and Liz learned that Sally had grown up near Guildford, played serious netball and had read Economics at Durham. She was bilingual in German and English because her mother was German and they had spent most holidays in Germany. 'That was why the Service accepted me, I'm sure. I am also fluent in Polish because my grandparents came from there,' explained Sally.

Goodness, thought Liz. MI6 must have thought she was a real catch. 'Is Berlin a good posting?' she asked.

Sally nodded. 'There's always something going on here. I mean, the Cold War may be over but this place is a real hub for spies – a bit like Vienna must have been after the War.'

'I know. There's a lot of it about,' said Liz wryly. She took another sip of her wine and hitched herself up in her seat; it seemed time to get down to business. 'About tomorrow.'

'Yes. As I understand it, your meet is in the Botanic Gardens. In the little café there.'

Liz nodded. 'Yes, but I don't want anyone else around. No minders. I don't want the target scared off. He may be nervous already.'

Sally said nothing for a moment, looking down at the table. Then she lifted her head, looked straight at Liz and said, 'There are some worries about security.'

'Really? What worries?' asked Liz.

'About *your* security.' Liz was about to respond but before she could say anything Sally went on, 'As I said, this place is a hotbed. The Russians have a huge presence here, including a large security team. They keep a sharp eye on each other. I've read the background to your operation and, as I understand it, it's not unlikely that your contact may be under investigation. The Russians are sure to be trying to find out how you got on to their Illegals operation in London and we don't know how far they've got with that.

'Your man may be under surveillance while he's here; we just don't know. So our instructions are to make sure that you are not walking into a set-up. After all, we haven't told the Germans you are here – or why. We can't rely on their help if things go wrong.' Sally paused, looking slightly uncomfortable.

Liz was taken aback. This modest-seeming young woman had turned out to be rather more formidable than she looked. 'Whose instructions are these?'

Sally looked at her as if this should have been obvious. 'Mr Arbuthnot, of course. He discussed it with my Head of Station.'

Fane – bloody Geoffrey Fane, thought Liz. He can't keep his fingers out of anything. But as she thought about it, she had to admit that there was a lot of sense in what Sally had been saying. It was true that Mischa might be under suspicion. He might even be under control and have been ordered to call this meeting so that his masters could create an embarrassing situation or, even worse, do Liz harm. The more she thought about it, the more she saw the sense in having some backup.

She looked at Sally who had been watching her closely, waiting to see how she would react. 'OK,' she said. 'I can see that. It makes sense.'

Sally let out a long breath, then smiled broadly. 'Oh good. They told me not to tell you about, and just do it. But I said I couldn't possibly. I thought it was dishonest and I wouldn't like it to be done to me. They said it would be my fault if you hit the roof. I'm so glad they were wrong.'

Well, well, thought Liz. Good for Sally. She said with a smile, 'If you ever want a job on my side of the river, just let me know. Now, what are you proposing?'

'We'll put a team out to look for any sign of surveillance on him when he arrives. We'll alert you by phone if that happens and you should abort and go straight back to the hotel and wait for me. If, on the other hand, all's clear and the meet goes ahead, then we'll be close by in case they intend to disrupt your rendezvous once it's begun. If there's any sign of that, we will intervene to let you get away – grab a taxi and go straight to the airport and catch the next plane to London. Is that OK?'

'Are you sure that's all necessary? If he sees you, he'll be the one to abort, and then we've lost the only source we've got on these FSB Illegals operations.'

'He won't see us,' said Sally confidently. 'We're very good. We have to be,' she added. 'It's tough working here.'

Liz looked sceptical, and Sally said, 'All we have to do is make sure you're safe. The hard part is up to you. Mr Arbuthnot said he didn't care if anything happened to your Mystery Man; he didn't care if he was arrested by the German BPOL or hauled in by the BND or assassinated by the FSB.' She laughed at the torrent of acronyms, but then her expression sobered. 'But he did say that if as much as one hair on your head was ruffled, my next posting wouldn't be London, but Outer Mongolia.'

Sally drained her glass of wine and Liz laughed. She liked this girl; she reminded her of Peggy. 'It's a deal,' she said, 'and I'll hold you to it. But there's one condition.'

'Oh?' asked Sally nervously.

'You can't tell "Mr Arbuthnot" that I caved in so quickly.' As she saw a look of relief spread across Sally's face, she raised a hand and motioned to the waiter. 'Let's have another glass of wine,' Liz said, uncertain whether she was more irritated or flattered that her personal safety seemed to be so important to Geoffrey Fane.

13

LIZ WOKE EARLY. AFTER her conversation with Sally the previous evening she was now feeling more nervous about the meeting with Mischa than she had before. She'd thought of Germany as a very safe place – comfortably Western European and friendly; a place where Mischa was the only one with anything to worry about. But after hearing Sally comparing Berlin to post-war Vienna and talking about abort plans, Liz knew she had better take the preparations for her meeting a lot more seriously.

She breakfasted in the hotel's small dining room, busy even at this early hour with couples and small family groups loudly chatting in various languages and planning their day. Liz had already worked out her route to the gardens, and since Peggy had researched the tram times and the location of taxi ranks, Liz knew exactly how long it would take her, so she took out her guidebook and studied it like the well-organised tourist Liz Ryder would be. After breakfast she paid her bill and left her bag to be collected later. If any of Sally's worst fears happened and she couldn't get back to the hotel, there was nothing in the small suitcase that Liz Ryder would not have owned.

At nine o'clock she left the hotel and walked to the Anhalter Bahnhof, where she caught a tram that took her halfway towards her destination. Getting off at the northern edges of the Friedenau district, she waited at a tram stop in a small queue of smartly dressed young people who looked as if they were going to work, though it seemed quite late for that. She abruptly pulled out her mobile phone, looked at the screen and, as though she had received a message, crossed the street to a taxi rank opposite the tram stop and climbed into the first cab in the line. As it pulled away, she glanced back and was glad to see the next taxi still parked and waiting.

It was a considerable drive to the south-west fringes of the city and though she tried to follow the route on the map on her phone she found it impossible to keep up with all the twists and turns. Once she spotted a stretch of the wall that had divided the city between the two opposing ideologies of the Cold War, though now it looked more like the graffiti-adorned walls the Eurostar passed outside Brussels than the frightening barrier it had once been. Although there was no wall nowadays, if Sally was right, East and West were still using Berlin as a jousting ground.

As directed by Peggy, she had asked the driver for an address several streets north of the Botanic Gardens. She got out and made a play of dropping her handbag and picking it up slowly while the driver drove off; then she walked through quiet suburban streets, passed by just a few cars and pedestrians. She was relieved to see no sign of Sally or her colleagues or indeed of anyone at all taking any interest in her. She walked on, circumventing the grounds, until she came to the southern entrance on Unter den Eichen. The gates were just opening to the public, and she joined a small group – a few middle-aged people, what seemed to be a class of young children with a couple of teachers, and a handful of older students with notebooks who got out of a small bus, talking earnestly. Liz wondered about them, but then it was her turn at the cash desk, so she paid her six euros for a day ticket and went in.

She meandered along a path through the arboretum, past what seemed acres of roses growing underneath tall trees. From time to time she examined the pamphlet about the gardens she'd been given along with her ticket, trying to look like her mother, who ran a nursery garden in Wiltshire and knew all about plants, and not like Liz Carlyle, whose interest in them was non-existent.

When she reached the glasshouses at the east end of the gardens she headed for the largest, the Grand Pavilion. It was an immense Art Nouveau-style building, an intricate cobweb of thin steel and glass panes. As she went in she was struck by a wall of heat and humidity that had her perspiring in seconds. A man in a green uniform was spraying the plants with a fine mist of water but otherwise there appeared to be no one around.

She sat down on a wrought-iron bench under an over-hanging palm tree at the end of a row of tropical plants. Someone had left on the seat a copy of the same leaflet she had been given at the gate. As she sat down she casually swapped it for her own. She examined the new brochure and saw a circle drawn around the little picture of the café. This was the 'All clear' signal from Sally – the only actual intervention she had agreed.

Five minutes later, Liz was inside the café, sipping a large black coffee at a table just by the door. Several tables were occupied. An elderly couple was chatting to the waitress, whom they clearly knew well. Liz put them down as regular customers and no threat to her or Mischa. She wasn't quite so sure about the four young people on the other side of the room. They were talking animatedly in German about some papers they had spread out on the table. She thought they all looked remarkably fit for students and hoped that if they were not what they seemed to be, then they were Sally's colleagues.

As she was speculating about a couple of young American women at another table, the door opened and Mischa walked in. He went straight across to the counter and gave his order to the waitress. Liz watched how his eyes took in the room as he saw her and came and sat down at her table.

'All clear?' he asked tersely. With his cord trousers and blue wool jersey, shirt collar visible at the neck below a two-day stubble, Mischa could have passed for a university lecturer. Though there was nothing reflective or thoughtful in his dark, restless eyes.

'Seems to be,' Liz replied, keeping her voice down.

'There was a car by the entrance when I came in – with a woman, a blonde, and a man. They were kissing, which seemed remarkable so early in the day.' He shrugged. 'But who knows? And they didn't follow me into the gardens; I made sure of that.'

That better not be Sally, thought Liz. 'So how are you?' she asked quickly, steering him away from the idea of surveillance.

'I am glad you could make it here. I leave in another couple of days. I needed to see you again.' Liz nodded and waited for him to go on. 'I am going back to Moscow. Meeting there would be very difficult.'

Yes, thought Liz. I certainly wouldn't want to be doing this in Moscow.

The café was filling up now, with elderly couples, young women with pushchairs and babies in prams. 'OK,' she said slowly, 'here I am. So, why did you want to see me – how I can help?'

'First of all, you should know the consequences of what happened in Britain.'

'You mean the Russian Illegals we exposed there?'

Mischa nodded. 'Yes. You sent them back to Russia, which was a big mistake.'

Liz happened to share his view, but she was certainly not going to criticise her own government to this Russian. The Foreign Office had been immovable in their opposition to putting the two Russians on trial, fearful of the damage to relations with Russia and the possibility that two British citizens would be put on trial in Moscow as a tit for tat. 'There were reasons for that,' she said.

Mischa shook his head in disgust. 'Not good ones.' He brought out a cigarette lighter from a pocket in his trousers and fingered it absentmindedly. 'You see, the couple you sent back were questioned thoroughly by their superiors in the FSB. What is that phrase – no stone was left untouched?'

'Something like that,' said Liz equably, not wanting to provoke him. He sounded on edge, and she remembered him from their previous meeting as nervy and irascible. As she was waiting for him to go on, the door of the café opened with unusual force and two uniformed police officers marched in.

Liz felt an icy wave wash up from her stomach to her head. She stiffened, clutching her bag. Thoughts flashed through her head: was this the disruption Sally had talked about? No one had bleeped her phone to warn her. Should she get out fast and leave the country?

The policemen had walked up to the counter, spoken a few words to the waitress and now turned to face the room.

She looked at Mischa. He was rigid; sitting very straight in his chair, motionless, the fingers clutching his lighter white and bloodless.

The room had gone silent. One of the policemen spoke, but Liz's German wasn't good enough for her to understand what he was saying. She watched Mischa and saw him relax his hold on the lighter. His face returned to normal and he looked at her with a small smile. The policeman stopped speaking and a babble of sound broke out in the café as the two men walked back to the door and left.

'What was that about?'

'It's OK. One of the children from a school group is missing, probably wandered off. They're asking everyone to look out for her.'

Liz let out the breath she seemed to have been holding for hours and said, 'I'd like another cup of coffee.' As she turned to wave at the waitress she noticed that the little group of students was no longer there. She felt increasingly uneasy but resisted the impulse to leave – at least until she had heard what Mischa had to say.

She turned back to him. 'You were saying that it was a mistake for us to send those two Illegals back.'

'Yes. The FSB think someone tipped you off. They think you have a source.'

Liz was tempted to point out that once the Illegals started meddling with members of British intelligence, as they had done, there was a fair chance they were going to get found out. Even without the information Mischa had given her. But she said nothing.

The waitress put their coffee on the table. Mischa blew on his and took a sip. Putting down his cup he said, 'Because of this suspicion, a full-scale inquiry has been launched.'

'Into how we got on to the Illegals?'

'Exactly. The FSB has decided someone inside its organisation – or with access to its information – told you about the operation in the UK.'

'Do they suspect anyone in particular?'

'Ha.' Mischa's laugh was bitter. 'You must not know the FSB. They suspect *everyone*. This means my brother and all his colleagues. And it means me, because of my position in the military and the fact that I travel abroad.' He waved a hand dismissively. 'If I sold automobiles for a living, they would leave me alone – though they'd still wonder about my brother.'

'I can see that's very worrying,' Liz said. 'But there's no reason to think they'll get any proof of anything. We've both been very careful.' She wondered if this was all Mischa wanted to tell her. She hoped not; she'd wasted her time if all he wanted to say was that he was scared of the FSB.

He looked at her angrily. 'It is much more than worrying. There will be no mercy if they discover my involvement. And none for my brother – even though he doesn't know I've been talking to you and the Americans. They would never believe him. Mother Russia is quite happy to execute those sons she believes have betrayed her.'

Liz nodded sympathetically. Mischa looked at her and continued, 'There have been some developments.'

At last, thought Liz. 'Oh?' she asked mildly.

'Yes, but first I need to know how you can help me.' Liz was thinking how best to reply when he held up his hand. 'I am not talking simply about money. I need to know that if they decide it is my brother who has been talking – or me – you will rescue us.'

Liz had heard this sort of appeal before from agents who were beginning to realise the increasing danger of their position. She had no ready-made escape plan up her sleeve for extracting from Moscow one or possibly two people under suspicion. It would be a very difficult, if not impossible operation. In any case, she wanted to keep Mischa in place so he could continue to provide information.

She also needed to weigh up how much interest there would be in Mischa as a defector. What would the Americans pay towards the costs; how much interest would there be from British defence intelligence? Not to mention the added complication that Bruno Mackay was off to Moscow with the intention of trying to recruit Mischa's brother; going, in his own words, straight to the horse's mouth.

Given all that, it was vital that Mischa remained well disposed to the British. His brother would almost certainly tell Mischa about any approach Bruno made, so it was important that Mischa confirm that the British were reliable.

She said carefully, 'I don't believe they would have allowed you to come here if you were seriously under suspicion. But we need a way of keeping in touch. For the moment you should continue to communicate with me via the address you have, as you did this time. But you need to let me know if there's a way I can safely get a message to you. I will consult colleagues about some faster means of communicating securely. If the inquiry starts closing in on you or your brother, then you must tell us. Meanwhile, keep your head down. We will work on a plan for if the worst comes to the worst.' She hoped this was sufficiently reassuring, though she had committed to very little.

It seemed to work. 'You're good at getting people out,' said Mischa with a small smile. 'I've heard about Gordievsky.'

Gordievsky had been the KGB Head of Station designate in London in the 1980s – and a British agent. When he fell under suspicion he was successfully exfiltrated from Russia by MI6 in the boot of a car.

Mischa said, 'His escape is still talked about.' He smiled again, adding, 'Though not by senior officials.'

'I bet,' said Liz. 'So, you know then that we look after our sources. But these things are not easy and need a lot of planning.'

'We would also need to know that we would be looked after once we arrived in your country.'

'That's a two-way process,' said Liz carefully, beginning to feel that too much was being asked and nothing given.

Mischa leaned back in his chair and looked up at the ceiling. When he brought his eyes down to the room, he kept them averted from Liz, as if slightly embarrassed by what he was about to say. 'I am sorry but that is not quite enough. I would like to feel you will be as generous as the Americans have been.'

'If you are talking about payment now, then I can confirm that while you remain in Moscow you will continue to get the same retainer, whether it comes from us or the Americans.' She was growing angry now at his avarice, and was keen to put an end to the bargaining. 'Provided,' she continued, 'that you are still useful to us.'

Mischa had picked up on her irritation and seemed to realise that he had got all he was going to get for the moment. Just then the door of the café swung open and a couple came in. Mischa looked at them, then looked away. 'The couple from the car,' he said through clenched teeth. When Liz glanced their way, she was relieved to see that the woman was definitely not Sally. The couple stood for a minute, talking to each other in German and looking at a menu the waitress brought to them before seeming to change their minds and leaving.

Mischa was looking nervous now. He spoke quickly, keeping his voice low. 'Very well. I will trust you and your colleagues, and yes, I have some further information. You will remember that I told you that the FSB were infiltrating Illegals with the aim of destabilising countries they regard as threats.'

'I do,' said Liz, hoping he would calm down. His agitation now was obvious.

'The American operation is over.'

'Over? Was it successful?'

'That I don't know. But you remember I told you the operation was on hold because the Illegal was ill. Now that's over.'

'Has the Illegal been replaced?'

'That's all I know,' he said.

Liz's disappointment must have shown in her face because he went on, 'There is more. You uncovered those two in the UK, as we know. But I think you did not discover all that they had been doing.'

'Really?' Liz was trying not to show her surprise. 'We investigated their activities thoroughly before we sent them packing.'

'There was something else,' said Mischa emphatically. His eyes were roving around the room now, full of fear and distrust. 'I don't know exactly; my brother hasn't told me. But I know the FSB is crowing because part of their operation is still in play – just without a local controller.'

'Please try and find out more. If you do, I think I can guarantee a bonus,' said Liz.

'I will try,' said Mischa. His anxiety was escalating.

'Anything else?' she asked.

'There is one more thing. When I told my brother I was coming to Berlin for three weeks, he was very amused. "Why Germany?" he asked.'

Why indeed? thought Liz. Mischa said, 'I explained I was here for three weeks' attachment to the Embassy. My real task is to form an assessment of NATO preparations if we Russians are ever to ... come west.'

'You have some sources here?' Liz asked, suddenly alert.

'Possibly,' said Mischa. 'But that is not what I have to tell you now. My brother said, "We have something going on in Germany too."'

'Did he say what or where?'

'No,' said Mischa. Liz saw his hands were starting to tremble and she decided not to press him. She sensed he was very near the edge.

But Mischa seemed to get hold of himself and re-engage with her. 'I think the German operation is connected to the one in the United States.'

'The one that is now defunct?' When Mischa looked at her, puzzled, she said, '*Kaput.*'

'Yes.' He was staring at Liz, then stood up abruptly. 'I need to go to the toilet.' He crossed the room and disappeared through a door marked WC. When he comes back, thought Liz, we'll go outside and sit on a bench in a quiet part of the garden where he can see that no one is following him.

But ten minutes later she was still sitting alone at the table, facing the fact that Mischa was not coming back.

14

T HE FOLLOWING WEEKEND IRMA was at home when Dieter Nimitz arrived from Brussels, and to his relief she seemed to be in a good mood. He went upstairs and showered and changed; when he came down, he found her in the kitchen preparing supper. She had never liked cooking and saw food as fuel rather than a source of pleasure. But though he was quite a good cook and ate well during the week in his Brussels flat, Irma didn't welcome him in the kitchen except for Saturday night, and so yet again they sat down to a bland supper of sausage, sautéed potatoes and green beans.

'How was your week?' he asked dutifully.

'Good enough,' she said, which as always discouraged further questions. He had learned not to press her – not if he didn't want to have his head bitten off. But all week he had been wondering about the letter he'd seen from the orphanage, asking about the young man who had gone on a Freitang school trip abroad and not returned. He couldn't have said exactly why he was so interested in the matter. Perhaps it was the rarity of learning anything about her work, since Irma was uncommunicative, and scrupulous about storing all her documents in a locked filing cabinet.

She said, 'Did you see the Commissioner this week?' She often asked this, as if his future depended on the Commissioner's favour, whereas it was Van der Vaart who would determine Dieter's future, and Van der Vaart who had made it crystal clear that Dieter's career was staying right where it was.

'No. He was visiting Austria – the refugee camp.'

'Any news from there?'

He shook his head. In fact, he and his colleague Matilda had been copied in on the Commissioner's email from Carinthia, reporting on what he had found. The situation was even grimmer than previously thought. The Austrian authorities seemed to be expending most of their energy on preventing more refugees from entering the country, rather than on looking after those who had already arrived.

But he didn't want to discuss this with Irma; she would have endless questions, and he was tired. What he most wanted at home was a complete break from the depressing rigours of his job, so he said nothing now about the Commissioner's report.

They had planned to go into Hamburg the next day to see a sculpture exhibit, but in the morning Irma cried off, saying she had some unexpected work from school to deal with. She insisted that he go on his own, however, and he left the house at about eleven o'clock. He walked to the train, stopping only to buy a newspaper, but at the station he found a group of people gathered outside. Two policemen stood blocking the entrance to the ticket hall.

'What's happened?' he asked a woman.

'There's been an incident,' she said. 'Someone jumped in front of a train. They've closed the station while they remove the body.' She looked at him, hesitating for a moment, then seemed to decide it was safe to add, 'It was a foreigner.'

He stood wondering what to do; it seemed unsympathetic to ask the policeman how long it would take to bring out the corpse. He supposed he could take a taxi into town instead, but it would be very expensive and Irma would complain. In any case, no cabs were waiting on the rank. He could take a bus, but that involved a bit of a walk, and he would have to change at least once on his way into Hamburg.

What a nuisance, he thought, then felt slightly guilty, remembering the poor soul who had caused this disruption to his plans. There was nothing for it, he supposed, but to go back home, where Irma would be working in her study, and he could make lunch for them both. The prospect was unenticing; no doubt she would want to ask more questions about how he'd spent his week, and when he was likely next to see the Commissioner.

He decided to have lunch out instead, and he found a café across the road, where he ate a bowl of pork and bean *Eintopf* and drank a small beer. Then he walked slowly home, wondering if Irma would allow him a brief nap that afternoon. As he turned on to his road he saw a car approach from the far end, near his house. It was a silver Mercedes saloon, travelling rather too fast for this quiet suburban street. As the car passed, Dieter stared at the man behind the wheel. He wore a jacket over a shirt and striped tie, and had a square, rugged-looking face, with an old-fashioned moustache that followed the curving contours of his upper lip. Intent on driving, he didn't even glance at Dieter.

At home as he opened the front door, Irma emerged from the back of the house. 'What are you doing here?' she demanded, as she came towards him.

He was taken aback by her tone. 'There was an accident. On the track. They cancelled the trains.'

'You might have told me,' she said, her voice rising.

'I'm sorry,' he said mildly. 'I didn't think it would make any difference. Is something wrong?'

She shook her head. 'I'm busy in the kitchen,' she said, and retreated down the corridor.

He went upstairs, but decided not to take a nap. He looked for the book he was reading, a novel by Günter Grass, but it wasn't by the bed and he couldn't find it in his little study. He went downstairs and called out to Irma in the kitchen. 'Have you seen my book? You know, the one by Günter Grass?'

'No. Isn't it upstairs?'

'I can't find it. Never mind, I'll look in the drawing room,' he said, and opened the door.

'No,' she cried out from the kitchen, but he was already in the room. It was rarely used except when they had visitors and was formally furnished, with Dresden china on a side table, two heavy armchairs with chintz covers and a deep sofa that might have dated from the days of the Kaiser. Irma had traditional taste, and this room was really hers and hers alone.

There was no sign of his book, but the room felt slightly different from usual. What was it? He sniffed – and smelled the faintest hint of cigarettes. Odd – Irma hated smoking and forbade it in the house.

He sniffed again just as she came in behind him. 'I think you will find your book upstairs,' she said sharply, and motioned him to leave the room.

He held up a hand. 'Don't I smell tobacco?' he asked.

'Not unless you have been sneaking a cigarette yourself.'

He sniffed again. The aroma was unmistakable.

She sighed. 'I know,' she said. 'It was the workmen when they painted the windows. The swine – I expressly told them to do their smoking outside.'

'Ah,' he said, nodding, though he thought – *the workmen left six weeks ago*. But he said nothing.

Later, after supper, as he swept the leftovers from their plates into the pedal bin, he saw something glinting. He reached down and found himself holding the stub of a dark brown cigarette with a gold filter tip. A special cigarette – a Sobranie, in fact, the sort he remembered the man in the Homburg hat smoking so many years before, one after another. For a brief second, he wondered if that man had been in his house, but he realised that was impossible – that man would have died years ago. But who had smoked it then, and what had they been doing here? And why had Irma lied to him?

He was the one used to hiding behind countless untruths: how many glasses of wine he'd had at lunch, who his friends were in Brussels – he made sure to mention Matilda only rarely – even the occasions when he had taken a taxi rather than public transport, and of course the big untruth, the secret he had told nobody, the secret of his real identity.

The nature of his relationship with Irma meant that he was the one who hid things, half out of fear of his wife's tongue, half from a need for some fragment of independence. The very concept of Irma lying to him was entirely novel. He felt he had lurched on to disturbing new ground and he did not know what it might mean.

15

M ATILDA BURNSIDE STOOD AT one corner of the Grand Place, ignoring the appraising glances of passing men as she waited for her husband Peter, who as usual was several minutes late. She was a tall woman with shoulder-length chestnut hair and the sort of strong features that are often called handsome but in her case verged on the beautiful.

She had been in Brussels for two years, working in the Migration department of the European Commission, and had been married for one. Her husband Peter was in the Foreign Office – or at least that's what he told people – and was based in the British Embassy, as Counsellor Economic, a job title that gave away nothing at all about his true responsibilities.

Matilda was a Home Counties girl who had discovered a flair for languages at school, and had studied French and Spanish at university, where despite an active social life and a passion for the cinema she had managed a stunning First Class Honours degree and promptly been snapped up by a multinational bank. The pay had been high, the prospects mouthwateringly attractive, but life in the City of London had proved repetitive and dull, and after eighteen months she had jumped at an offer of a position with the European Commission working on the problem of refugees and migrants arriving in unprecedented numbers from North Africa and the Middle East.

The money wasn't bad, though it didn't compare with the bank's offer when it tried to keep her, and the bureaucracy was stifling, but at least her days were spent trying to help people who needed help, rather than padding the already comfortable coffers of the wealthy. And lest she sounded too pious about the merits of her new posting, it had also provided her with a husband – a tall, intelligent and, yes, slightly dashing kind of husband – though one who was always late, she thought with a flicker of annoyance. It was raining slightly and the lights were just coming on in the square. From where she stood just under the arcade in front of the Palais du Roi she could see their reflection sparkling in the wet cobbles. It was beautiful, which certainly could not be said of much of modern Brussels, particularly not of the buildings in the area where she worked.

Her colleagues liked to joke that the B in Brussels stood for 'boring'. But if anything, Matilda Burnside thought it should be for *bouffe* – as in 'nosh' or 'grub'. Never had she eaten so well or so much; her husband, Peter, said the food here was better than in France. There were restaurants everywhere and when they met after work in the Grand Place, as they did at least once a week, without walking more than a few steps they could take their pick from haute cuisine in a restaurant with Michelin rosettes to pizza in a bar.

But tonight she fancied nothing more complicated than *moules frites* eaten at a long wooden table in the cellar bistro of one of the old buildings in the square.

Her mind these days was flooded by images of the refugee camps in Syria and Libya, and increasingly in Italy as well – though at least on the European mainland the refugees were fed. What haunted her most were the children, shrunk like African famine victims, trapped in the Middle East and North Africa, beyond reach of anything she could do, vulnerable to the worst of humanity – the traffickers, the rapists, the killers. And hungry, hungry all the time. Increasingly, Matilda found herself feeling quite ill at the prospect of another splendid meal.

She'd shared this feeling with Dieter Nimitz, her colleague at work; it was unusual for her to share her feelings with him – it was almost always the other way round, especially when he was battling with their department head, the dour Dutchman Van der Vaart. Sometimes, despite being twenty years younger, she felt like an older sister to him. He often seemed stressed, as he had done this week – so much so that today she finally asked him what was wrong. He had started to say it was nothing, then he'd changed his mind and said, 'It's Irma,' in a voice that was barely more than a whisper.

Matilda knew very little about his wife. Dieter might tell her every detail of Van der Vaart's latest stupidities, and moan at length when Accounts questioned his expenses, but he very rarely talked about his home life. Matilda knew that though married, he was childless, and that he went back home most weekends and seemed very proud of his wife, who was the headmistress of a school in Hamburg. But she knew little else, so what he had then said about her was unprecedented – and also rather strange. His wife's school had seemingly lost one of its pupils – or at the very least allowed one of them to stay behind after a sponsored visit to America.

78

That in itself seemed mildly peculiar, but Dieter's account of his wife's mysterious visitor last weekend was also odd. At first, Matilda thought silently that his wife was simply having an affair – not too unlikely given that she was on her own all week. But the photos she'd seen on Dieter's desk of Frau Nimitz did not suggest a woman given to philandering; nor, to be blunt, a woman likely to receive approaches. What was odd was that Dieter didn't seem at all concerned about his wife's possible infidelity but rather, for reasons she couldn't understand, he was worried that the visitor had something to do with the missing student.

She'd decided to tell Peter about it. He would know if she was making a mountain out of a molehill; he was always very good at that. And there he was, she thought, seeing the tall figure walking briskly across the square, holding a large, striped golf umbrella. As he tipped it back slightly and saw her, he grinned broadly and she forgot her irritation at his lateness.

'Hello hello,' he said and kissed her on the cheek. 'What a horrible evening. Let's go somewhere warm. Do you know, I really fancy a nice plate of *moules frites*.'

'You must be a mind-reader! That's just what I want.'

'Come on then,' he said, grabbing her hand.

She laughed, and they set off at a trot, sending a pigeon that was pecking at something beside their feet off with a wild beating of wings.

When they were sitting at a table in the cosy restaurant with bowls of steaming *moules* and a large plate of *frites* in front of them, he asked, 'How's our German friend?' Peter had never met Dieter Nimitz, but he liked to hear about his contretemps with Van der Vaart, and also delighted in Dieter's many sayings, expressed in excellent but idiosyncratic English, which were often unwittingly funny.

'He has what I believe are called domestic difficulties.'

'Oh no,' said Peter in mock-alarm. 'You'd better not be the shoulder he wants to cry on.'

'Don't be an idiot,' she said with a smile. 'It's not like that. He rarely mentions his wife, so this was quite unusual. She's very successful – the headmistress of a school in Hamburg. But he thinks she's been behaving strangely.'

'How so?'

She explained about the letter Dieter had found. Peter said, 'There could be all sorts of explanations, you know. All of them perfectly innocent.'

'I know. But that wasn't all. She had a meeting with someone in the house when Dieter had gone out. But he came back early and she tried to conceal the traces. He's pretty sure it was a man he saw driving away when he came back to the house.'

'Ah, so maybe she's the one leaning on an extra-marital shoulder?'

'I don't think so; at any rate, it isn't what Dieter is worried about. He seemed to think it might have some connection with her work – and with the letter he found.'

'Why?'

'He couldn't say why exactly. He made some reference to the Russians.' She noticed she had all of Peter's attention now. 'But when I pressed him, he just mumbled something about a cigarette.'

'And that's all he said?'

'Yes. I suggested he try and find out more about this missing student from the school. It didn't sound right to me.'

'Good thinking,' said Peter. Though his voice retained its lightness there was a professional crispness to it as well. 'Now tell me some more about Dieter's wife.'

16

AUTUMN WAS COMING TO New England, and even on this sunny afternoon there was a slight edge to the air. It was still too early for the annual fireworks display of the region's maple trees – with their palette of vivid scarlet and gold – that drew visitors from all over the world, but the advantage for Harry Fitzpatrick was that he didn't have to wait in a queue at Burlington airport's car-hire desk, and there was virtually no traffic as he drove to the university for a second time.

He was following up a request from the FBI office in the London Embassy that had originated from MI5. They'd learned that a young immigrant living in Germany, who had been on a school educational visit to an American university, had not returned to Germany with the other students. For some reason, they seemed to think there was something sinister in his disappearance. It seemed that some bright spark in MI5 had read Harry's report of his enquiries at the university following the death of the man called Petersen, the man suspected of having been a Russian Illegal. They had noted what Harry had learned, that Petersen taught on a summer course for visiting foreign schoolchildren. Now they were wondering if the course the missing student had been on might possibly have been the course in Vermont. It all seemed a very long shot to Harry but he was secretly rather flattered that his initial report had aroused such interest and so he was happy to do as he was asked and try to find out more.

He had started by ringing the head of Petersen's department from his office in FBI HQ in Washington, but had found him impossible to reach – thanks to a Cerberus-like secretary, a dry old stick from the sound of her voice, who on three separate occasions was adamant that the professor was too busy to speak to him. The fourth time he rang, Cerberus announced that the professor had left on a recruiting trip to the West Coast, and had asked Angie Emerson, the woman Harry had met previously, to deal with him. Emerson was also away, at a conference in Cleveland, but due back on Tuesday. Taking no chances on further delays, Fitzpatrick had made an appointment to see Emerson on Tuesday and booked a flight to Burlington.

This time, Angie Emerson was more smartly dressed than on their previous encounter – in neat black trousers and shiny black loafers, though her hair was still precariously secured in a fragile bun with wisps poking out. She got up from her desk to shake Harry's hand, then motioned him to sit down. She said, 'I'm sorry the boss isn't here.'

'Well, I have to say he didn't seem very eager to see me.' He explained about the rebuffed phone calls.

Angie Emerson looked slightly embarrassed. 'Miss Thurston – that's his secretary – can be a bit off-putting. And I'm not surprised the prof didn't want to see you. He's strongly socialist. I think he was a communist in his younger days. He's probably allergic to the FBI; he may have thought you wanted to see him about that.'

'Well, he'd have been wrong. Hoover's been dead a long time. This is a follow-up to what we were talking about when we met last time. So I'm glad to be talking to you again rather than having to explain it all to him. If you remember, when I called on you, you told me that sometimes high-school students came here to take IT courses during the summer vacation.'

'That's right. It's a good use of the facilities, since otherwise they'd just sit unused for three months of the year. And, frankly, for some of us it's a much-needed supplement to our salaries. You don't become an academic to get rich,' she said with a grin.

'And some of these students come from abroad?'

'Absolutely. They're not the majority, but there's always a group from overseas. This year they were from a high school in Germany – I'm pretty sure it was Hamburg. Though they weren't German-born – refugees from the Middle East. Syrian mainly.'

'So they all went back to Hamburg?'

'That's right. They flew from JFK so they could have a couple of days to see the sights in New York.'

'Did any of them stay on?'

Angie looked puzzled. 'How do you mean?'

'You know, stay on for further studies, enrol as students in the university.'

'No, they're too young – only sixteen, maybe seventeen. They'd have had to apply for next year, not this one. Presumably they would have to get visas, leave to remain, something.'

'So no one connected with the summer course stayed on?'

Angie shook her head. 'No one stayed as a student here.'

He hadn't flown up here to leave stones unturned, so he persisted. 'Or stayed to do anything else?'

She began to shake her head again, then stopped. 'Well, no one,' she conceded, 'unless you mean Aziz. But he's not a student: he works in IT. He's the assistant to the division's tech head. He was a bit older than the others. He's probably twenty now.'

'Where can I find him?'

It proved easier to learn about Aziz than to locate him. His office was on the top floor of an adjacent building and easy to miss. By the time Harry Fitzpatrick found it and knocked on the door he was almost breathless, having gone up and down the stairs several times in his search.

To his relief, a voice called out from inside, 'Enter please,' in accented English. He pushed open the door, which just missed colliding with the chair on which a youth was sitting, his back to the door, in front of an oversized Apple monitor. The room was tiny.

The young man turned to face Harry and smiled shyly. Even sitting, he looked small, quite frail, with short black hair and thick glasses. He wore a sweater over a white shirt with a frayed and crumpled collar. 'Professor Galloway? I'm sorry you've been having problems with your machine. Did you bring it with you?'

Harry shook his head. 'No,' he said. 'But that's because I'm not Professor Galloway.'

Aziz looked surprised. Harry said, 'I'm from the Federal Bureau of Investigation – the FBI.' He took his badge from the side pocket of his suit jacket and flipped it open. 'My name's Fitzpatrick and you, I take it, are Aziz.'

'That's right,' the youth said, attempting a smile.

'OK, Aziz. I'd like to ask you some questions. That all right with you?'

For a moment, Fitzpatrick thought Aziz might actually say no. So obvious was his agitation that if the path to the door hadn't been blocked, Harry thought he might have made a run for it. Aziz put both hands on the desk and clasped them tensely. 'OK,' he said, as if sentence had already been passed.

Over the next twenty minutes the story that emerged was harrowing, though it grew vaguer and less dramatic the closer it came to Vermont. Aziz had been among the first refugees from the civil war in Syria; he fled with his parents and siblings after their village had been among the recipients of an Assad-ordered air strike. On the coast, Aziz's father paid with the last of their savings for the family to join a fishing boat that would take them across the Mediterranean. When the time came, there was only room for one of them in the packed craft; as the eldest boy, Aziz was delegated by his father to take the sole place – the family would follow in another small boat due to arrive the following day.

The journey took two fraught days. It rained throughout and the boat leaked; the soaked passengers were forced continuously to bail the accumulating water. Then a squall blew up in the pitch black and the boat was thrown about like a toy on a spring. For the second time in his life, Aziz had been afraid he would die, and this seemed confirmed when the boat collided in the dark with something hard and immoveable. But it was the beach on Lesbos. Aziz had survived.

He waited the next day for the rest of his family to arrive in the second boat. Waited and waited and waited some more. It took three days for the news to arrive: the boat had set sail as planned, but sank in the tail-end of the squall that Aziz's own transport had barely survived. There were no survivors.

For a month he had lived in a refugee camp on the island, then he'd been moved to another larger camp on the mainland. Aziz was consumed by grief and confusion over what now awaited him. No one suggested he or any of his fellow immigrants were welcome in Greece; instead, local members of Golden Dawn harassed the inmates of the camp continuously, and one afternoon Aziz saw a fellow Syrian beaten to death by the Greek fascists. It was then that he decided to escape from the camp and take his chances.

After that, his account grew hazy – Harry Fitzpatrick gathered that the boy had worked his way north, then crossed the German border illegally. He had been passed around various German agencies until he landed up at an orphanage on the edge of Hamburg, a world away from the small Syrian village where his life had begun.

Here Aziz had a stroke of luck. A staff member at the orphanage who spoke Arabic and English had befriended him and lent him a computer and they had talked about his interests and ambitions. This man had found him a place at a school that specialised in teaching refugee children who had a special talent for IT. In response to a question from Harry, Aziz said it was called the Freitang school.

Aziz told Fitzpatrick with obvious pride how he had come top of his year in coding HTML. He was hoping to go to university, and after graduating from the school had spent the previous year studying to get his German to a sufficient standard, while working as an assistant at the school.

By now Harry Fitzpatrick's investigative antennae were alive and alert. 'Why were you included in the group of students who came here last summer?'

Aziz replied, 'I have always wanted to see America.'

'Yes, but it couldn't have been your decision. You weren't paying, after all. So why send someone older, someone who'd already graduated?'

Aziz shrugged. 'The headmistress asked me if I'd like to go. I said, "You bet."'

Harry tried not to smile. It was hard not to like the boy, especially when you considered what he'd been through. 'So did you enjoy the course here?'

'Well,' he said hesitantly, and Harry Fitzpatrick saw that his nervousness, which had subsided while he told the story of his flight from Syria, had now returned. 'I already knew much of the curriculum.'

'Really? So you came all this way only to find you knew what they were teaching already? Bit of a waste of time then, for you and the university.'

'No,' Aziz said sharply, stung by this. 'I was given special tuition.'

'I see. Who with?'

'Professor Petersen.'

Bingo, thought Fitzpatrick, now persuaded he'd been right to come in person. He would not have found this out over the phone. 'I've heard of him,' he said neutrally.

'He died last month,' said Aziz.

'Yes, I know that. But tell me what you expected when the headmistress at Freitang asked if you wanted to come here.'

'I didn't know what to expect,' said Aziz, his eyes widening. There was a dark spot of sweat on his shirt collar now. 'But when Mr Petersen saw that I already knew what the others were learning, he gave me a test for software developers to see if I had a special skill. He said it showed I had a natural gift for cyber surveillance – or counter-surveillance.'

He's talking about hacking, thought Harry. That's what this is about. Cyber attacks. Perhaps this young man really did have a special talent – he was obviously very clever – or perhaps Petersen just wanted to make him think he was special, so he could control him. That was half the battle in suborning someone like this innocent kid; if he was told he had a special gift for something, he would be much more inclined to go along with any instructions to use that talent…

Aziz explained, 'You would know it as hacking.'

'Is that what he was teaching you to do?' Fitzpatrick asked with feigned surprise. 'That's illegal.'

'No, no,' the boy protested. 'It was to *detect* hacking, and expose it.' He continued anxiously, 'It was *anti*-hacking work.'

'Oh, I see,' said Harry, hiding his scepticism. There was no point in making the boy feel too nervous or he would clam up. 'So tell me exactly what he taught you.'

Harry Fitzpatrick could not in a month of Sundays have begun to recount with any accuracy what followed as Aziz launched into what Harry thought of as techno-babble. He seemed entirely unable to explain to a layman what he was talking about. But Harry was pretty sure he was getting the gist and it was very worrying.

It appeared that under the guise of teaching Aziz to detect unauthorised computer intrusions, Petersen had actually been teaching him to penetrate networks without leaving any trace. They had even set up a dummy corporation, Aziz told him proudly, for Aziz to practise on. If indeed the dead Petersen was a Russian Illegal, as seemed to be the opinion of FBI HQ and the Brits, then something very sinister seemed to have been taking place, involving not only the university but also the school in Germany. What and why and whether it was still going on, given

Petersen's death, Harry wasn't in a position to say. But as he listened to the young man in front of him it seemed to him improbable that he was a knowing accomplice.

Finally, Aziz finished his account. Fitzpatrick said, 'Thank you. That's all very clear. But let me ask you, who were you doing this for? I mean, was it just to give you some skills so you could get a job back in Germany?'

Aziz looked offended by the suggestion that his training was nothing but a certification process. 'The professor said he was doing confidential work and wanted me to assist him. He was the one who first said it might be possible for me to stay on.'

'What, here in Vermont?'

Aziz nodded. 'Yes, he said I could become an American.'

'He would get you a green card?'

'In time,' said Aziz. 'If my work was satisfactory.'

Fitzpatrick could imagine the situation; how Petersen would have played the boy along, offering the carrot of a green card with the stick of deportation should he fail to comply with his instructions. Fitzpatrick sensed that any mention of his employment status now would be unnerving. Aziz would probably be here on a one-year student permit, and Petersen's death made his future status uncertain. Presumably he could always go back to Germany, but the situation there was becoming more difficult for immigrants by the day.

'You mean, the work you were doing here on hacking?'

'Yes, though I would need to have a position in the department. He arranged that – helping teachers and students with their computers is my job. And printers – printers seem to be very difficult for everybody,' he added, with a shaky smile.

Fitzpatrick didn't smile. 'So your job here would be a cover for the work he wanted you to do.'

Aziz stared sadly at him. 'I had not thought of it that way. It is real work. I do help people with their computers.'

'Did Professor Petersen say who he was working for? And who you would be helping?'

Aziz shook his head. 'I did not think it was for me to ask. But...' He paused while Fitzpatrick waited, barely concealing his impatience.

At last Aziz said with obvious reluctance, 'Since I am in America, I thought it must be the FBI.'

17

I T WAS A BEAUTIFUL September day in Moscow: mild, windless and with bright sunshine – no hint yet of the chills of winter to come. Bruno Mackay was sitting in the coffee shop on the ground floor of the smart new block where he had taken an apartment. He was unrecognisable with his floppy blond hair now brown and fashionably short, horn-rimmed spectacles hiding his eyes – once blue, now green – and trendy stubble and smartly casual clothes instead of his usual suits. As he sipped his coffee and consulted his latest-model iPhone, he looked the perfect hedge fund executive, which was what he was pretending to be. He felt as comfortable as an MI6 officer undercover in Moscow can.

He was confident that his back story would stand scrutiny. There was an Ireland-based office of Quoin Capital Management, staffed by a competent young woman with a degree in Modern Languages from Warwick University. She spoke fluent French and Russian and was well briefed to answer any questions about the company or about 'Alan Urquhart', currently in Moscow researching investment opportunities. The office in Dublin was Bruno's communication link with Vauxhall Cross, and with the MI6 Station in the Moscow Embassy, with whom he had no overt contact at all.

Bruno's job was to try to get alongside Mischa's brother. He was under strict orders to do no more at present; he was to do his best to get acquainted with the brother, but he was to make no move at this stage towards a recruitment pitch. The CIA Station and the MI6 Station, working together, had managed to identify Mischa and his brother as Mischa and Boris Bebchuk. Mischa was in the army, Boris an FSB officer working at FSB HQ in Moscow. Further work had also produced an address for Boris and the location of the school attended by his six-year-old son.

In his first couple of weeks in Moscow, Bruno had lived in a hotel and under the pretext of flat-hunting had got to know the district where Boris and his family lived. Once or twice he just happened to find himself outside the school at going-home time, and he observed those waiting to pick up the children – young women mostly, nannies and mothers and the occasional grandma. A few children were picked up by a uniformed driver or an obvious security guard, for this was a pretty opulent area of town. He didn't know which one was the Bebchuk boy but he noticed that several of the children lived in a small group of new, expensive-looking apartment blocks a short walk away from the school. So it was in one of those that he had taken a flat, and he had chosen the one with the coffee shop on the ground floor.

It was quite in keeping with his cover story that he should spend a couple of hours most mornings in the coffee shop, having breakfast and working on his laptop and his phone. Quoin Capital Management had no office in Moscow; Alan Urquhart was there to decide if there were sufficient business prospects to justify setting one up. For the moment, the smart coffee shop could credibly serve as his office. But it also served as his observation post. He had noticed that some of the mothers regularly stopped in the coffee shop after they had deposited the children at school. Most sat in a group chattering loudly in Russian, but in the second week of his vigil his eye had fallen on a woman who always sat by herself. After a couple of days, he'd greeted her with a friendly 'Good morning' in Russian. She'd smiled and replied in heavily accented Russian, so he'd asked where she was from, only to discover that she was Parisian. This was a stroke of luck for Bruno, who spoke fluent French, having served in the MI6 Station in Paris for several years.

Bruno, at his most charming, soon had her talking freely about herself. As luck had it, she was lonely and unhappy. Her name was Michelle. Separated from her husband, she was forced to carry on living in Moscow, which she hated, because he was blocking all her efforts to get a divorce and take her one child to live in Paris. He was a wealthy oil man with enough money and know-how to work the legal system to his advantage. He didn't care what she did and was quite happy to pay for her very comfortable lifestyle, she said, but he wanted the child, even though he only saw them at the weekends.

From then on Bruno and she met regularly in the mornings and sometimes for a leisurely lunch in one of the nearby restaurants. Bruno was beginning to feel that he must capitalise on this relationship before it turned into a full-blown affair. She was clearly very willing, but he needed to avoid any chance of getting involved in a divorce suit or even getting a bullet in the back from one of her husband's henchmen. So one day after lunch Bruno suggested he should walk with her to pick up her child since he had a later appointment in that direction.

Michelle smiled at him, a little surprised. She touched a strand of her blonde hair, which she had trimmed – and coloured, Bruno cynically concluded – every week at the chic local salon frequented by oligarchs' wives. She said, 'That would be very nice. I have told my son all about you. Are you sure?'

'Absolutely.'

It was the scene Bruno had observed when he was recceing the area before he moved there. Mothers and nannies, some on foot already waiting, others sitting in massive four-wheel-drive vehicles and large saloons, several with chauffeurs wearing peaked caps, and a smattering of dark-suited security guards with dark glasses and earpieces.

A car pulled up next to them. It was far less grand than the others – a modest Lada that stood out for its normality. But when the driver got out – a tall man with dark slicked-back hair, wearing a knee-length leather coat – Michelle poked Bruno in the ribs. 'Mind your manners,' she said, and gave a small laugh.

'What do you mean?'

'The man who just got out of the car...'

'What about him?' asked Bruno, looking at the man more carefully. He seemed self-assured, confident, as he lit a cigarette and leaned casually against the bonnet of his car, smoking and watching the entrance to the school. 'Isn't he one of the parents?'

'That's not all he is. The mother of one of my boy's friends told me he's a spy.'

'Really?' Bruno didn't have to feign surprise.

Michelle nodded knowingly. 'She told me he is an officer in the FSB.'

'FSB?' asked Bruno, as if he had never heard the acronym before.

'You know, the secret service. What the KGB used to be.'

'How does she know that?'

'She's friends with his wife. The wife told her that she wasn't very happy with her husband. Apparently, he drinks.'

'That's awful!' said Bruno, with a grin. They had just shared a bottle of wine over lunch.

'No, I mean *really* drinks. Shouts at her until he passes out.'

'He must be pretty senior if he's got children at school here. It has to cost the earth.'

'There's only one child,' said Michelle. 'The apple of his eye, apparently. They live very simply, so they can pay the fees.'

'Maybe Mrs Godunov has money of her own.'

'Godunov?' She looked at Bruno, then smiled when she realised he had just made the name up. 'That's not their name,' she said. 'Though the real one sounds just as silly.'

'What is it?'

She laughed. 'He's called Boris Bebchuk.'

He laughed too, trying to disguise the adrenalin he felt coursing through his veins. He knew his orders: get as close as you can without raising any suspicion, while Liz Carlyle gets what she can out of the brother. Bruno had to play his next cards very carefully. If he got it wrong and this guy Boris got suspicious, MI5 would lose their source. Mischa would panic and disappear. But a piece of good fortune like this didn't land in your lap very often and when it did you had to pick it up.

So he said, 'I've been thinking of having a drinks party to meet some people – I don't know anybody here yet really. Perhaps you'd like to invite your friends from the school and maybe ask them to bring a friend or two.'

He waited slightly nervously while Michelle thought about this. Had he pushed for this too quickly? But then she said, 'I think that is a marvellous idea. And I know just the caterer for you.'

18

It was Saturday afternoon and Dieter was at home by himself. Even though he knew that Irma would be gone for at least another hour he was keeping an anxious ear out for the sound of her key in the front door. She was leading a day retreat for the teachers of the Freitang at the school itself – no off-site away days for Irma, he reflected with a thin smile. Her familiar parsimony would ensure a meagre lunch of sandwiches prepared by the kitchen staff, pressed, reluctantly, into weekend service.

He felt extremely uneasy snooping around his wife's study, though he knew it was the only way he would discover whether his growing suspicions were justified. His colleague and now confidante Matilda in Brussels had been very reassuring when he'd explained his worries; he had felt immense relief that she hadn't dismissed his concern or thought him a fantasist. On the contrary, she had listened with interest, and the next day had raised the subject again herself.

'You know, Dieter,' she'd said during their coffee break in the canteen, 'I'm sure Irma isn't doing anything wrong. But there can't be any harm in finding out for sure; it would put your mind at rest. And who knows? Perhaps she's got involved in something without realising it. Perhaps she's being taken advantage of.'

Knowing Irma as he did, the chances of her being victimised were remote, but he took Matilda's point that knowing what was going on would reduce his anxiety. The difficulty was there was only one way he could think of to find out more about Irma and the Freitang school – search the filing cabinet in her study upstairs at home.

The cabinet was always locked but that was not actually a problem. The year before both Irma and their house-keeper had come down with flu, and the cleaning had fallen to him. One weekend he had set about vacuuming and dusting. He had found it not only a boring chore but also rather more complicated than he had thought. In his efforts to hoover the cluttered floor of Irma's study to her high standards, he had managed to wedge the vacuum's nozzle between the back of the filing cabinet and the wall. Hard as he pulled, it wouldn't budge. At last he had turned off the vacuum, then edged the filing cabinet away from the wall by a couple of inches, freeing the nozzle. It was then he saw the small key taped to its steel back. Trying the key in the lock of the cabinet, he found it turned easily, and it was with a mixture of apprehension and private delight at discovering the hidden key that he re-taped it to the filing cabinet, before shoving the cabinet back in place.

So the problem wasn't access to the cabinet, though previously he would never have dreamed of using the key to look at the contents. He couldn't imagine what Irma would say or do to him if she ever found out he had looked inside.

Now as he turned the key and gingerly pulled open the top drawer, he found his hands were shaking. He stared nervously at the neat line of file pockets hanging on the rails, each individually tagged with tabs inscribed in the dark Gothic hand Irma favoured.

Each pocket contained several files in buff-coloured folders. They all concerned the Freitang school. One folder contained a set of minutes of governors' meetings; another seemed to be accounts going back several years. There was a pocket of files containing annual performance reports on teachers and other staff members. Further back in the top drawer were files containing papers about various pupils. They looked like reports of interviews with the children detailing how they had come to be in Germany, their journey from their homeland and what their family circumstances were. They were all orphans, their parents having died before they set off or disappeared somewhere on the journey. To each report was attached the results of an intelligence test and what looked like some sort of technical aptitude test. The only remarkable thing was that the marks were all very high. As Dieter knew that the school specialised in computer studies, he assumed that the tests were part of some sort of selection process. It all looked much as you might expect.

He opened the drawer below it, and to his surprise found it virtually empty. The first few files inside contained articles from education magazines on teaching German to foreigners and others concerning trauma among orphaned children. There were some papers about post-traumatic stress among refugees and others along similar lines. It wasn't until he came to the last few files that his interest was aroused. In a folder he found a brochure from the University of Vermont and attached to it some correspondence dated the previous April about a group of children from the Freitang school who were to visit for the summer school in computing studies. On a separate paper was a list of names alongside dates of birth and nationalities. They all seemed to be fifteen or sixteen years old, though he noticed one who was older – nineteen.

The file behind this one contained a brochure from a school in England, the Bartholomew Manor College, near Southwold, Suffolk. There was a picture on the front of a grand house in what appeared to be extensive grounds. He took it out and flicked through it. The school was for children from thirteen to eighteen. It called itself an 'international' school, and claimed to specialise in preparing children for entry to the top universities of the world with a special focus on modern technology. Though he didn't have much experience of international schools, the fees seemed very high to Dieter and he wondered why Irma should be interested in their prospectus.

He was puzzling over this, turning the pages of the glossy brochure looking for an explanation, when he heard the front door close loudly. Christ! He had lost all track of time. He stuffed the brochure back into the file and the file back into the metal cabinet, then closed the drawer as quickly and quietly as he could, turned the key still sticking out of the lock and pocketed it, shoving the cabinet back against the wall.

He had just got things back in place when he heard Irma coming up the stairs; he looked around wildly, trying to control his panic. He grabbed a book from the bookshelves and sat down heavily in the room's only armchair, doing his best to breathe normally.

'Dieter,' Irma called out as she came down the corridor and stopped at the bedroom door. Not finding him there, the footsteps restarted, until they reached the doorway of the study, where Irma saw him apparently sitting quietly, engrossed in a chapter of *Buddenbrooks*, a book he had read at school and not enjoyed.

'What are you doing?' Irma demanded as he looked up from his book, trying to stay calm.

'What does it look like?' he said with a broad smile, holding the book up.

'You never read in here,' she said accusingly.

'Sometimes I do,' he said weakly. 'When you're out.'

She stared at him for a second, seeming to weigh things up. Then she snorted. 'Honestly, Dieter, if you want to sit in my study you only have to ask.' But he could see there was suspicion in her eyes – as if, like him, she had seized on something plausible to say, something at odds with what she was really thinking.

19

SEVERAL DAYS LATER, LIZ was sitting with Peggy as rain lashed the windows of her Thames House office. There was a lot to follow up. She had briefed Peggy on her meeting with Mischa and his sudden disappearance; they had heard nothing from him since. In Liz's absence, a note had come from Geoffrey Fane, relaying a message from Peter Burnside in Brussels about a school in Suffolk named Bartholomew Manor. It seemed that Irma Nimitz may have been in touch with it.

Now Liz was thinking how best to divide the tasks. Peggy said, 'I'll be happy to go and look round this school in Suffolk, if you like. We didn't get much more than its name from the MI6 Station in Brussels, but I've done a little research.'

'Actually, I was thinking you should go to Germany. It would be good for you to get some experience abroad.'

'Really?' said Peggy, looking pleased.

'Yes,' said Liz firmly. Peggy wouldn't have any credible reason to visit Bartholomew Manor College, since she was far too young to pose as a prospective parent. Liz reckoned she herself could just about get away with it. 'I'll take Suffolk. What have you found out about the place?'

'Not a lot, frankly. It used to be a private residence, then twenty years ago it was bought by some local people and run as a sixth-form college. It catered mainly to middle-class children who needed A Levels but were struggling in their normal schools.'

'Like these tutorial colleges in London. Little Jonny mucks up his GCSEs, the independent school wants him out because his A Levels will drag their ratings down, so off he goes for cramming to an expensive sixth-form college.'

'If you're saying that the clientele was rich and stupid,' Peggy said with a smile, 'you're probably right. But...'

'Yes?'

'Something's changed. Either the school was bought or the owners changed tack – either way, they've got a new Head and a new admissions policy. They are actively recruiting overseas students to come and specialise in IT. It sounds as if they only want the clever ones now – there's an entrance exam. There's a prospectus on their website; the fees look exorbitant to me.'

'Do we know how many foreign pupils they've got? The proportion of British to foreign?'

Peggy shook her head. 'There's nothing in the prospectus about that.'

Liz thought for a moment. 'I know somebody who might be able to give us a lead. You remember the Chief Constable of Manchester – Richard Pearson? He's moved to Suffolk now. I'm going to ring him.' She reached for the phone on her desk.

Peggy asked, 'Do you want me to stick around?'

'No need,' said Liz. 'But come back later, will you? You can help me with my cover story for this college.'

*

Even in busy Manchester he had often answered his own phone, so Liz was not surprised when Chief Constable Pearson picked up at once. 'Hello. Pearson speaking.'

'Good morning, Richard. It's Liz here. Liz Carlyle. I'm sorry to be slow replying to your message. Work has just been frantic recently. How is life in Suffolk?'

'Hello, Liz,' he said warmly. 'How nice to hear your voice. It's surprisingly busy, actually. It's not the holiday camp you might imagine. But I'm starting to get used to the odd ways of East Anglia. And I love the countryside, especially the coast.'

'Where are you based?' She remembered passing a large, ugly police building somewhere outside Ipswich.

'For the moment I'm renting a cottage in Bury St Edmunds. I couldn't find anywhere I wanted to live in Ipswich. What's the point of coming to a rural area if you're going to live in a big town? So I've set up my office in the police station in Bury. It's caused a bit of eyebrow-raising but it suits me.'

'Good,' said Liz. Pearson was easy-going but always seemed to know his own mind.

He went on, 'At the moment I'm still finding out about the county so I'm travelling around a lot, visiting the different areas. There's some lovely coast in this county. How do you fancy coming down some time? I've found a first-rate boatyard and I'm thinking of commissioning a small boat.'

Liz smiled to herself at his enthusiasm, remembering that he had told her how he would go out at weekends with his brother-in-law, a commercial fisherman. It had been a sort of escape; he'd take his phone with him, knowing that after a short time he'd be too far from shore to receive any calls. Hearing him talk now, Liz remembered how much she enjoyed his company. She realised that she'd actually wanted to ring him after he'd left his message weeks before; she wasn't quite sure why she hadn't. But now she was glad to have found a work excuse to get in touch.

Pearson went on: 'To what do I owe the pleasure of your call? I have to say I was giving up ever hearing from you again.'

'I'd better warn you it's business,' said Liz, and she heard Pearson sigh. 'Well, only partly,' she added. 'Something's come up in an investigation that seems to connect to a college in your patch. I don't suppose you've ever heard of it. It's a sixth-form college about ten miles west of Southwold called Bartholomew Manor.'

There was a pause, then Pearson said, 'Now, that is really interesting. I don't think it can be a coincidence. This college has crossed our radar here, and just a few days ago. I'd love to know what your interest in it is – if you can tell me.'

'I will,' said Liz, 'but you go first.'

'I was talking to one of my senior colleagues the other day and he mentioned it. A friend of his wife had gone to look round. Her husband is being posted to the Middle East for a couple of years and they want to leave their sixteen-year-old son in Britain to take his A Levels. So she went to look round a couple of boarding schools – one in Southwold, and Bartholomew Manor College. She found it so strange that she told my colleague about it. She thought the place was positively sinister, and she got the clear impression that they didn't want her boy there and couldn't wait to get rid of her. To tell you the truth, she wondered if it had something to do with child exploitation – she mentioned paedophilia. My colleague thought she was being overdramatic. But it certainly sounded odd.

Most of these places are only too keen to welcome parents – and their cash.'

'That's interesting,' said Liz. 'Have you taken it any further?'

'A little. Our child protection team did a bit of research on the place. Apparently, it was taken over about nine months ago, with the intention of setting it up as an international school – it's not clear what that means exactly but they have been bringing in their teachers from abroad. We received a tip that some of them may not have any qualifications or have the proper documents to work here. I gather they're not all EU citizens.'

'Are you following that up?'

'We will be, probably through the Home Office and possibly the Department for Education. But we need something a lot more solid first. Now it's your turn. What's your interest in the place?'

'It's even vaguer than yours, I'm afraid. It's just that the name of the school came up in an investigation that seems to link in some way to that Illegals case we were both involved in last year – when you were in Manchester.'

'Don't tell me the Russians have penetrated rural Suffolk.' He laughed. 'Is it anything to do with our air bases?'

'I doubt it, though it could be anything – or nothing – at this stage. I'm intending to go to the school myself in a few days. I'll be a prospective parent and see whether my reception is similarly unwelcoming.'

Liz paused, wondering how to suggest that they might meet up as well. I am terribly out of practice, she thought. I can't even ask a man for coffee.

'If you're coming this way, then let's meet up,' he said quickly. 'We could have lunch or dinner, depending on what's convenient. I'll look forward to hearing your impressions of the place – and to seeing you, of course. Deal?'

'Deal,' said Liz firmly, pleased that he had taken the initiative. She hadn't learned much more about Bartholomew Manor, but she was very glad she would be seeing Richard Pearson again.

20

'THIS IS OUR BRAND-NEW IT centre,' Miss Girling
announced. There was unconcealed pride in her
voice. Liz could see why, since every other part of
Bartholomew Manor College was thoroughly outdated
and in need of a complete overhaul. What had once been
a charming manor house, built of mellowed brick with a
pair of fine Dutch gables, was now a rundown building
that bore little resemblance to the photographs that
appeared prominently in the school's prospectus.

It had been a frustrating drive from London. Liz had
left late enough in the morning to miss the rush hour and
had made it to the M25 in only half an hour. The A12 had
been clear, and she had sailed through Essex and circled
Ipswich without any delay. But once she had started to
follow her GPS through the smaller roads of rural Suffolk,
everything slowed down: a tractor creeping along, a traffic
light at roadworks that took forever to turn green, and a
fork in the road where the GPS said no such fork existed.
Inevitably, Liz chose the wrong branch, and five miles later
had had to turn around and retrace her route, only to over-
shoot the small sign at the top of the lane that led to
Bartholomew Manor. She thought she had left herself

time to spare when she set out that morning, but by the time she turned into the gravel drive of the college and parked next to a smart new blue Mini she was twenty minutes late. Under the archway of the college's entrance, the woman who turned out to be Miss Girling stood ostentatiously consulting her watch with an impatient look on her face.

Like the manor house itself, Miss Girling was not in her prime. Her hair was grey and thinning, her spectacles were of a little-old-lady sort, and she was dressed in a worn skirt of grey herringbone tweed and a thick woollen cardigan with large wood buttons. She explained to Liz that she was to show her around before her interview with the headmaster.

'I understand your son is sixteen,' she said.

'Yes, George is sixteen,' replied Liz. 'And he's not my son; he's my stepson.' She and Peggy had decided this was more plausible than pretending to be the boy's mother, and it seemed to satisfy Miss Girling, who nodded. 'Should we also expect a visit from the boy's *natural* mother?' she asked, with just a trace of cattiness.

Liz shook her head. 'No,' she said shortly. When Miss Girling seemed to expect more – perhaps an account of a bitter divorce? – Liz said mildly, 'She died several years ago.'

To Liz's satisfaction, Miss Girling looked rather embarrassed. 'I am sorry,' she said faintly.

Throughout the brief tour that followed, Miss Girling talked non-stop, as if from a memorised text and as though she had given this tour a hundred times before.

'Where is everyone?' asked Liz as they walked through the deserted corridors.

'Term starts late this year,' explained Miss Girling. 'They're all still at home.'

'Even the foreign students?'

'Yes. And the students don't live here at the manor anyway. For those who board we have an accommodation block at a nearby estate.'

For all her chatter, Miss Girling could not disguise the sad state of the college's classrooms. They contained rows of old-style wooden desks and mismatched chairs. One room was what Miss Girling referred to as 'our language lab', a series of wooden tables supporting large, antiquated tape recorders; another was 'the science hall', benches with sinks and old Bunsen burners, where clearly no science had been done for years. Miss Girling diligently showed each room to Liz, talking all the while and seemingly unaware of the impression the place was making on Liz. The occasional glimpse of an elegant cornice or a fireplace still with its ornate surround was the only evidence that this had once been a distinguished private house.

'Now I'll show you the IT block,' said Miss Girling as they emerged from a door at the back of the main house. Behind the manor was a line of brick outbuildings on the far side of a courtyard – what had perhaps once been the stables. As they approached them, Liz could see signs that the old buildings had been recently restored.

'Here we are,' said Miss Girling, flinging open the door and standing back so Liz could get the full effect. It was totally unexpected. Striplighting suspended from the ceiling cast a pale glow over row upon row of smart new work stations, separated by low wooden dividers. Liz counted thirty places before giving up.

'How long has this been ready?' she asked. It all looked barely touched, like a showroom with no customers.

'Just a few weeks.'

'Will all the students get to use it?'

Miss Girling shifted uneasily. 'Not at first. I believe it's only meant for those taking advanced computing.'

'Are there many of those?'

The older woman hesitated, then said, 'I'm not sure. That's something to discuss with the headmaster.'

'I was wondering, too, how many of the students here are from abroad. The brochure wasn't very clear.'

'They used to be all English children, mainly from local Suffolk and Norfolk families,' said Miss Girling, sounding slightly wistful.

'And now?'

Miss Girling puffed out her cheeks, then took a deep breath. She seemed unsettled by the question, and Liz waited for whatever she was about to say. But she just looked at her watch and said, 'I think it's time I took you to the Head; he'll be expecting you.'

21

M ISS GIRLING LED LIZ back into the main house
and into a small anteroom. As they came in a young
man stood up from behind a half-sized partner's desk. He
was short, slim and athletic-looking, with close cropped
black hair. He wore a black jacket, black jeans and a collar-
less black T-shirt. The outfit seemed more suitable for a
trendy part of London than deepest Suffolk. His face was
saturnine and expressionless.

'Cicero,' said Miss Girling, 'this is Mrs Forester. She has
an appointment with Mr Sarnat about her son, George.'
She turned to Liz. 'Very nice to meet you,' she said stiffly,
and was gone before Liz could thank her for the tour.

Cicero gestured towards a large oak door opposite his
desk and said, 'Mr Sarnat is ready for you now. Please go
through.' He spoke in an English so flat and accentless
that Liz concluded he must be foreign. She smiled at him
but he didn't smile back, and as she went to open the door,
he sat down again, eyes intent on his monitor.

Mr Sarnat had chosen the room that had probably been
the dining room of the manor house a century before. It
was long and comparatively narrow with tall sash windows
looking out towards the courtyard at the back of the house.

In the centre of the ceiling was a beautiful plaster rose from which hung a dusty crystal chandelier. Wide polished oak floorboards were scattered with Persian rugs, and two antique side tables held a pair of Chinese lamps. The Head's desk was centred against the far end of the room, its back to a wall-wide spread of white cornice-topped bookshelves. Unlike his assistant, Mr Sarnat came out quickly from behind his desk, smiling to greet her and shake hands. 'Mrs Forester, how good to meet you. Please do take a seat.'

Liz sat down in front of the desk while Mr Sarnat resumed his seat. 'I hope you have enjoyed your tour of our premises,' he said. 'Miss Girling has been here for many years, longer than any of us, and she knows the place inside-out.' His lips hinted at the faintest of smiles. 'As you may have noticed, she is also rather old school.'

'Yes, but she seemed very proud of your new IT block.'

'Did she now? I am glad to hear it.' His English was perfectly inflected but again Liz suspected he was not a native speaker; she wondered if he and Cicero were products of the same language school – though he could not have looked more different from his assistant. He was tall and broad-shouldered, with blond hair combed to one side. He had regular features, with a straight long nose and dull blue eyes capped by the palest set of eyelashes Liz had ever seen on a man his age – she estimated he was in his early forties. He wore an expensive well-cut suit, and a yellow silk tie with a cream-coloured shirt. He could have passed for an international businessman, prosperous and perhaps a little complacent. There was none of the slightly harried look one usually found in a schoolmaster.

'I'd like to hear a little about your boy. George, isn't it?' he said, looking down at some papers on the desk in front of him. Slowly interlocking his hands, he sat back in his leather chair.

Liz gave him the account of her non-existent stepson George that she and Peggy had devised. She explained that they lived in Geneva where her husband worked, but that both she and her husband were English and intending to return in the next year or so. They wanted George, who was just sixteen, to finish his schooling back at home and go to a British university. George was being taught well at the school he attended in Geneva (Liz could have supplied its name if pressed) but he was a highly intelligent child whose interests weren't altogether catered for by the rather old-fashioned curriculum obligatory in that country's cantons.

'What interests are those?' Sarnat asked with mild interest. Liz still could not place his accent; he might have been Dutch or German or even Scandinavian with his blond Aryan looks.

'George is very keen on computers,' Liz said, and for the first time there was real interest in Sarnat's eyes. 'He learned programming at a very early age – "coding", I think it's called. Other boys seem to like football, but George has never enjoyed sport – he's always much preferred sitting in front of a screen.'

'How interesting,' said Sarnat, and he sounded as if he meant it. He leaned forward in his chair. 'Do you know what languages he likes to code in?'

Liz opened her hands, palms out, Italian-style. 'I haven't a clue about these things, I'm afraid. George likes to say I don't know Coffee from JAVA, if that means anything to you.'

'It does, actually,' said Sarnat with a brief smile. 'You've seen our new IT centre. I think your son might use it very profitably. We do have an exam for the students we take from abroad, but from the sound of it young George would pass with flying colours. Most of it is computer-related.'

'Really? I'd have thought you'd be mainly concerned that their English was up to scratch.'

'Not necessarily. You see,' he said airily, 'the world these days is more and more interconnected through technology rather than spoken or written language. People like to say the international lingua franca is English, but I'd say it's digital.'

'So some of your students don't know English at all?' Liz did her best to sound surprised rather than inquisitive.

'I wouldn't go that far, and since we want them to feel at home here, we do offer remedial classes for those who don't have much English when they arrive.'

'Where do most of them come from?'

'All over the world,' Sarnat said, then perhaps sensing Liz would not be satisfied with such a vague reply he added, 'We try our best not to classify our students in any way. That's why we are most reluctant even to describe their nationalities. The world here at Bartholomew is seen as one nation, one people, linked by one sense of self.'

'Goodness, you make it sound almost like a religion. I didn't see a chapel on my tour,' she added with a little laugh.

'There is no chapel, nor any religion; we discourage our students from attending any kind of organised services. The faith we want them to have instead is in themselves, and in the common purpose we as their teachers try to inculcate.'

'I see,' said Liz, but she didn't really. It sounded remarkably airy-fairy for a school Head hoping to impress a prospective parent. But maybe he didn't want to impress her.

There was a knock. Turning, Liz saw Cicero in the doorway. Sarnat stood up, 'If you'll excuse me for a moment.'

He left the room and Liz sat still for a minute or so until, hearing two sets of footsteps leaving the anteroom, she stood up. Taking a step closer to the desk, she studied the titles of the books that sat on the shelves. There was some history, some biography, a complete set of Shakespeare and, at the end of one shelf at Liz's eye level, several books on, of all things, Confucianism. Curious, she stepped around the side of the desk, reading their titles with an ear cocked for Sarnat's return. *Confucius: A Personal History, Confucianism in Taiwan, Taiwan and the Confucius Synthesis.*

What was the fascination with Confucius? she wondered. And with Taiwan? Taiwan had a superb technical education system, she knew – she'd remembered that at one point in the not so distant past Silicon Valley had been full of Taiwanese hardware and software engineers.

As she scanned the books, she noticed a gap in the tightly packed shelves, presumably where a book had been taken out and not returned. Something glinted in the opening. Moving a neighbouring book, Liz took a closer look. She saw a metal protuberance, shaped like a tennis ball, attached to the back of the bookshelf. At the front of the 'tennis ball' there was a little glass eye, and when Liz looked more closely the eye opened and shut, then opened again. She could detect a very faint whirring sound.

Hearing footsteps in the corridor, she quickly put the book back and returned to her chair. Moments later, Sarnat came back in. Their exchanges now became entirely conventional and focused on the usual topics discussed by parents and a prospective school – term dates, tuition fees, and the application form Sarnat took from his desk drawer.

But when they had finished their business and said their goodbyes and Liz got into her car again, she was cursing herself. She had fallen for the oldest trick in the book – leave someone alone in a room and watch what they do. There was something very strange about this place. To find CCTV or its equivalent in a school wasn't odd in itself but to put a hidden camera in the headmaster's room, focused on the visitors' chair, and then to leave them alone so you could watch what they did was not only unusual, it spoke of a suspicion and distrust that were positively sinister. What was the school trying to hide?

22

THE CROWN AND GREYHOUND was an ancient coaching inn on the outskirts of Diss on the road from Bury St Edmunds. In recent years it had been cleverly converted into a gastropub without sacrificing any of the old-fashioned charm of its cosy public bar or losing any of its traditional patrons. As Liz walked in through the bar the sight and sound of the locals – gamekeepers and farm workers in boots and overalls, with well-behaved dogs lying on the floor beside them – reminded her how far she was from Pimlico. At the back, behind the bar, a new annexe had been built for a dining room, and there she found Chief Constable Pearson, sitting at a table for two near the inglenook fireplace, where one of the season's first fires was blazing.

He stood up as he saw Liz approach. Pearson was a tall, lean figure with blond hair that was going slightly grey at the edges and striking green eyes.

'Liz,' he said with a big smile.

'Hello, Richard.' They kissed cheeks and Liz sat down, suddenly feeling rather shy.

'It's lovely to see you. Not our usual sort of meeting place,' he said, waving a hand at the surroundings.

'No. But it's good to get out into the countryside for a change. Remind myself that it's all still here.'

'I feel the same,' he replied. 'And how were our mysterious friends at the college? I can't wait to hear all about it.'

She described her visit, making him laugh with her account of Miss Girling and the rather grim Cicero. But when it came to Sarnat and the man's odd mix of technophilia and weird philosophising, Pearson frowned.

'The oddest thing of all,' she said, dropping her voice, 'was that I discovered there was a camera hidden in the bookcase in the headmaster's study, with the lens trained on the visitor's chair. They left me on my own for a little, while Sarnat went off to do something. I think it was deliberate – to see what I did. I didn't think. I suppose I was lulled into carelessness, assuming it was just an odd kind of school. So I got up and looked at the books and found the camera. I'm sure they photographed me snooping.'

'That sounds extraordinary,' Pearson said. 'I made a few inquiries, and you're right to think the man's not your average schoolmaster. Most of the college governors have resigned since he came in – they weren't forced out, but they no longer had any say in the running of the place. Initially, the new Head made a great show of consulting them but then he seems to have just forged ahead regardless. As you say, he's changed the whole thrust of the institution: he's concentrating on foreign students with a total focus on IT.'

'But who owns the place now?'

'The ownership's not clear. It used to belong to a local family, but when Sarnat took over as Head and some of the governors complained about his behaviour, they got short shrift from the family – they didn't want to hear it. Either the family's given Sarnat their approval or they've sold the place and don't want to admit it – or possibly they've signed some sort of confidentiality agreement. Perhaps they've sold it to Sarnat himself.'

'We need to try and find out more about him. I couldn't make out his nationality – Dutch possibly, or German. But it was impossible to tell for sure.'

Pearson glanced at Liz. 'Can I ask what he's doing that you're interested in?'

Liz looked around the room. There was no one in earshot, but when she spoke it was in low tones that Pearson had to lean forward to hear. 'You can ask, but I can't give you a very coherent answer. Not because it's confidential; it's just that we don't know.

'We uncovered something similar in the States, where someone was sent in to train young people in aspects of computing, probably some form of hacking or cyber disruption or even espionage. We just don't know. But the man doing it there died, so the whole thing seems to have aborted before we could be sure what it was all about. We've had some information since then suggesting the same manoeuvre might be under way in other countries, including the UK. The name of Bartholomew Manor College came up in what seemed to be the same context but without any more detail.'

'This isn't being done by the Dutch or Germans, surely?'

'No. More likely the usual suspects.' She looked at him and he nodded to show he understood. 'But anyway,' she said, her voice back to normal, 'thanks for the info. It gives me a very good idea where to look next.'

They'd ordered their dinner by now and while they ate, Liz asked Pearson about his new role.

'I'm the lead Chief Constable for coastal security,' he explained. It seemed the East Anglian coast on the North

Sea was proving particularly vulnerable to a range of intruders. 'In this part of the country we're getting everything you can imagine,' he went on. 'The Kent coast is the easiest to reach from Europe – Calais to Dover is what, fourteen miles? – but it's heavily policed and it's a relatively small body of water. Plus there's so much shipping in the area that it's dangerous for small craft to cross that way – especially since they keep their lights out.

'But the stretch of coast from Harwich to Cromer in Norfolk is about a hundred miles long, with lots of beaches, all deserted at night and some of them miles from anywhere. Boats can come in from any number of places: Dunkirk all the way up to Denmark. Border Force is doing what it can with the resources it has and so are the police forces all round the coast. But we need a more coherent strategy. It's my job to work with our immediate continental neighbours as well as our agencies and come up with something better than we have now. So you can see why I said I was busy.' His voice trailed off as he contemplated his task.

'Is most of the traffic refugees?'

'A lot of it is, poor sods. People who've managed to escape the violence in their homelands, risked their lives crossing the Med and travelled across half of Europe, only to end up drowned in the North Sea or getting dumped on some lonely East Anglian beach with not a clue about what to do next. If they actually get this far, they're the lucky ones.'

'Do you ever catch the smugglers?'

'Occasionally. But it's haphazard. That's why I'm trying to improve collaboration and resources. Then, of course, there are the drugs and the weapons. They come in this way, too. Still, I don't mean to moan. It's a job really worth doing if I can make an improvement.'

'Are you glad you've moved south then?'

He thought for a moment. 'Yes, I am. It's been a big change for me, with plenty of adjustments, but I am sure it was the right move.'

'I have to say I was a bit surprised. You'd done so well in Manchester, after all.'

'I think I was starting to feel I needed a change. New challenges and all that.' He paused before adding softly, 'And no ghosts.'

Liz nodded. They had both lost partners, and shared an understanding of what each other had gone through.

'I do go back north now and then. To see my brother-in-law and my wife's parents – they're still hanging on,' he said fondly. 'But what about you? Have you ever wanted to make a change?'

'Sometimes,' said Liz. There had been moments when she had wanted to up sticks and go somewhere new and start a completely different kind of life. Especially after Martin had been killed in Paris; for a while she had thought very seriously of chucking in her job and just travelling the world. Eventually she had concluded that she would just be running away from her grief, when she knew that inevitably it would follow her wherever she went.

She said, 'I have moved into a new flat,' and grinned at the absurdity of claiming this for a life-changing event.

Pearson smiled sympathetically. 'That's not nothing. Moving house was the worst part of it for me. I couldn't believe how much stuff I had accumulated over the years. It took me a month to sort the wheat from the chaff. Even then a lot of chaff came south in the removal van.'

*

Outside the sky was cloudless and full of stars. Pearson walked Liz to her car, where she turned to say goodbye. They went to exchange a kiss on the cheek but got slightly out of synch and ended up kissing on the lips instead. Pearson drew back. 'Sorry about that.'

'That's all right,' Liz said with a smile.

'Is it?' He was smiling too. 'Then maybe I should do it on purpose this time.' And he kissed her again, very tenderly. Putting his hands gently on her shoulders he looked her in the eye. 'It's very good to see you again, Liz Carlyle.'

'Likewise, Chief Constable.'

'I'll be coming to London the week after next for a few days. Any chance of a repeat performance?'

'The dinner or the kiss?'

'Both, if you're willing.'

'We'll have to see about that,' she said teasingly. 'Why don't you ring me tomorrow with your dates?'

They said goodnight for real this time, and Liz got into her car and drove off, waving to Pearson as he unlocked his saloon. She realised it was going to be quite late by the time she reached Pimlico and that she had an early start the next day.

But it didn't matter one whit, for she felt happier than she had in a long time. So happy, in fact, that she drove in a mild sort of daze. When she reached the roundabout where her road joined the A11 she had to wait in a short queue to let a line of lorries go through. It was only chance that made her glance in her mirror and notice that two cars behind her there was a blue Mini waiting in the queue.

It was the same model she had seen that morning at Bartholomew Manor, with a man at the wheel. As his car inched forward he was highlighted by a streetlamp. He looked the spitting image of Cicero, Mr Sarnat's glowering assistant. If the car behind her hadn't honked impatiently for Liz to join the roundabout, she would have been able to take another look and make sure.

23

Bruno Mackay had firm views about parties, particularly the ones he gave himself. Simple entertaining was usually better than complicated efforts that could easily go wrong, but he also knew better than to cut corners. If you were going to offer food and drink it should be special food and drink – particularly on occasions like this when he was out to make an impact.

It was with this in mind that he ordered the refreshments – this would be a drinks party and then some, he told himself. For the drinkers he would serve pink champagne from France and ice-cold Russian vodka; for the faint of heart (he didn't expect many), there would be elderflower cordial.

He had booked a caterer who was half French and understood that for an international mix of guests, it made no sense to serve only local food. Instead of caviar, which his well-heeled guests would be accustomed to, he opted for smoked salmon flown in from Scotland, served on squares of black rye bread, and trays of devils on horseback.

Two girls had arrived to help set up and tour the room as it filled up, making sure glasses were kept full and canapes circulated regularly. This was not going to be a cheap party, Bruno realised, but his cover as international invest-ment banker required only the best.

Since the party was ostensibly being held to allow Michelle to introduce her friends to Bruno, the guest list was largely left to her. Bruno added a few acquaintances of his own, partly to repay the hospitality they'd shown him, and partly to provide cover for the one invitation he abso-lutely needed to have accepted. When he had shown Michelle his own much smaller list, she had barely scanned it, and didn't seem to notice that Mr and Mrs Boris Bebchuk were on it.

Now Bruno stood impatiently while the two waitresses finished their preparations. Where was Michelle? The party was due to begin at any minute. As if in answer, the front door buzzed, and when he opened it Michelle bustled by him, carrying two large bouquets of flowers, one in each hand. 'Men,' she said with mock-annoyance, looking around. 'They never appreciate the decorative in life. Your flat is *très gentil*, Alan, but it needs a bit of colour. You there,' she said sharply to one of the waitresses, with an imperiousness she must have learned from her Russian husband, 'can you find a vase?'

'Let me look,' said Bruno, and by the time he found a couple of jugs that would do, several of Michelle's friends had arrived and were happily drinking the pink cham-pagne and munching the smoked salmon. The ice was already broken, thought Bruno, and soon the room was filling up as more people arrived.

He made a point of circulating, meeting as many of his guests as possible. The women were all friends of Michelle and most of them had brought a husband or partner. Bruno knew none of them. He introduced himself to two of the men, who were standing by the window. One was Jens, a

Norwegian, involved in selling oil-refining equipment to Gazprom, if Bruno understood correctly. The other was a Scot called Henderson who worked for whisky distillers selling Scotch to the Russians – they were less voracious buyers than the Chinese but equally keen on the more expensive products.

'That's a wonderful view,' said Jens, and they spent a few minutes admiring the outlook from Bruno's apartment before moving on to the standard topics of Moscow expats – the daily encounters with Russian bureaucracy; the best getaway places for the weekend; new restaurants, new coffee houses, and so on. Throughout Bruno was keeping an eye on the door, more hopeful than expectant. He was about to give up his wait and make a host's tour of the room when the buzzer went.

He decided to wait and let Michelle greet the new arrivals. A woman came into the room, and he recognised Bebchuk's wife from the photographs supplied by the Americans. Michelle greeted her warmly, and Bruno saw with disappointment that she seemed to be on her own, when suddenly a man came in behind her.

Bingo! It was Bebchuk, dressed smarter than at the school gates, in a grey suit and brown shoes, and looking slightly grumpy – he must be wondering what his wife had got him into, thought Bruno, dragging him to some foreigner's drinks party. Bebchuk shook hands politely with Michelle, but was clearly ill at ease.

Bruno excused himself and ambled towards his new guests, playing the part of a casual but attentive host. He approached them with his hand out, saying, 'So pleased you could come. I'm Alan.'

'I am Boris,' said the Russian as they shook hands.

Mrs Bebchuk said, 'And I am Bella.'

A waitress came towards them with a tray of drinks and the Russian couple each took a glass of champagne.

'Your hair looks wonderful,' Michelle said to Bella.

Bruno seized his opportunity. 'Come and meet some people,' he said to Boris, 'while the girls talk about hairdos.' Boris smiled and followed Bruno to the window, where Jens and Henderson were still standing, now talking about salmon fishing on the Kola Peninsula.

Bruno introduced Boris, and for a little while the other two made more general conversation to include him. They explained what they did for a living and why they were in Moscow, and Boris remarked that he was a civil servant who worked on regional transport policy. Then they discussed the view from Bruno's window again, until Henderson said something to Jens about the size of a fish he caught on the Spey the summer before, and Bruno turned quickly to Bebchuk. 'Do you fish?' he asked quietly, as he heard Jens say something to Henderson.

Bebchuk looked puzzled, and Bruno imitated the casting motion of a fly rod with one hand. Bebchuk laughed. 'No, I do not fish.'

'Neither do I,' said Bruno, shaking his head and smiling. 'So what do you do in your free time?'

'I like football,' said the Russian. 'And movies.'

'What kind of movies?'

'All movies,' said Bebchuk easily; he'd drunk most of his glass of champagne and was relaxing a little. 'But especially French films.'

'What's your favourite?'

Bebchuk hesitated. '*Belle de Jour*,' he said, naming the Buñuel film starring Catherine Deneuve as a bored housewife who finds work in a brothel. 'But don't tell my wife. I don't want her getting any ideas.'

Bruno laughed. 'You can count on me,' he said, taking another glass of champagne from a passing waitress and handing it to Boris Bebchuk.

Boris said, 'I didn't quite hear you when we were talking with the other gentlemen. What is it that you do here?' His expression was friendly, but his eyes steady and probing.

'Well, when I want to impress people I say that I'm in capital investment. But that's just a fancy term for taking rich people's money and buying things that will make them even richer. I suppose that makes me a kind of trader.'

'Traitor?' said Bebchuk, his eyes widening.

'No, no,' said Bruno hastily. 'Trader – a buyer and seller.'

'Ah. That I understand. What do you like to do in your spare time?'

'Nothing so intellectual as watch Buñuel. To be honest, I love to eat – especially lunch. I play a game with myself: I try to eat in a better restaurant each time I go out than the last one I went to. It doesn't have to be expensive; it just has to be good.'

'And there are enough of these places in Moscow?' Bebchuk sounded sceptical, which amused Bruno. Usually the Russians would bristle at any suggestion that the Moscow version of something – from art to light bulbs – was inferior to its Western counterpart.

'There seem to be – I've been on a pretty good run lately. And I've lined up another place this week.'

'Where's that?'

'Near the Kremlin, believe it or not. It's not much more than a hole in the wall but I'm told the dumplings, the *pelmeni*, are truly special.'

'You like *pelmeni*?'

'I do,' said Bruno firmly. 'Don't you?'

'I *love* them,' said Boris emphatically. 'But I would think for a foreigner they were not to your taste. When are you going to go to your hole in the wall?'

Bruno paused as if to consider his coming diary of appointments. 'I thought of going on Thursday.' His face suddenly lit up. 'I don't suppose you'd like to join me? I enjoy this little game of mine, but it's always nice to have company when I go to a new place.'

Bebchuk was watching Bruno carefully. Eventually he said, 'Thursday. It could be possible. Give me your card and I will telephone you to confirm this lunch. I am sure I would enjoy it,' he said, though the expression on his face was unreadable.

24

PEGGY ARRIVED AT THE British Embassy in Berlin promptly at nine o'clock. She had flown in the evening before and, anxious to do well on her first mission abroad, she had resisted the temptation to explore Berlin, eaten a modest supper in her room at the hotel and been in bed by ten o'clock.

The Embassy, at the north end of Wilhelmstrasse not far from the Brandenburg Gate, was within walking distance of her hotel. She had never visited Berlin before but she had seen pictures of the city during the Cold War, and it gave her a thrill to know that she was walking in what had once been Communist East Berlin. She had no difficulty in recognising the Embassy building – it was huge, forbidding and, to her eye, rather prison-like with its rows of recessed windows. It was blocked off at the street entrance by concrete bollards. In the reception area a policeman stood guard, armed with a Heckler & Koch automatic.

She was relieved to find Sally Mortimer already waiting in the foyer. Her warm welcome immediately dispersed the chilly feeling of the place. 'I thought I'd drive us to the BfV,' she said amiably. 'My car's garaged just down the road. It will take a while to get there but that gives us plenty of time to discuss tactics in the car.'

Peggy was soon admiring the deftness with which Sally manoeuvred her car through the crowded streets of Berlin. As they threaded their way confidently through the morning traffic, Sally said, 'I'd better tell you about this man we're going to see. His name is Lamme, Abel Lamme, and he's pretty senior in the Service. I've had dealings with him before and he's what my mother would call an S-H-I-T.'

'Oh God,' said Peggy, her thoughts of a pleasant morning disappearing. 'What's his problem?'

'We are, I'm afraid. He's supposed to be very clever and good at his job but he can't deal with women at work – all his colleagues say so. He actually refers to his secretary as "the girl", even though she's about sixty. I wonder she doesn't slap his face, but she's too polite and well brought up.' Sally shifted gear smoothly as she glided around a taxi dropping off a fare. She went on, 'I can't tell you how glad I am you're here. Maybe we can pull his leg a bit. Don't worry,' she said as Peggy started to demur, 'I know we want to persuade him to do something for us; he's simply far too pleased with himself to notice we're winding him up.'

'Are all the men in the BfV like that?' Peggy asked, curious. 'Are they all sexist?'

'No. Not really. On the whole it's not too bad,' Sally replied. 'No worse than the average. And don't get me wrong, I like it here – the city's wonderful, and the work is fascinating. No complaints there.'

She paused, and Peggy waited. Finally Sally asked, 'Are you married?'

Peggy shook her head.

'Boyfriend?'

Peggy said, 'No.' She hesitated, then added, 'I had a long-term partner, but he did something stupid and embarrassed me. We were living together, but he moved out about four months ago.'

'I'm sorry. Though if he let you down then perhaps it's for the best.'

'Definitely,' said Peggy. 'How about you?'

Sally gave a small groan. 'That's the bad side of this posting. There simply aren't any available men. The ones at the Embassy are either married or, to be frank, only interested in getting me into bed. The German men are friendly enough but hard to meet, and they're all so *formal*.' She said in a thick German accent, '*Vould Fräulein Mortimer care to accompany Herr Stuger to the opera this Saturday?*'

Peggy laughed. 'Perhaps they think that's the right way to treat a foreign diplomat.'

'I know,' said Sally, 'but sometimes it's positively painful.'

'How about back home?' asked Peggy. 'Is there anyone there?'

'Not really. I was very keen on someone in the Service. We went out a bit. He's older than me and he has a bit of a reputation. He's never married; been on a lot of postings at the sharp end and I think he finds it difficult to commit to anyone. On the surface he's the kind of man everyone warns you off. But he's actually very kind and completely charming. He could make me laugh more in five minutes than anyone else could in a month.'

'So what's happened to him?'

'Well, just when things were getting quite serious, I got posted here. He came out for a couple of weekends – then the silly bugger went and got himself sent on some secret undercover job. Now I don't know where he is.'

A lorry pulled out and Sally braked hard. 'Idiot,' she said sharply, her eyes on the road. A good thing too, thought Peggy, since otherwise Sally might have seen the surprised expression on her face; she had just realised that the man Sally was talking about could only be Bruno Mackay.

From Sally's account, Peggy had pictured Abel Lamme as an old-fashioned caricature of a male chauvinist – middle-aged, a bit overweight, moustache perhaps, tweed suit, possibly a cardigan. So she was surprised to find him not much more than forty, and smartly dressed in a faux-Armani suit with an open-necked shirt. He was tall, over six feet, with dark brown hair and a handsome face. He might have been an articulate footballer or a TV presenter, thought Peggy. He stood up to greet them, shaking hands and half bowing with elaborate courtesy.

'Good morning, ladies,' he said in only slightly accented English. 'What an honour it is to have two such beautiful young persons call on me. Please sit down and tell me how I can be of service.'

'No, no,' replied Sally, with equally exaggerated courtesy. 'The honour is all ours. We must apologise for disturbing you but as my colleague from London, Fräulein Peggy Kinsolving, will explain, it is a matter of some importance to both our countries.'

She turned to Peggy who was having difficulty not laughing during this exchange. She took control of herself and set about describing the complicated situation they had uncovered in Hamburg.

'Dieter Nimitz is an official with the European Commission in Brussels, where he works on immigration issues. His wife, Irma, is the Head of a school in Hamburg that specialises in educating immigrants. The fact that they both work with immigrants may be pure coincidence, of course.'

Peggy paused. Lamme was leaning forward in his chair, listening with his hands pressed together in a steeple against his dimpled chin. He said in a neutral voice, 'Go on.'

Peggy continued: 'Recently Dieter confided in a colleague at the Commission that he was concerned about his wife. He said she had been in contact with educational institutions in the US and UK about sending some of her students to study there.'

She paused, but Lamme was now looking up at the ceiling. She went on, 'We have reason to believe, through information from a third country, that she may be placing particularly talented immigrant children in these institutions for training in advanced cyber espionage.'

'And who is Frau Nimitz doing this for?'

'Our best information at this stage is that it may have a Russian connection. That's why we are here – we'd like your help finding out.'

Lamme lowered his head and stared at Peggy. 'Let me see if I understand this correctly. A German citizen, a Herr Nimitz, with a home in Hamburg, works on immigration policy at the European Commission. Poor fellow, I'd say – his job can't be much fun these days. His wife is a schoolteacher who teaches immigrant children in Germany, some of whom may go abroad to take courses in computer science at other institutions. Herr Nimitz, for whatever reason, is unhappy about this, and has complained to a colleague. As a result, the British intelligence service sends two officers – highly experienced, no doubt, and both extremely attractive,' – and he bowed his head as if in obeisance to their beauty – 'to ask for help from the BfV in …

what exactly? Stopping Irma Nimitz from sending students to study abroad?' He shook his head dismissively. 'I don't think it's the BfV that's required in this case; I'd say it was a marriage counsellor.'

'That's not all Nimitz told us.' Peggy was growing angry now. 'Apparently, when he was back at home for the weekend, he was meant to go into the city. But instead he returned home unexpectedly early, only to discover that a man had been visiting his wife. He said this was unprecedented.'

Lamme shrugged, with a condescending smile. 'So perhaps his wife has a "special" man friend, one so captivated by her charms that he was not willing to wait for her husband to return to Brussels before visiting her. Indiscreet? Of course. "Unprecedented" – I doubt it. This just confirms my view that a marriage counsellor would be more useful in this situation than the BfV. My dear Fräulein Kinsolving, my colleagues in counter-terrorism have many urgent investigations on hand. They would laugh at me if I asked for resources to investigate such a matter.'

'If I may finish,' went on Peggy coldly, 'there is one more piece of information that you might find carries some weight. A third country with whom we are working on this case has good reason to believe that the Russians are involved.'

'Hmm,' snorted Lamme. 'If your third country is the USA, as I suspect it is, you will soon learn what everyone knows, that they see Russians under every bed.'

Peggy could see from the corner of her eye that Sally Mortimer was getting red in the face and looked about to explode. Peggy, on the other hand, was feeling an icy anger. She didn't mind disagreement, or even open opposition, but she could not stand being sneered at, especially by an arrogant man not much older than she was herself.

She said firmly, 'What we're asking from you is very specific and very limited.'

Lamme widened his eyes as if to say, 'Is that so?' He looked amused.

'We cannot of course conduct any surveillance of our own here,' continued Peggy.

'Certainly not,' said Lamme sharply, the smirk leaving his face.

'But you can, and we'd like you to. We would like the Nimitz house watched while the husband is in Brussels during the week. Their house is in Blankensee, by the Elbe just outside the city—'

'I know where Blankensee is,' snapped Lamme. 'But tell me, who issued this request? Forgive me, but I am assuming it did not initiate only with you.'

Sally burst into life, like a kettle boiling over. 'Geoffrey Fane,' she snapped.

The other two had almost forgotten she was there, so wrapped up in their own contest, and they turned to look at her. Lamme seemed startled. It was obvious he knew who Fane was.

'And if I say no? What then? Perhaps you should telephone Mr Fane and let me explain the reasons.'

'He's on holiday—'

'Ah, I see, Mr Fane is unavailable. How convenient.'

'Not at all,' said Sally. 'I have his mobile number and instructions to ring him if there is in any problem. I think he'll be surprised to hear from you, since he seemed confident our request would be granted with no difficulty. But be my guest.' And she took out a notebook, apparently ready to read out a telephone number.

Before she could do so, Lamme put up a hand. 'Hold on,' he said, and he seemed to be thinking hard. 'If we were to agree to help, for how long would you expect the surveillance to continue? Our resources are very stretched.'

Peggy said, 'Today is Friday. Dieter should be coming home tonight, and usually leaves on the very early flight on Monday morning. So it would be from then until his return next Friday – in the first instance, that is. Then, depending on what happens, we could review it. We are looking to find out who it is who visits Irma Nimitz.'

'A working week? That is quite a long time.'

Peggy said nothing and was glad that Sally stayed quiet as well. The silence seemed to make Lamme uneasy. He shifted a bit in his chair, then seemed about to stand up, sat still instead, and finally slapped one knee with his hand.

'Very well, a week it will be,' he declared, as though the time frame was his own devising. 'Though I trust that, if we ask some day in the future, your Mr Fane will return the favour.'

'Of course,' said Peggy, before Sally Mortimer could reply. They both knew full well that Geoffrey Fane had no direct control over surveillance in the UK, which was in MI5's bailiwick, but Peggy was happy to let Lamme think he'd achieved a draw if that meant the Nimitz house would be under surveillance. Mission accomplished.

25

AFTER THE TWO WOMEN had left, Abel Lamme went back to his desk and sat down heavily. He was angry, and worse than that he felt stupid. He had been outmanoeuvred by a couple of over-excited English girls and he didn't like it. What's more, he thought their case was ridiculous. He didn't believe for a moment that there was some sinister Russian connection to a schoolteacher in Hamburg and the immigrant children she taught. The story of children being taught computer skills for evil ends sounded ludicrous to him. His colleagues would think he'd gone soft in the head if he made such a case for diverting scarce surveillance resources from counter-terrorist operations.

But he had to do something, having said he would. What was the minimum he could do to satisfy those girls and get them out of his hair? He sat drawing angry patterns on a piece of paper on his desk, reviewing the options. CCTV, he thought. That's what we'll do. If this Irma Nimitz woman does get a male visitor during the week, we'll photograph him and his car. Then we can identify him and if he turns out to be her bit on the side, he need never know. If by any remote chance he's a Russian, as the girls seem to think, we'll recognise him and his car if he's stationed here in Germany. In any case, if there is a regular visitor, we can set up some mobile surveillance next time he calls and find out where he comes from and what he's up to. That will have to do, he thought grumpily, though I'll bet even that is a complete waste of time.

So on the following Sunday the residents of the Nimitzes' street would have noticed men from the telephone company up various phone poles along the street. If anyone had asked, which they didn't, they would have been told that a fault had been reported and the lines were being checked. On Sunday evening Lamme was phoned and told that the system was in place and test pictures were being simultaneously received in the BfV operations room in Hamburg and at Headquarters in Berlin. They showed a wide-angle view of the street outside the Nimitzes' house, and close-ups of the garden at the back and the entrance to the house. The cameras were programmed to trigger if a car stopped in the street outside or if the front door opened or anyone walked through the garden.

Lamme's instruction to the operations room was that on Monday he wanted to see still photographs of the two occupants of the house, Dieter and Irma Nimitz. He then wanted to see a daily log of movements at the house, again with still photographs. If there was a male caller at the house who was clearly not a tradesman or the postman, he wanted to be told right away. What he didn't tell the Ops Room is that he didn't expect this to happen.

On the Monday morning Lamme was sitting at his desk looking at a set of photographs. In one, a rather plump woman in her early fifties was coming out of the front door carrying some shopping bags. Another, timed one and a half hours later, showed her unloading full bags from the boot of a car. There were also several pictures of a tall, thin, grey-haired man, presumably Dieter Nimitz, coming and going – the last one, timed at six that morning, showed him leaving the house carrying a small overnight bag and a briefcase.

Lamme rang Sally Mortimer at the British Embassy.

'Good morning, Miss Mortimer,' he said, his voice without warmth. 'I have the first pictures from our little operation. They show the two main characters. Do you wish to have copies?'

'Yes, please. I would like to see all the product.' She paused and then added, 'I am very grateful to you for your help in this.' What no one saw was that after she had said it she stuck her tongue out at the telephone.

As the week wore on, the surveillance operation proceeded as Lamme had predicted. Each morning there was a packet of photographs on his desk showing all the usual comings and goings at any normal suburban house. Irma left every morning at about eight; the cleaning lady arrived at nine and left at one; the postman came every morning; once there was a delivery of what looked like a parcel from Amazon. Each day, Irma returned at about four thirty, once nearer five with shopping. In the evening all was quiet and no one came or went.

But on Thursday the pace suddenly changed. At two o'clock, the phone on Lamme's desk rang. The Ops Room officer said, 'Just heard from Hamburg. Your lady's come home early. They're wondering if she's expecting a visitor.'

'OK. I'm coming up to watch.' He was curious despite his scepticism.

In the Ops Room one of the large monitors on the wall was blank. Nothing was moving at the Nimitz house so the cameras were inactive. One of the Ops officers brought up on another screen the feed from fifteen minutes previously; Lamme watched the figure he recognised as Irma hurrying up the path and opening the door with a key.

Nothing more happened for a time, and Lamme grew restless, and started pacing round the Ops Room. He had been sure the English girls had been imagining things. Was he going to be proved wrong? He waited, glancing from time to time at the blank screen, his jaw clenched.

The screen flickered into life, showing a black Mercedes saloon pulling up outside the Nimitz house. The digital clock in the corner of the screen read 14.45. The car door opened and a heavyset, dark-haired man in a leather jacket got out. He collected a briefcase from the passenger seat, slammed and locked the doors and marched up the path to the front door of the house. Before he could ring the bell, the door opened and Irma Nimitz welcomed him inside.

'Oh no,' muttered Lamme under his breath. He knew who the man was. Igor Leonov, identified FSB officer, undercover as a cultural attaché at the Russian Consulate in Hamburg and the target of many an unsuccessful surveillance operation.

Whatever was going on at this house in Blankensee was bad news. And even worse, from Lamme's point of view, was that he was going to have to admit to the English girls that they had been right all along.

26

'H AS ANYONE SEEN PEGGY?' Liz was standing at the door of the open-plan office. Heads turned from screens but no one nodded.

'I don't think she's in yet,' said a voice. 'Her coat's not here.'

'That's strange,' replied Liz. 'I was expecting her for a meeting ten minutes ago. She must have forgotten. Will you ask her to look in when she gets here?'

Really odd, thought Liz, as she walked back to her office. Peggy never forgets. She had reached her door when the phone started ringing. Suddenly concerned, she hurried to pick it up.

'Hello, Liz,' said a familiar voice; there was a lot of noise in the background.

'Peggy? Where are you? I was expecting you ten minutes ago.'

'That's why I'm ringing. I'm on a train – I've been trying to get through but we keep going into tunnels and the WiFi's not working. My mother had a fall in the night; she's been taken to hospital. I caught the first train north as soon as I heard this morning. I'm sorry about our meeting.'

'Don't worry about the meeting; it can wait. But I'm so sorry. How is your mother; is she all right?'

'I think so. Apparently they took some X-rays and nothing's broken. But she's got some cuts and bruises and is quite shaken up, so it's just as well I'm going to see her.'

'Absolutely. You met let me know how she is.'

'I will. How was Suffolk?'

'Very interesting. I'll tell you all about it when you're back.' She knew Peggy wouldn't expect her to go into details over the phone, though she would probably welcome the distraction from worrying about her ageing mother, who was becoming increasingly fragile. She knew Peggy was worried that her mother might not be able to look after herself for much longer. Liz's own mother remained hale and hearty.

Peggy went on, 'I had an interesting time in Germany, though our German counterpart was a true dyed-in-the-wool chauvinist – thought Sally Mortimer and I were a couple of English airheads. But Sally sorted him out – she threatened him with Fane. You should have seen him wilt! Anyway, he's going to do what we asked. So you may get something from Six if anything happens.'

Liz was laughing. 'Well done. I can just imagine the two of you tackling a chauvinist.'

'It was Sally really. She'd dealt with him before so she knew how to pull his strings. She's a good egg. Even if her choice in men is a little suspect.'

'What do you mean?'

Peggy tried but failed to suppress a giggle. 'She's been having a fling with our favourite member of Vauxhall Cross.'

'Not Geoffrey Fane? I can't believe it! She must be nearly thirty years younger than him.'

'No, not Fane. Bruno Mackay.'

'Oh God. Poor girl. She's doomed to heartbreak. In any case he's disappeared off the map under deep cover.'

'I know. She's not happy about it. Well, I'd better go. We're nearly at my station. I hope to be back tomorrow but I'll keep in touch.'

'OK. Good luck and best regards to your mother.'

Liz put the phone down. She hoped Peggy's mother would be all right. She lived in Doncaster. It would be difficult for Peggy to look after her adequately while working in London.

The following afternoon Peggy was back, much reassured by her mother's recovery, to find a message from Sally Mortimer via Vauxhall Cross. There had been a Russian visitor to the Hamburg house. He was a known FSB officer.

Hearing this, Liz said slowly, 'It makes sense, I suppose. Especially as it seems to have been the Russians behind this boy at Vermont University.'

'But…?' When Liz looked at her, Peggy said, 'I sense you have your doubts. About the Russians, I mean.'

'Well, we need better evidence than a single visit to a German headmistress. But that's not the only reason I'm sceptical. Let me tell you about my visit to Bartholomew Manor.'

She told Peggy about her trip to Suffolk and the strangeness of the school – Miss Girling, the bizarrely named Cicero, then the enigmatic figure of the Head himself, Mr Sarnat. She described Sarnat's study and the books she'd seen, as well as the trap she'd fallen into, being caught by a hidden camera. She didn't mention her dinner with the Chief Constable, but told Peggy how she thought she'd detected Cicero in his Mini behind her on her way home. At this, Peggy's eyes widened and she said, 'I don't like the sound of that at all.'

Liz shrugged. 'It could have been a coincidence. Or I could have been mistaken and it wasn't Cicero's car. Anyway, the point is, there was a very odd atmosphere about that place – what my mother's friend Edward would call "distinctly rum". The books in particular struck me – why this odd Confucian stuff, and why Taiwan?'

'Did you find out who the owners are?'

'No; just that the owners have changed.'

Peggy nodded. 'Let me do some digging then.'

She was back to Liz by the next morning, sooner than expected. From the contented look on her face, Liz knew she had discovered something. 'OK,' she said, 'let's have it.'

'I've had a team working on this as it's pretty complicated. The school, which like most schools used to be a non-profit charitable trust, is now a private company. It changed status three years ago. Now it belongs to something called Elkhorn plc.'

'Should I have heard of them?'

'I don't think so. Very mysterious this Elkhorn. A Jersey company that turns out to be a shell – for another company in the Virgin Islands called Daubisson Assets.'

'Who are?'

'A holding company – this time for a Swiss company, registered in Geneva. With a board composed – as far as we could tell – of unremarkable local businessmen.'

'That's a bit odd. Why would a bunch of Swiss burghers want to buy an obscure school in a remote part of Suffolk?'

'I'm not sure they do. It smacks of token directors – not the power behind the throne.'

'Who is the power then?'

Peggy looked down at her notes. 'My candidate is one Simon Lee, an owner of half a dozen language schools in the Far East. British passport holder, Hong Kong born but now a resident of Taiwan. Interestingly, we noticed that in some document he claims a degree from a university in Leipzig. That was at a date before the Wall came down – when Leipzig was in East Germany.'

'Hang on a minute. You're saying the real owner is a Taiwanese businessman?'

'Well, he's not Taiwanese. He seems to be British but he lives in Taiwan now. He's the only candidate we've got and he seems to have a very unusual background.' She looked again at her notes. 'Jacques Millier, François Didier, Henri Palotin – none of these gentlemen seem to have either the assets or international experience to drive the acquisition of the school. It just doesn't make sense. Simon Lee, on the other hand…'

Liz sat and thought for a moment. Peggy said, 'Shall I pursue our Mr Lee some more? He seems the one lead we have.'

Liz shook her head. 'I'm not sure I agree. By all means look him up; see if Six have anything on him; do a police check. But I think we should be concentrating on the school itself and what exactly is going on there.'

'How do we do that? Won't they find it peculiar if you ask for another visit? And you said yourself, I can't really pass as a prospective parent.'

'No, you can't. But there may be other ways we can learn about the place.' She smiled at Peggy. 'I have an idea.'

27

B RUNO THOUGHT THAT IF he arrived at the restaurant about ten minutes late it would convey the right air of nonchalance. So he deliberately dawdled through Red Square, pausing to admire a bride being photographed in her wedding finery, and took his time ambling down the side street leading to the restaurant he had suggested for their lunch.

Nikita's was not quite the hole in the wall that Bruno had described to Bebchuk, but it was very small, with no more than a dozen rough pine tables. It had the air of what in London or San Francisco would have been a pop-up restaurant, though Bruno knew from a previous conversation with the owner that it had been open more than a year.

Bruno found Bebchuk at the back at a table for two, stabbing at his phone and looking irritated. He stood to shake hands and Bruno said extravagantly, 'A million apologies. My choice of restaurant but I'm the one who got lost.'

'I was about to give up and order some food,' said Bebchuk with a forced smile. The tone of his voice suggested he wasn't given to listening to excuses.

They both sat down and Bruno added, 'Actually, I would have been on time but I came via Red Square. Just my luck – there was about a battalion of soldiers trooping through and the police wouldn't let us cross the square until they'd passed.'

'In Russia, the military gets priority,' said Bebchuk, smiling thinly.

'Were you a military man?'

Bebchuk shook his head. 'My father was an officer in the Red Army.' His English was accented but very good.

'Didn't he want you to follow in his footsteps?'

'Of course,' said Bebchuk simply, 'but it was OK – I persuaded my little brother to enlist instead.' He gave a wolfish grin and Bruno laughed.

A waitress appeared. 'This is my shout,' Bruno declared, remembering the speciality of the place. '*Pelmeni*, don't you think?' he asked Bebchuk, and the Russian nodded. Bruno looked at Bebchuk's glass and said, 'Water for me too.'

Bebchuk said, 'This is not water. And I'll have another one.'

'Make that two,' said Bruno.

As the waitress departed, Bebchuk said, 'And were you a soldier? One of the Queen's Guardsmen perhaps.'

'Not at all.' Bruno gave a self-deprecating laugh. 'I'm a lousy shot and can't read a map. I would have been continually lost on manoeuvres.'

Bebchuk smiled but he was watching Bruno closely. 'Did you also have a brother who is a soldier?'

'No brothers; just sisters – three, in fact. I was the only son.'

'These sisters of yours, they spoiled you?'

'Absolutely,' said Bruno. Most of what he was saying was true, which was always best for a cover story.

'Is this what they mean when they speak of a lady's man?'

'Well, I don't know about that, though it gives one a head start, I suppose. With three sisters I had a pretty good idea of what girls look for in a chap.'

The *pelmeni* arrived: two large bowls full of sombrero-shaped dumplings, with little side dishes of sour cream. The filling was a spicy mix of beef and pork, and utterly delicious.

'What do you think?' he asked Bebchuk.

The Russian speared a dumpling and chewed thoughtfully. 'Excellent. Not as good as my mother's, but a close second. But speaking of the ladies, how long have you known Michelle?'

'Oh, not long,' said Bruno. 'But I like her very much.'

'She must like you too. She was most insistent that her friends come to meet you the other night.'

'That was kind. I don't know many people here yet.'

'You like Moscow then?'

'Yes. There's so much energy here. Exciting times.'

'Where else have you lived?'

Bruno had used cover stories for most of his professional life. He was quite capable of discussing the relative merits of life in Pakistan, North America, most of Western Europe and even, if pressed, the Outer Hebrides. Now he put into service his most recently concocted CV, much of it based on his own considerable travels. He told the mandatory story of having his pocket picked in Rio de Janeiro, related an amusing account of trying and failing to bribe a Customs inspector in what had then been Yugoslavia. But that was all when he was younger, he added. In his present job as an investment banker he had to be a model citizen; trust and probity, he said, were his USP.

'USP?' asked Bebchuk, frowning.

'Unique selling point,' explained Bruno. 'In my business we distinguish ourselves from the competition by our reputation and our performance.'

'So I understand that you are exploring opportunities for business here. Do you intend to stay here some time?'

'Could be,' said Bruno amiably.

'Michelle told my wife you were planning to apply for permanent resident status.'

Experienced in concealing surprise, Bruno merely opened his eyes a little wider. 'I don't know if permanent is quite right. But I have no plans to leave unless something wonderful comes along that takes me back home.' Seeing an opening, Bruno went on, 'Would you ever want to live abroad?'

Bebchuk took his time replying. 'Possibly,' he said cautiously at last. 'If the conditions were right.' He was still staring at Bruno.

Bruno looked down at his bowl and scraped absent-mindedly at it with his fork. 'You know, as a state official, you have great value to people trying to do business in Russia.' He lifted his eyes but let them rove idly around the room. 'Russia remains a mystery to us in the West. People who understand the inner workings of this place are rare as gold.'

'As gold? You exaggerate, my friend.'

'Not at all.' Bruno allowed himself at last to meet Boris's gaze. 'Though obviously it depends on how much the person knows about the inner workings of things.'

'Obviously,' said Bebchuk. It was hard to tell if he were amused, interested or simply bored.

Bruno sipped his vodka, trying to stay patient. 'To some extent it would depend on what this person in the know wanted to get out of it. Financially, I mean,' he added.

'There is that,' Bebchuk acknowledged. 'There are also other issues, no?'

'Are there?'

Bebchuk raised his hand at the waitress and signalled for another vodka. She looked at Bruno, and he decided he had better match Bebchuk, so he nodded, though he was going to drink it very slowly. He badly needed to keep his wits about him.

Bebchuk sighed. He said, 'You know, in Moscow since the time of Yeltsin, many people have made lots of money. So much so that people forget that money does not always make you secure. What is the point of a billion roubles if the government can take it away? Just like that.' He snapped his fingers for emphasis.

'I suppose the wise ones have their money abroad,' Bruno commented. 'Somewhere safe, so that even if they become enemies of the government, they have their money out of harm's way.'

'"Harm's way" – I like that,' said Bebchuk. Then his voice hardened. 'But what good is safe money if you are not safe yourself? Without that, there can be no security. Except perhaps for the widow of the man who thought a billion roubles made him safe.'

Bruno was silent for a moment, then, emboldened by the vodka, he said as soberly as he could, 'I suppose there are always ways to keep people safe, as well as their money. Provided there is trust, that is.'

'Trust. The magic word, is it not? But many of those who trusted your country are no longer alive.'

Bruno said nothing, and Bebchuk smiled enigmatically. Then he said, 'I thank you for an excellent lunch. I would stay for coffee, but I need to get back to the department. Perhaps we can have another lunch sometime. I will choose the restaurant perhaps – if you trust *me*.'

The Russian left and Bruno called for the bill. He was in no doubt that his message had got through to Bebchuk. What he felt less confident about was how it had been received.

28

MATILDA BURNSIDE HAD BEEN surreptitiously observing Dieter Nimitz all morning. The two of them shared a large office on the fifth floor of the Berlaymont building, the headquarters of the European Commission, and from where she sat by the window Matilda could see Dieter clearly without seeming to be looking at him, though this morning she doubted he would have noticed even if she had been staring right at him. He seemed completely withdrawn, wrapped up in himself.

She had noticed when he arrived for work that he looked more than usually haggard. His face was always thin and rather grey but this Monday morning his cheeks seemed to have fallen in and his eyes were glazed. He hadn't been looking well for weeks but now he looked positively haunted. She was uncertain whether to try to get him to talk or whether to wait and hope that he would say something of his own accord.

Her husband Peter had asked her to tell him if Dieter said anything more about his wife, but not to raise the subject herself, ask questions or seem to be prying. On the other hand, simple human kindness seemed to demand that she tried to help her colleague and friend. She sat quietly, getting on with her work but conscious of the cloud hanging over the other desk.

Finally, as the clock moved towards midday, Dieter cleared his throat and spoke for the first time since he had said a gruff 'Bonjour' on arrival that morning. 'Matilda, will you come and have some lunch with me? There's something I'd like to discuss with you but I'd rather not talk in the restaurant here.'

'Love to,' said Matilda. 'Let's go now before it gets too crowded.'

Soon they were installed at a quiet table in the little local bistro, each with a glass of wine in front of them and their lunch orders given. Dieter looked straight at Matilda and said, 'I want to tell you a story – my story. I am putting myself into your hands. I think you will know what to do.'

She looked at him, her eyes full of sympathy, but said nothing.

'I was born in the GDR,' he began. 'Not in a village between Munich and Salzburg as I have always claimed. My name then was Dieter Schmidt. My father worked for the Stasi. When I was seventeen I was visited by two men, one a Russian. They asked me a lot of questions and later I was told that I had been selected for undercover work. East Germany was in the Eastern bloc, of course, so I felt greatly honoured.

'After my school exams were over I was sent to Moscow and given a new identity, Dieter Nimitz, and trained in all the details of my new background until I wore them like a skin.

'That was in 1974. After six months' intensive training, I was sent back to say goodbye to my family; then I went to West Germany with a student group on an exchange visit. I was the one member of the group who stayed behind.

'I don't know how it was arranged but no questions were asked and overnight I became Dieter Nimitz, freshly graduated from a *Gymnasium* in Bavaria. I was given a place at Hamburg University to study languages. Everything had been arranged for me, including my accommodation, and no one asked any questions or doubted my authenticity. I had learned my lessons well.

'After I graduated I was instructed to accept a job offer I received from a small import–export firm in Hamburg. I worked there for seven years, hearing nothing at all from my controllers. I was convinced they had forgotten all about me when suddenly I received an instruction to apply for a post here at the Commission. I started here in 1987.'

He stopped and reached for the water jug to refill his glass but his hand was shaking so much that he couldn't grasp it. Matilda reached out and gently took the jug from him and refilled both their glasses. She had a thousand questions to ask, but she knew he had more of his story to tell, so she just smiled at him encouragingly and waited. The waiter came with their food, but Dieter only poked with his fork at the plate in front of him.

'I've worked here for almost thirty years,' he went on eventually. 'And I have heard nothing from the Russians except when they told me to apply for this job. I had no idea what their plan for me was or even if they had one. When the wall came down and the regime in Russia changed, I assumed that as everything was in turmoil I had been forgotten. Maybe priorities had changed. But recently I have wondered. Wondered whether the plan was something very different from anything I imagined and whether I have been playing a part in it all these years without even knowing.'

This was even more intriguing than the first part of his story. Matilda, who had been eating while he had been talking, mainly to cover her surprise at his story, now put her fork down and leaned forward, her elbows on the table and her chin on her hands. She spoke for the first time but just to say, 'Go on.'

'I met and married my wife Irma while I was working in Hamburg. Friends of the owner of the company introduced us. I hadn't had much to do with women and when she made it very clear that she wanted to get married, I agreed right away. We were married less than a year after we met. We had a small ceremony. I said I was an orphan. It didn't seem strange at the time as there had been so much upheaval in Germany.

'I never told Irma about my real origins and she never asked about my past life. Frankly, I never asked much about hers. It sounds strange to say that now, but it didn't seem so at the time. She's always been the dominant one in our marriage.' He gave a long sigh. 'But recently I have begun to wonder about my marriage, and about Irma, and I have now become convinced that it was all arranged – that Irma was under instructions to marry me.'

'Instructions from whom?'

'From the same people who had turned me into Dieter Nimitz,' said Dieter, as if it were completely obvious. 'I think perhaps they decided that I don't have the right temperament for secret undercover work, so they used me as a convenient and respectable cover for whatever they have had Irma doing instead.

'I am now sure, from everything I have noticed recently, that she is involved in some sort of plot involving the immigrant children at the school. I don't know exactly what's going on, but from what I have discovered now it seems to involve your country as well.'

He stopped talking and took another long gulp of water. For the first time that day he looked straight at Matilda. His face had relaxed and his eyes looked brighter. He said, 'So, now you know my story. I have never told anyone before but it was time and I feel relieved. You must do whatever you think right with the information but please do something. I don't want whatever Irma is doing to succeed. I am sure it is wrong and damaging and I don't want the children to be harmed.'

'Thank you for telling me,' said Matilda simply. 'I do know who to talk to and I can guarantee that we will do everything we can to find out what's going on – and to prevent any harm coming to these children.'

29

Florence Girling stood in the kitchen of the cottage she had shared with her mother for many years and, since her mother's death, now lived in alone. For the third time, she was reading the letter that had come in the post earlier that morning. It had been lying on the mat inside the front door when she came downstairs, along with the usual assortment of fliers for cheap pizza in Southwold, double glazing, bargain spectacles and a plastic bag to fill with old clothes for a charity. She noticed the letter at once. It was marked SUFFOLK POLICE.

She found this rather alarming as she had never had any dealings with the police. When she opened it her alarm was joined by confusion.

Dear Madam,
Records show that you are the registered holder of a Driving Licence Driver Number GIRLI 588214F99SV, valid from 19 10 1985 to 22 08 2028, in the name of Florence Girling.

A document with these details was discovered at the scene of an incident in Oswestry which is being investigated by the Shropshire Police. We note that you have not reported your licence as missing and we need to establish how it came to be in Oswestry in the above circumstances.

Accordingly, we would be grateful if you would present yourself with this letter at the Southwold Police Station on the Saturday following the date of this letter at 10:30 a.m. The address is Mights Rd, Southwold IP18 6BB. Please ask at Reception for Ms Diane Kingly.

Should you be unable to attend this appointment please telephone the number at the head of this letter.

Yours sincerely
R. T. Vollman

Although thoroughly upright – there had never been the faintest whiff of scandal in her life, not to mention any trouble with the law – Miss Girling was not unflappable. And now she found herself in what her mother had always called an absolute tizz. Standing in the kitchen with the letter in her hand, she wished her mother were still alive: the elderly Mrs Girling had been a rock in times of crisis. What would she have done now, Miss Girling wondered plaintively, then instinctively switched on the kettle.

As she sipped a cup of tea, Florence felt reason return. First things first, she decided, and found her purse. There she was relieved to see her licence, which had sat in more or less the same position, untouched, unused, for over thirty years. She pulled it out, put on her glasses and peered closely at it, carefully reading the line of tiny letters and figures. Yes. It was the same as in the letter. How had it been found in Oswestry when it was here in her hand?

Florence had passed her driving test years before, in a fleeting show of independence from her mother, but had never owned a car. When she had discovered the cost of buying and running a vehicle, she had thought better of it, and in any case she didn't need one. A bus took her each morning from the stop at the end of the road right to the top of the lane that led to Bartholomew Manor, and a bus brought her home each evening. There was a small general store and post office in the village which answered most of her needs. She wasn't much of a traveller. Once a year she went to London to have lunch with an old friend from schooldays, and for this she splurged on a taxi to Darsham station where she caught the train to Liverpool Street. A car would be a nuisance rather than a help, and an expensive one at that.

As good sense overcame her initial fears, Miss Girling found herself increasingly puzzled. Someone, somehow, must have found out the details of her unused driving licence and had been driving around pretending to be her.

She had read about identity theft in the paper and had heard them talking about it on Radio 4 but she had no idea how it was done. She thought it had something to do with internet banking but she didn't do that; she used the branch of Barclays in Southwold. In fact, she didn't use the internet at all. She used the telephone if she wanted to get in touch with anyone. So how could someone have stolen her identity? A mistake must have been made by someone – perhaps because she hadn't used her licence, they'd issued her number twice? It wouldn't have surprised her in the least. It was bound to be due to computers in some way or another, even if it wasn't the internet.

She held a profound mistrust of computers. She knew that people younger than her, which meant virtually everyone at Bartholomew Manor, would dismiss her views, call her a dinosaur and point to the benefits computers were bringing to mankind. Name one, Florence Girling thought sourly. There was nothing they could supply that she wasn't happy to do without. For her, the benefits of technology had ended with the invention of the wireless and the telephone.

It was not a view she thought it wise to share at work. Not since everything had changed at Bartholomew Manor. Once she had left home each morning full of enthusiasm for the day ahead. She had spent twenty entirely enjoyable years in what had been the most traditional private second-ary school in this part of the country, helping to educate what she was certain would be the cream of the young men and women of their generation.

But over the last few months her job at Bartholomew Manor had become a nightmare. Once she had taught Geography and helped with the administration. Now she didn't teach at all; indeed, there weren't any pupils left to teach. Local families had all taken their children away.

Her job now was a sort of dogsbody role, and consisted mainly of showing prospective parents around. She was ashamed of the dilapidated state of the main school. The classrooms needed a thorough overhaul – painting, new furniture and general updating. Even she could see that. The only area where money had been spent was on the technology suite the new owners were so proud of. She had so far managed to mask her alarm at the computer-focused curriculum the school now offered, and tried to show to the prospective parents a pride she didn't feel in the gleaming equipment. Not that there were many of them and none of them seemed to want to send their children there. She didn't blame them. As far as she could understand it, the school seemed now to be rely-ing on an intake of new students shortly to come from abroad.

The new owners remained a mystery to her, but she was certain they were foreigners, though she couldn't have said where they were from. The Head was a strange man, much given to philosophising, with his assistant, the oddly named Cicero, whom she found sinister and frightening. She felt increasingly out of place and she sensed that they were just waiting for an opportunity to get rid of her. But she had decided to hang on as long as she could, since she knew they would have to pay her something to leave and she was also due her pension. Although she somehow sensed that if they moved against her first, she might be left with nothing at all.

30

Miss Girling knew most of Southwold like the back of her hand, but the address she had been given for the police station was a road on the outskirts of the town, on an unattractive 1950s housing estate which it had taken her two buses to reach. She got off the bus, cautiously looking round her. She dreaded meeting anyone she knew as she didn't want to have to explain that she was out here visiting the police.

As she walked from the bus stop, looking for the number she had been given, she could see nothing that looked like her idea of a police station. She remembered the old one in the centre of the town, which had been closed for several years now. It had been a rather imposing red-brick double-fronted building with steps up the middle and a blue lamp over the door. But this was a street of single-storey buildings, some with small gardens in front and others with concrete for parking cars.

She found the right number house with no difficulty. The strange thing about it was that it looked very little different from all the other houses in the street except that its windows were covered with a fine metal mesh. As she approached, she could see that the building had been extended considerably, using all the space where the back garden had once been. Its front garden was concreted over and two cars were parked there, one an ordinary-looking silver car and one a police car. She walked up to the front door and noticed with some relief that underneath the bell was a small plate that read *SUFFOLK POLICE*. She rang the bell and the door clicked open.

Inside was a square hall with a low table and a couple of upholstered upright wooden-armed chairs – rather like the visitors' chairs in a hospital ward. In one of these a young woman was sitting reading a magazine. As Miss Girling came in, she put the magazine on the table and stood up.

'Miss Florence Girling?' she asked smiling. 'Do come in. I'm Diane Kingly. Thank you for coming. I hope you had no difficulty finding this place. It is a bit off the beaten track, I'm afraid.'

'I had no difficulty,' replied Florence, somewhat taken aback by the warmth of the welcome.

'Well, if you'll follow me, we'll go somewhere a bit more comfortable.'

Florence followed the young woman along a corridor past several closed doors until she led Florence into a comfortable sitting room with chintz-covered armchairs and a two-seater sofa. Against the wall by the window was a small polished dining table on which stood a cafetière of coffee, cups and saucers and a plate of biscuits.

'I should think you could do with a cup of coffee after trekking out here,' said the young woman. 'Do you take sugar? Biscuit?'

The coffee organised and delivered, the young woman sat down. By now Florence Girling had had a chance to sum her up. She looked most unlike a policewoman but

Florence was modern enough to know that they came in all shapes and sizes these days. The young woman was wearing slim black trousers with ankle boots, and a soft grey cowl-necked sweater. Her hair was a shiny brown and held by a clip at the back of her head. She had very blue eyes.

'Please call me Diane,' said Peggy Kinsolving. 'It's a very strange story about your driving licence being found in Oswestry. Have you brought it with you and the letter I sent you, just as formal identification?'

Florence scrabbled in her bag and produced both documents. 'Can you tell me what this is about? You see, I don't actually own a car, and I haven't driven one for over twenty years. So my driving licence has hardly ever been out of my purse since I got it and I've never been to Oswestry.'

'Well, I'm afraid I think it's likely that someone has been using your licence – or should I say a copy of it, or a fake licence with your details on it.'

Peggy examined the licence carefully. Then to Miss Girling's relief, she smiled, and said, 'It seems to be the genuine article.'

'So how did my details come to be used in Oswestry? And how did the police get the false licence?' asked Miss Girling. She was feeling more confident now that it looked as though no one suspected her of anything. She was genuinely interested to know what had been going on.

'That's what we're hoping you can help us with. Do you know anyone in the county of Shropshire?'

'Goodness no,' said Miss Girling, for whom Shropshire might as well have been in Africa. She was Suffolk born and bred, and could count on the fingers of one hand the people she knew who, like her old schoolfriend now in London, had been foolish enough to move away from the county.

'All right,' said Peggy, 'then I think our best bet is to assume that someone took down your details for use elsewhere.' She saw the look of alarm spreading across Miss Girling's face, and added sympathetically, 'Without your knowledge, of course.'

'But who could it be? I haven't been burgled, and –' she paused, recognising the grimness of her confession – 'I don't have many visitors.' Not a single one in recent weeks, she realised, other than her next-door neighbour.

'What about work? Could it have been there?'

'I wouldn't think so,' said Miss Girling, though she was discomfited by the suggestion since it matched her own earlier speculation about her employers.

'Tell me about your place of work, if you don't mind. I gather you work at a school.'

Miss Girling wondered momentarily how this woman knew where she was employed but was soon distracted by her own account of the place. She explained how she had first come to work there many years before, on the recommendation of her mother's oldest friend, and how much she had enjoyed teaching the students at what had then been a high-class private secondary school. She was pleased to find Miss Kingly nodding with interest as she talked about the school back then, the support it had had from the local community, the spirit of the place, evinced in the general good nature and willingness of both staff and students.

'And now?' asked Peggy quietly.

Miss Girling exhaled. 'Don't get me started,' she said.

'Go on,' encouraged Peggy. 'Is it as bad as all that?'

'Worse,' said Miss Girling.

She was beyond discretion by now, and found herself throwing caution to the wind since this young woman seemed so sympathetic. A year's worth of stored-up resentment came out, in a long and highly specific account that reflected what she really thought about the place in its new incarnation. At one point, as she was describing the sinister Cicero, she realised that Miss Kingly was taking notes. But did that matter when Miss Girling was only telling the truth?

It was as she was describing Mr Sarnat – he of the businessman's suits and Confucianist reading – that Miss Kingly interrupted. 'Is Mr Sarnat the owner of the school?'

Miss Girling thought for a moment before shaking her head. 'I don't think so.'

'Who is then?'

'I don't know,' she admitted. 'Though I'd dearly like to.' If only to give them a piece of her mind, she thought to herself.

'And these new foreign students? When are they arriving?'

'It's unclear. Or at least no one's told me,' she admitted. 'But it must be soon, or they won't be here for the start of term.'

'Do you think you could find out, Miss Girling? And possibly who the new owners are as well? You must be the school's resident memory, after all. No one knows as much about it as you do.'

'I suppose that's true,' said Miss Girling, pleased by the compliment. For once it felt nice – and useful – to be old. If only all young people were so polite and understanding as this Miss Kingly.

'I wouldn't want you to do anything that would get you into trouble,' said Miss Kingly soothingly. 'It's just that you're in a position to find things out that even the authorities can't uncover.'

'Do you think this has anything to do with my driving licence?' asked Miss Girling, puzzled.

'We can't be sure,' said Miss Kingly pensively. 'Put it this way, Miss Girling: there have been suggestions made that all is not what it seems at Bartholomew Manor. The evidence points to the owners possibly skirting a line close to the edge of the law. If that's the case, then pilfering an innocent civilian's particulars from a driving licence would seem to them mere child's play.'

'But that's monstrous,' protested Miss Girling.

'It is indeed. But these are awkward customers we're dealing with.'

'Criminals?'

'Who's to say? But it's not impossible.' Miss Kingly looked suddenly abashed, as if she had given away much more than she had meant to. 'I hope I can trust you to keep this conversation strictly in confidence, Miss Girling.'

'Of course,' said Miss Girling, unsure what conspiracy she had enlisted in, but finding it oddly exciting to be part of it.

Miss Kingly went on, 'Which means that this will not be our only conversation. If you wouldn't mind I'd like to keep in touch. That way if you discover anything about the ownership of the school, you'll be able to let me know. When the students do arrive, I'd be very interested in knowing what they are like and, most important, where they come from. In fact, if you could keep me posted about anything unusual going on, that would be very helpful. I'd leave it to you to decide what constitutes "unusual", since you are the expert on Bartholomew Manor,' she said with a smile. She added after this had sunk in, 'Would that be all right?'

'Oh yes,' said Miss Girling, finding it refreshing to be asked to do something off her own bat for a change, even if it came from someone young enough to be her daughter.

'Then let me give you my card. You can ring the number on it at any time – day or night. I may not answer personally, but they will promptly relay any message to me.' She handed over a small calling card, which Miss Girling deposited in her handbag. She could study it on her way home on the bus.

Miss Kingly continued, 'But don't ring from a phone at the school or anywhere where you could be overheard. At home is best. And I don't want you to feel you have to do any of this. If you feel uncomfortable in any way, do let me know. But I can assure you that my colleagues – and not just at Suffolk Police – would be very grateful for any information you can provide. As I am sure you have guessed, I don't always work on stolen driving licences.'

'I gathered as much,' said Miss Girling, though truth be told, this was the first time it had occurred to her that, much like the peculiar Mr Sarnat but in an altogether healthier way, Miss Kingly was not absolutely one hundred percent what she had appeared to be. And now she thought about it, the young woman never had claimed to be a police officer.

31

IT WAS NINE THIRTY in the morning. Chief Constable Pearson was sitting at his desk in Bury St Edmunds trying to write a speech he was to deliver at the Chief Constables' conference the following week. It wasn't going well. His subject was the police role in the prevention of illegal immigration but he didn't feel he had a good story to tell. In his view, far too little resource was being devoted to the problem. The press would be in the audience, all too ready to catch him out with their questions – the left alert to anything that could be construed as an abuse of human rights, the right anxious to expose anything that indicated the police were 'soft' on immigration. His task was to craft something that avoided both these potential pitfalls, and any others, and he was finding the task almost impossible.

As he drank the cup of coffee that his secretary had just brought in, he let his mind wander over more pleasant subjects. He'd emailed Liz the day before and they would be meeting for dinner on the first night of his stay in London. He sensed she was as hesitant as he was about their growing closeness, but hoped she shared his underlying conviction that theirs was a relationship worth pursuing. It was not merely that he was lonely, though he was, but he was also genuinely attracted to Liz.

There had been other opportunities and even a few, usually terrible, 'dates'. Well-meaning friends and even his sister and brother-in-law had been eager to introduce him to eligible women, often divorcees, sometimes single women who had simply never met the right man. How often he had sat through dinner parties which had the subtext of finding someone for 'poor Richard'; how often he had tried to parry the post-party enquiries as to whether he would like the phone number of Victoria, or Eleanor, or Amanda.

With Liz there was none of that; he had met her on his own, thank God, and more to the point, she had suffered a loss equivalent to his. Who knew what would come of it? But for the first time since his wife's death, he had a real interest in finding out.

He had just reapplied himself to the speech when his secretary came in again to say apologetically that one of the officers from the Immigration team wanted to have an urgent word with him about a report of something suspicious at Dunwich beach.

'Ask him to come in,' said Pearson, pushing his speech away with relief.

Inspector Gurwant Singh was the only Sikh in the Suffolk force. He was a tall man, and with his neatly rolled beard and pale blue turban he made an impressive figure.

'Come in. Sit down and tell me what's happened.'

'Well, sir,' Inspector Singh began, 'I have a source that I've known for several years. He has a small boat-building yard at one end of Dunwich beach. He's been keeping an eye out for me on that bit of the coast and I've asked him to ring me if he sees any stuff on the beach, unidentified boats or anything that might indicate an unauthorised landing.'

Pearson nodded but said nothing.

'He rang me at eight this morning,' went on Singh. 'He said that he had been disturbed in the night by what sounded like a lorry or a bus. He has a cottage just by the gap in the dunes where the path goes up from the beach to the track that leads through the marsh to the coast road. He said he thought it was strange but he didn't get out of bed to look and just went back to sleep. He's quite an old man, over seventy now,' Singh added, as if to explain this failure of his source. 'But this morning when he went down to the boatyard he saw that the shingle was all disturbed and there were signs that people had been walking there. Quite a few people – it couldn't have just been a couple of twitchers, sir. The tide was still quite high when he first went down to the beach but as it fell he saw signs that some sort of a boat had come in. At this time of the year it's usually pretty deserted down there during the week and always at night. I wondered, sir, if you would care to accompany me to interview my source.'

'I would indeed, Inspector,' said Pearson, pushing his chair back and standing up. 'Let's go straightaway. What's his name?'

'He's called Geoff Gumm, sir. He's getting on now, as I said. But he's got all his marbles and he can still build a fine boat.'

'I'll look forward to meeting him,' said Pearson. 'I've been thinking of buying a boat since I arrived in Suffolk. Sailing used to be my favourite form of relaxation. My brother-in-law is a great sailor but he sails in the north and since I've been down here in Suffolk I've not been out on the water.'

It took them over an hour to drive to the beach. They parked at the edge of the marshes and scrunched their way across the wide expanse of shingle beach to a fenced-off area where two small fishing boats were standing on wheeled trailers, their brightly painted hulls a splash of colour against the grey pebbles of the beach. As they approached they were greeted with a volley of barking from a black and white sheepdog, which bounced out from behind the fence with a ball in its mouth. It dropped it at Inspector Singh's feet, then lay down, furiously wagging its tail, until the policeman picked up the ball and hurled it across the beach.

'That's Judy,' said Singh as the dog rushed after the ball. 'If you throw her ball for her she's your friend for life.'

'Not much of a watchdog, then,' said Pearson.

'Not fierce,' agreed Singh. 'But she does bark.'

They found Geoff Gumm in the large wooden shed that served as office and workshop for his one-man boat-building business. He was sitting on a stool crouched over some planks he had been sanding down. He uncoiled himself, took off his eye shield and stood up as the two police officers came in.

'I thought it was you when I heard Judy,' he said. 'I can tell from her bark whether it's someone she knows or a stranger.' Gumm was almost as tall as Inspector Singh and stood surprisingly straight given his age and the fact that he must spend a lot of his time bent over his work. He was lean, almost thin; his face and his sinewy arms were like dark brown leather and his hair was startlingly white in contrast.

'Come and take a seat in the office,' he said after Singh had introduced the Chief Constable. 'Have a glass of my home-made lemonade.' They sat on tall wooden stools round a high oak table covered with sheets of drawings and sketches while Geoff Gumm went to a fridge in the corner and got out a wine bottle from which he poured lemonade into three glasses.

He sat down to join the two visitors. 'Cheers,' he said, raising his glass. 'How can I help you?'

'Cheers, Geoff,' replied Singh. 'Would you tell the Chief what you told me on the phone this morning about what happened last night?'

'Well,' said Geoff, 'it was about four thirty this morning. Judy woke me up. She has a special bark in the night. Not like when you arrived just now, more a warning sort of growl – though it's enough to wake me. I heard the sound of a heavy vehicle – not a car but something bigger. Then I could hear footsteps on the gravel and a few voices.

'We do occasionally get parties at night down on the beach but it's a bit late in the year for that now. My bedroom's at the front of the cottage so it looks over the path that comes up from the beach through the dunes. It's just behind the boatyard, over there' – he waved an arm towards the back of the shed. 'I have very thick curtains to keep out the draughts when it's windy in winter and not much light gets in, so I didn't see any vehicle lights, if it had any on. Anyway, I'm sorry to say I didn't get out of bed to see what was going on. I'd had a pretty busy day and I just went back to sleep when I heard it drive away.

'But then when I went down to the yard this morning I saw all the shingle on the beach stirred up and as the tide dropped – it was high tide at about four last night – I saw marks of a boat having come in. Quite a substantial one too: some sort of decent-sized dinghy, I'd guess. It could have landed people from a larger vessel standing off the shore. That's when I decided to ring Inspector Singh. I'm sorry now I didn't look out of the window.' He rubbed one brown hand through his hair ruefully.

'Thank you,' said Pearson. 'That's very helpful.' He turned to Singh. 'Shall we go and look at what tracks this vehicle has left? Then I think we should get a forensic team down here to examine them and the boat traces on the beach before they get obliterated. Meanwhile we can get someone from Southwold down here to tape off the lane and that part of the beach.'

While Inspector Singh made some phone calls, Pearson and Gumm walked through the gap in the dunes to the track beside the cottage. Near the cottage tyre marks were clearly visible in the sand as well as a number of footprints. 'Those prints look like whoever made them was wearing trainers,' said Pearson. 'Not that that tells us much. Most people do nowadays, especially on beaches.'

'These tyres were made by some kind of small lorry. Big treads, but not so big it would get stuck,' said Geoff thoughtfully.

'Could've been a small bus,' Pearson replied. 'More likely, if it had come to pick people up. Anyway, our forensic guys will know what it was.'

By now Inspector Singh had joined them, having finished his calls. 'They're all on the way,' he said. He too was looking at the tyre marks and the footprints. 'Have you noticed?' he asked after a moment. 'There's no marks of little wheels.' The other two looked at him.

'Little wheels?'

'You know. When people travel anywhere now they all have bags with little wheels that they pull behind them. So perhaps these people had no luggage.'

'Maybe it was on their backs,' Geoff said. 'Backpacks.'

'That could mean they were young,' said Pearson, frowning. He turned to Inspector Singh. 'What traffic cameras are there on the roads round here?'

'Not sure exactly, sir. I know there's one on the road into Southwold.'

'Get on to Southwold right away. Let's get CCTV checked on all the major roads with a ten-mile radius. That early there wouldn't have been much traffic.'

'Will do, sir. I'll tell them we're looking for a small bus or a van – transit van or a bit bigger. Possibly a small lorry. There shouldn't be too much to choose from at that time in the morning.'

Pearson turned to Geoff Gumm. 'Thanks very much, Geoff, for your quick action on this one.'

'Not at all. I'm kicking myself I didn't get out of bed to have a look. That would have been a lot more helpful.'

Pearson shook his head. 'You've helped a lot; don't worry.' He smiled. 'I'd love to come down one weekend and talk to you about boats. Here's my card. I used to do a lot of sailing when I was working in the north. I'm missing it now and thinking I might get something small myself.'

'I'd be very pleased to help. You know where I am and I'm nearly always here.' With a handshake and a nod, Geoff Gumm went back to his sanding. Pearson was silent as he and Inspector Singh walked back to their car. The coast here was increasingly used as a landing place for illegal immigrants, but this example seemed unusually well planned. For what possible purpose?

32

LIZ HAD BEEN MORE spooked than she liked to admit by her visit to the school – the pathetic Miss Girling clinging to the glories of the past in the face of change, the strange headmaster, the camera hidden in the bookshelves, but above all Cicero, the headmaster's assistant, who she thought had followed her car as she drove away. She had been a lot more observant since then of the people and cars around her but so far she had detected nothing to indicate that anyone was taking a particular interest in her.

She hadn't told anyone she was feeling uneasy – nervous was too strong a word for it – nor had she said she thought she might have been followed. Of course, in her account of her visit to the school she had mentioned the hidden camera but her colleagues didn't find it particularly worrying that the school now had a photograph of her. Her cover as a prospective parent had been good and there was no reason to think that it hadn't been taken at face value. Everyone agreed, though, that she would have to keep clear of any dealings with the school in future.

As she drove through Pimlico towards the M4 on Friday afternoon, she was keeping a sharp eye on the traffic behind her. But she saw no blue Mini or anything else to cause her concern. As she left London behind her, she began to relax and look forward to seeing her mother for the first time in several weeks.

'Darling! I wasn't expecting you for hours.'

Susan Carlyle was watering the potted fruit trees in the back courtyard of the plant nursery she still helped to run. It was next door to the Bowerhouse, the small gatehouse of the large estate where her father had been the manager. Her father had died unexpectedly young, but the estate owners had let Liz's mother stay on, and when the estate itself had been broken up – the outbuildings sold, the land leased to two local farmers – she had used her savings to buy the Bowerhouse outright.

With an empty nest when Liz left home, Susan Carlyle had time on her hands, and she had gone to work in the new nursery when it opened. Within two years she was running it; now being well past retirement age she had moved to part-time hours but refused to quit work altogether, despite Liz's urgings.

Liz said, 'I left early to beat the traffic. Getting out of London on Friday gets worse and worse.'

'Well, it's a nice surprise. Give me two seconds and I'll be finished. Edward should be back any minute now; I sent him out to buy supper. You're a nice excuse for a proper meal – most evenings we seem to fall back on scrambled eggs and toast. And you've picked a good weekend to come down; there's nothing on at all. Just the three of us.'

Part of the reason Liz hadn't often visited Bowerbridge in recent months was a fear of being a spare wheel. The other part was that when Martin Seurat was alive, they had spent many happy times here. Martin had come to love the local Wiltshire countryside, and to appreciate the resonance that certain places, like the Nadder river where her father had liked to fish, still held for a grownup Liz. He had got along comfortably with Liz's mother, and famously well with Edward – since they both shared a love of travel. So after Martin's death in Paris, memories of their time together here had been painful for Liz.

But something must have changed – Liz found herself happy to be back in the embrace of her childhood. She still missed Martin, and there was a pang when she went into her bedroom and saw the framed photograph that Martin had teased her about of a very young Liz sitting on her pony. But the veil of sadness that had hovered over even the prospect of this kind of visit had somehow lifted.

She made the most of it. On Saturday morning she helped her mother in the nursery where the early autumn sale was on, then in the afternoon took a long solitary walk along the Nadder. When she came home she found her mother and Edward standing together by the Aga in the kitchen, her mother wearing a striped cook's apron and Edward dressed in corduroys and a fisherman's sweater. The radio was playing big band music, and to Liz's amusement Edward was singing along to 'Take the "A" Train'. Seeing her, they both laughed, then conscripted her into helping with the venison stew they were making. Soon she was chopping carrots and mincing garlic, and she felt, as she had done when Martin was there, that she was joining in.

They had a long delicious supper, fuelled by two bottles of Chianti that Liz had brought down with her, and after dinner they sat in the low-beamed sitting room. Edward had lit the first fire of the autumn, made with ash logs cut from a tree that had come down in the previous year's big storm. When her mother yawned and announced she was going to bed, Liz stayed up to talk with Edward.

'I've got something special,' he announced, getting up to poke the fire before bending down to open the cupboard in the corner of the room. Reaching in with his long arms, he brought out a bottle in one hand, and two small glasses in the other. 'I hope you're joining me,' he said.

'Why not?' asked Liz.

He poured out an inch or so of dark liquid from the bottle and gave Liz the glass. 'It's Armagnac,' he said. 'I bought it when your mother and I were in Quercy. We had such a lovely week that I wanted something to remind us of it.' He poured an inch into his own glass, then put the bottle down and gave the fire another poke before sitting down across from Liz.

She said, staring at the flickering fire, 'You remember how Martin loved Armagnac?'

'I do indeed. It's thanks to him I developed a taste for the stuff.' He chuckled. 'Though with Martin, one didn't have much choice.'

Liz smiled. Martin's zest for life had been infectious. On the surface, he had been a reserved man – well dressed, proper in manner, punctiliously polite. But once relaxed, he would grow passionate about his latest enthusiasms – which could be anything from Armagnac to Simenon's Maigret stories. Martin was always on the lookout for a new interest, which had made life with him continually unpredictable, and fun.

Edward seemed to sense what she was thinking. 'You must miss that energy of his.'

'I do.' She laughed. 'I was never sure what would be next – a restaurant, a favourite film, a singer he had discovered on French radio. Once he fell in love with the Jubilee line on the London Underground. Don't ask me why – it was something to do with its name, I think.' She kept herself from laughing again, sensing it might soon make her cry.

Edward didn't say anything for a minute. He sipped his Armagnac and stared at the fire. Finally he said, 'You know your mother's worried about you.'

Liz sighed. 'If it's because I haven't come down much lately, then I hope she'll realise I've just needed some time to myself.'

'Completely understood. But no, it's not that.'

'Oh dear, I hope it's not because of my job. Mum's never been happy with my working in London. You must know that.' Her mother had never seemed to rid herself of the conviction that at some point Liz would see the light, leave London and her mysterious career, and come home where she would meet her prince, preferably a landed prince, disavow any further career ambitions and settle down to be a wife and mother like countless generations before her. It would have been infuriating if it had not been so inconceivably far from anything Liz was ever likely to do.

'To be fair, I don't think it has anything to do with your job,' Edward said, looking directly at Liz. He had startlingly blue eyes, which had not weakened or paled with age. Much more than her mother, he seemed to have a very clear sense of what Liz did. He had spent much of his life abroad, working for non-governmental organisations in the Third World, and had inevitably been involved with the UK government's foreign activities, including – at least peripherally – its intelligence services. He said, more gently, 'I think it's just she doesn't like to see you so alone.'

Liz sat back, slightly startled. She wanted to protest, but at the same time felt the truth of her mother's concern. Since Martin's death, Liz *had* felt alone, terribly alone – even here, on her rare visits to her childhood home.

She could not deny it, but at the same time she felt certain that this was no longer the case. Why? The image of Richard Pearson as he leaned forward to kiss her in the pub's car park was suddenly as vivid as her view of Edward. That was what had changed.

She took a sip of Armagnac and smiled at Edward. 'I can understand why she's been worried. And she was right to be, I suppose. But not any more. Can you somehow let her know that? It's early days, if you catch my drift, and I don't want to say anything more, but please reassure her if you can. Will you?'

And Edward, who for all his rumpled country style, was a man of considerable subtlety, gave a slow and appreciative smile. 'Count on me.' He reached for the Armagnac bottle, then leaned forward to refill her glass. 'And fingers crossed for you.'

Liz drove back to London on Sunday evening, late enough to avoid most of the returning weekend traffic. She felt relaxed after the weekend and it wasn't till she got back into central London that she thought again about Cicero in his Mini. She parked around the corner from the flat, removed her overnight bag and locked the car securely. She looked around to see if anyone was lingering nearby, but no one was. In the entrance hall of her building she collected her post from her letterbox – two bills and a pile of junk mail – and climbed the two floors up to her flat. As she opened the door she sniffed the air. There was a slight smell – faintly spicy, a sort of combination of perfume and curry. She thought back: had she cooked something spicy before she left? No. It must be coming from one of the neighbours' flats. She dropped her bag in the hall and went into the kitchen. To her surprise she saw that the door of the freezer compartment of the refrigerator was wide open. She couldn't have shut it properly before she went away. The smell was coming from some Indian ready meals that had thawed out, as had everything else in the freezer compartment. There was a pool of nasty-looking water at the bottom of the freezer and some was dripping out on to the floor.

It took her over an hour to clean up the mess in the freezer and on the floor. Finally, tired out and cross with herself, she poured herself a glass of wine, went into the sitting room and cheered herself up by looking at the view of the square below. Its plane trees were illuminated by the street lights, their leaves just beginning to brown at the edges as they responded to the advance of autumn. Finally, exhausted, she took herself to bed and fell asleep straightaway.

She woke as usual at six fifteen. Her bedside clock radio was set for six thirty, and she usually woke a little before then, waiting for the calm voice of the Radio 4 newsreader with the six thirty news. She always listened to the *Today* programme while she got dressed and had her breakfast.

A blast of pop music bellowed at maximum volume from the radio. She shot up in bed and slammed her hand down on the stop button.

She sat on the edge of the bed. What on earth had happened? That wasn't the *Today* programme, and why was the volume so high?

Had there been a power cut while she'd been away that had reset the radio? No, that didn't make sense; the correct time was showing on the clock. If there'd been a power cut it would have been flashing. What else could have happened? She looked at the dial on the radio and saw that it was set to Radio 1 – she never listened to Radio 1 and what about the volume? How had it got turned up to maximum? As she asked herself these questions she remembered last night – and the open freezer door.

A cold fear washed over her. Someone had been in the flat and done these things. Who and why? Then she gasped – what if they were still here?

She stood up, trembling, and went into the kitchen. Everything looked just as she had left it last night. She opened the door of a tall cupboard in the corner and seized the iron; it was the heaviest thing she could see. Then she went back into her bedroom and flung open the wardrobe doors. No one there. She looked under the bed – no one. She went into the spare bedroom and did the same thing, gradually calming down as she searched every place in the flat where a person could conceivably be hiding.

There was no one there. The front door was locked and bolted as she had left it last night; all the windows were closed and locked.

She went back to the kitchen, made some coffee and sat down to think. She was calmer now but the flat felt less safe and comfortable than it had. Could someone have got in over the weekend? If so, who and why? The locks were secure – at least she had thought so; but she had no burglar alarm and a really sophisticated person could get through any lock, as she knew. But nothing had been stolen. Whoever had been in had just wanted to frighten her; to let her know that they knew where she lived. Who would want to do that? Her mind kept returning to one person. Could Cicero have been in her flat? Her flesh crawled at the thought. If that's who it was then there was something very disturbing going on at Bartholomew Manor.

33

'A BABE IN ARMS could have got through this lock,' said John Ashe the following morning. Liz had reported to the personnel security team the strange events at her flat, saying that she was sure someone had broken in while she was away over the weekend. Now a team led by her old friend John Ashe was swarming over her flat, putting in alarms, a door camera linked to the Security Centre, movement sensors and the latest thing in window and door locks.

'You should have had this done before you moved in. We would have been able to get a look at them on the camera.' John Ashe took a great pride in his work and she knew he would have had every case officer's accommodation wired up if he'd been in charge.

'I couldn't have justified the expense,' replied Liz. 'I didn't have any reason to think anyone knew where I lived.'

'Hmm.' Ashe was not impressed. 'Well, you were wrong. I don't know who you're after this time, but they're obviously nastier than you think.' He went off to help his team lift the carpet in the hall to hide the wires for the panic buttons.

Liz left them to it and went to the office, feeling sad that her new home, which she had felt so pleased with, had now become a fortress controlled by the Service. She was none the wiser about who the intruder had been, or what the message was meant to be – other than to scare her – but her mind kept going back to Cicero and to what John Ashe had said about whoever she was dealing with being nastier than she thought. It seemed to her to make the investigation of Bartholomew Manor even more pressing. She knew Peggy's meeting with Miss Girling had put the old lady firmly on their side, but it could be ages before she discovered anything useful. It might be better to make a move before then – this time perhaps an official visit from the authorities. But which authorities and on what grounds? She was due to see Richard Pearson here in London the following week, but this was urgent. She decided to ring him today to ask his advice.

In her office she was about to pick up the phone to do so when she noticed the brown envelope on her desk. It must be another communication from her cover address. Inside the brown envelope was another postcard addressed to Liz Ryder at the cover address she had used when she'd visited Tallinn to meet Mischa for the first time. It had been posted in Germany.

The picture was of a stretch of beach. Beyond it there was a lake of vivid blue – you could see the trees of the far shore quite clearly. Turning the card over, she found the caption at the bottom of the card: *Strandbad Wannsee, Berlin.*

Liz read the handwritten message, written in the slashing strokes she recognised, and in the same dark blue ink: *Please come for a swim.* Above that were numbers which this time she quickly deciphered, discovering the proposed meet was in two days' time, at eleven in the morning. Liz groaned at the thought of making the journey at such short notice when she urgently wanted to address the mystery of Bartholomew Manor. It had better be good, she thought, wondering if Mischa had some new, though no doubt expensive, information to impart. Or was he just stringing her along in the hope of keeping on the payroll?

Still, she knew she had to go. This time when she reached for her phone, it was to ring not Richard Pearson but Geoffrey Fane.

The leaves on the trees lining the shore of the lake known as the Greater Wannsee were only just starting to turn. A light breeze hinted that summer's full warmth was over, but otherwise it could still be August. There was a regatta in progress, and Liz stood by the railings and watched as a yacht shot its spinnaker, bright red and balloon-like, high up in the air.

She was on the ferry from Kladow to Wannsee, in the south-west corner of Berlin. Earlier that morning Sally Mortimer had collected her from near the Brandenburg Gate in the heart of the city, where Liz had spent a sleepless night in a quiet, inexpensive hotel that suited her cover identity as Liz Ryder.

Sally had driven her to Kladow on the outskirts of the city, an oddly village-like neighbourhood full of old timber houses. There, Liz had walked over to the small harbour, where she just managed to catch the ferry – she was deliberately the last passenger to board, which meant no one followed her on. There might well be watchers already aboard, but hopefully only the British ones arranged by Sally. Back in London, Liz and Geoffrey Fane had decided not to tell the Americans about Mischa's request for a meeting, fearing it might inadvertently expose Liz's mission.

It took the two of them longer to decide not to tell the BfV, and it had been a harder decision to make. They had already broken the cardinal principle that a friendly intelligence service was always informed when operating on their territory when Liz last met Mischa in Berlin. Having heard about Abel Lamme from Peggy, Liz was adamant that he should not become involved. Let him continue the surveillance of the Nimitz household, but any involvement with Liz's mission had too great a likelihood of scaring off Mischa. If the Germans insisted on putting out surveillance and if Mischa spotted the watchers, he would abort the meeting.

She had read her guidebook thoroughly and turned now to look to the shoreline west of her. She saw the large mansion set back behind a line of trees. It slightly resembled the White House, she thought, though its stone was darker. Nowadays it was a Holocaust Museum, but in 1942 it had been the site of the infamous Wannsee Conference, which Eichmann himself had attended to help plan the Nazis' Final Solution. It seemed surreal to be so close to it, especially in such a tranquil setting.

The ferry was drawing close to shore, pulling into a marina full of moored yachts of various sizes. When it reached the jetty, the other passengers disembarked quickly, meeting family and friends waiting for them at the end of the long pier. Liz took her time getting off, and once on dry land stopped to admire the view of the Greater Lake before ambling slowly up to the street. She was carrying a canvas bag that held a swimming costume (borrowed from Sally Mortimer), a pair of flip-flops, a beach towel and a bottle of suntan lotion.

It was a walk of over a mile through an affluent suburban neighbourhood of villas, the grander ones closest to the lake. She took her time; the avenue was virtually empty – a postman ahead of her on foot, a woman in her garden pruning roses with a pair of bright orange secateurs. At last Liz turned left, down towards the shore and her destination.

If not quite Germany's Riviera, the open-air lido known as the Strandbad Wannsee was still remarkable. You approached from the road, passing a building that resembled an enormous hunting lodge but had stands selling frankfurters and soft drinks, with a restaurant inside. As she neared the beach, through a line of tall trees, she came upon a long row of low Art Deco brick buildings, running parallel to the shore, built, her guidebook told her, in the late Weimar days, just before the rise of Adolf Hitler.

As she reached the beach itself, Liz slipped her shoes off. The sand was fine and soft underfoot; ahead of her, the water of the lake looked very blue and inviting, and part of her wished that the swimming costume in her bag was for use and not just for cover. But swimming was not what she was here for.

Although it was late enough in the season for the children to be back at school, there were still plenty of people here, a few of them out in the water. The beach was dotted with strange white wicker seats, shaped like small boats tipped on their ends, their back and sides covered, their front open and facing the water. They were seats designed for protection from the wind but they also offered a fair degree of privacy for a quiet conversation.

Liz walked down to the water's edge and strolled along the shore, casting a casual eye inland at each of the wicker contraptions. Most contained couples; two of them young women who had obviously been swimming and were wrapped in towels. She saw no solitary men until finally, quite far along the beach, she saw the one she was looking for and walked towards it. Putting down her canvas bag, she sat down next to the man already inside.

Mischa was not dressed for the beach. He wore a blue blazer, white shirt, light cotton trousers and smart brogues. Since he did nothing to acknowledge Liz's presence, she sat beside him in silence at first. Finally she said quietly, 'Did you have to give a reason for coming to Berlin?'

'No, my trip was planned. There is a conference here I was long ago asked to attend. A good coincidence.'

'All clear on your way here?'

'Yes, I was very careful. I trust you were too.'

Liz ignored this, irritated by Mischa's usual suggestion of incompetence. She said instead, 'So here I am, Mischa.' She hoped this was important, given the time and effort it had taken to get her here.

He seemed to read her thoughts. 'Don't worry; I have not brought you all this way for nothing.' He was staring straight out towards the water as he spoke. 'I have news, and I am afraid it is not good.'

'OK,' said Liz, a wave of anxiety washing over her as various scenarios flashed through her mind. Had Mischa been indiscreet? More likely, it was something to do with his brother Boris – she knew from Geoffrey Fane that Bruno undercover in Moscow had made contact with him. 'So, what's happened?'

Mischa turned to look at her. 'Let me first explain. There is working in the FSB a couple – a man and wife – who returned to Russia several months ago. They were deported from the UK.' He paused, then added, 'You know who I'm talking about.'

'You know I do.' said Liz, suddenly concerned. Karpis and his wife had been expelled from the UK, where they had been working as Illegals, after their cover had been exposed. Liz had interrogated each of them; neither had given up anything of consequence about their efforts to suborn an MI6 employee, or about anything else they may have got up to. 'Why?' she asked.

'Because they seem to know you.'

'What do you mean?'

'It seems you visited an institution last month. One located in the east of your country, near the North Sea.'

Liz tried to control her surprise. 'How did you know that?'

'I didn't. My brother's colleagues did. Apparently you were filmed during your visit there.'

The secret camera she had discovered at Bartholomew Manor. 'Why would your brother's people know that?' she said innocently.

Mischa said simply, 'Because they are involved in the school.'

'How?'

He shook his head. 'That I do not know. What I know for certain is that you went there and were caught on film. And this film, my brother says, was shown to many FSB officers, including the couple I mentioned – because they were recently in the UK and were questioned by members of your Service, it was thought they might recognise the woman who visited the school. And they did. It was you.'

'And?'

He was taking his time. 'The couple recognised you at once. You told the school you had a son you wanted to place there. But the couple said this was not true. They said you were an agent of British intelligence.'

Liz was stunned. All she could think was that she should have broken the bloody camera when she'd uncovered it – then no one sitting in Moscow, like the Karpis couple, could have identified her.

She realised Mischa was waiting for her to respond. She said mildly, 'This is bad news, I agree. I don't suppose you have anything more to tell me.'

He smiled wistfully. 'No, I do not. I have only worries to discuss.'

'And they are?'

'Your presence at this college was discussed at length. Why were you there? Did you know it is not what it says it is? How could you have learned it was being used in a new way? Things like that.'

'And what were the answers?'

'That someone must have talked. But not at the college – that made no sense. Someone closer to the planning control room, which, as you now understand, is in Moscow. With the FSB.'

'They think the leak came from within?'

'They do.' Having turned his gaze to the beach he returned it now to Liz. 'Which we both know is true.'

'Is your brother in danger?'

'More than ever before. I have never seen him so… agitated. He feels he is a fish – once too small to be caught, but now with a very fine net over his head. And the net is tightening.'

'What does he want to do, then?'

Mischa did not answer right away. Liz thought of the possibilities: Boris might want to be exfiltrated with guarantees about what would happen to him in the West – he'd demand a certain style of living, she was sure of that. If for any reason he didn't want to leave

Russia, then she felt confident there would be a demand for 'danger' money – and that Mischa would want some for himself as well.

But Mischa surprised her. 'Nothing. He does not want to do anything at all. You see, there is no direct link between Boris and your Service when it comes to the information that has been disclosed to you. The link is me – and I am his brother. Boris rightfully trusts me. There is therefore nothing for his superiors to discover. Boris is nervous, as I say, but confident he will be cleared, provided...'

'Provided what?'

'He's afraid the Americans may try to approach him. He doesn't trust you – the English – and he's worried that you will inform the Americans that Boris is your source. If the Americans then approach him, the result could be disastrous – for Boris and for me.'

'So Boris knows you have been talking to us?'

Mischa looked discomfited but did not speak. Liz added, 'But he doesn't know you talked originally to the Americans?' She sounded incredulous in spite of herself.

This time Mischa managed a shrug, which Liz took to be an affirmative. She sat back against the wicker back of the chair. 'Tell me, Mischa, if your brother just wants to be left alone, what do *you* want?'

'I want my brother to be safe. That is all.'

'Really? That's it? What about you?'

'If Boris is safe, then I am safe too.' He turned towards her and she noticed that in line with his smart dress he had spruced himself up – his hair had been cut, and he had shaved that morning. 'But we will both be most *un*safe if the Americans act like they do: you know, go in like elephants – which means, approach my brother. Do you understand me?'

Liz nodded. 'Yes, I do. And I give you my word that the Americans will leave your brother alone.' She looked at him.

He held her gaze a long time, as if conducting a kind of visual polygraph. Seemingly satisfied, he nodded and looked away towards the lake. He said, 'So that is my news. This college is obviously very important to them and they have spotted you. I would take care.' He looked at his watch. 'Now I must leave. I would like you to wait here for some time before you go.'

'That's fine,' said Liz, hoping the surveillance team operating around them would not be worried when she didn't emerge from the wicker pod. She was about to say goodbye to Mischa, but he had already sprung to his feet and was striding away, his brogues slipping on the soft sand.

Liz sat watching a small yacht and thinking about this conversation. She supposed she should feel alarmed that the Russians knew she was on to Bartholomew Manor, but it was other things that were niggling at her. How had Boris known that the woman identified in the video footage from the school was the same woman whom Mischa had contacted? Previously, Mischa had always portrayed his brother as simply indiscreet rather than actively aware that what he was telling his brother was promptly relayed to a British intelligence officer. Why had that changed? Or had Mischa not come clean from the start about his brother's real intentions in these disclosures? And what was all that about the Americans and the warning that they must not approach his brother? It was Bruno who had got alongside Boris, not the Americans. Had Boris sussed him out and did he think Bruno was an American agent? If he had, Bruno must be warned and quickly, as he was in danger.

34

DIETER NIMITZ HAD COME home early. It was a Wednesday and 'home' today was the one-bedroom bachelor apartment in an anonymous block in Woluwe Saint-Pierre, the Brussels suburb he lived in during the week. He'd lived there for ten years but it was no more homely than the day he had moved in. He never invited visitors there. On the rare occasions he entertained, he took his guests to one of the many excellent restaurants in the area. It would not have occurred to him to invite them back to his flat.

But tonight was different. As he made some preparations – a tray with coffee cups and milk and sugar, a cafetière – he glanced around, embarrassed by the bleak soullessness of the place. It didn't normally bother him that there were no pictures on the walls, no cushions on the beige-coloured chairs and sofa, no ornaments of any kind. He still thought of the house in Blankensee as home, though as life with Irma became more chilly and difficult, he increasingly found himself regarding his Brussels apartment as a refuge.

He opened the cupboard where he kept some bottles of wine and spirits. Should he offer his guest a Scotch or a cognac? He wasn't sure. He felt nervous. He knew that when he had talked to Matilda Burnside, his office colleague, about his background – told her the secret that he had kept concealed all these years – he was taking an irrevocable step; that he was starting on a journey into the unknown from which there was no turning back. Where it would lead he didn't know, but he was about to find out what the next stage would be.

As he dithered, holding a bottle of cognac in his hand, the bell rang. He hastily returned the bottle to the cupboard and went to open the door. A good-looking man in his mid-forties stood outside. He was wearing an open-necked blue check shirt and a navy blue pullover and he looked friendly and informal.

'Good evening, Dieter,' he said holding out a hand and smiling. 'I hope I'm not too early.'

'Hello, Peter', replied Dieter, shaking hands. 'Of course not. Come in.'

He had met Matilda Burnside's husband a few times before, at the annual garden party given by their director, and once at a British Embassy cocktail party he had been invited to. He rather admired the man – he always seemed relaxed, open and confident – all the things Dieter would like to have been, but wasn't. And of course he was married to Matilda. Lucky him, thought Dieter, because unlike Dieter, Burnside had made an obviously happy marriage. Dieter had sensed early on that Burnside was more than Counsellor Economic at the British Embassy, and this had been confirmed when the 'help' Matilda had offered turned out to take the form of her husband.

Burnside came into the flat and Dieter motioned to his guest to sit down in one of the living room's beige chairs. Hovering by the sofa, he asked if his guest would like coffee, but the Englishman said no. 'Cognac?' offered Dieter, thinking it would give him a few moments to calm his nerves while he poured out the drinks. But again his guest declined.

There seemed no further way to delay the conversation, so he sat down on the sofa and looked at Burnside. He was just about to thank him for coming when Burnside said, 'I was very interested in what Matilda told me about your circumstances. I'm here to offer you whatever help I can.'

'Yes. She thought you might have some ideas about it all—'

'I certainly do,' he broke in, smiling disarmingly, and Dieter relaxed a little.

'Has Matilda explained my situation? Is there anything more you need me to tell you?'

'I think it would be helpful if you told me your story as you told it to Matilda, just to be sure I have all the details correct.' So Dieter went through the tale again: about how he had been recruited at an early age; how he had been directed into his job in the Commission; how he had met and married Irma, and his increasing uneasiness about her and what she was now involved in.

Peter Burnside listened intently as Dieter spoke, leaning forward in his chair and watching him closely. When he had finished, he said, 'Thank you. That's all very clear. That is one of the most fascinating stories I have ever heard. Your life almost epitomises the changes in Europe over the last few decades. But it must have been very hard, so I hope I can do something to help now.'

'I am glad I have told you,' replied Dieter. It was such a relief to meet somebody who seemed to understand, and who could also help him get to the bottom of what had happened to him.

'The first thing to say,' said Burnside, 'is that I don't think you personally have anything to worry about.' Dieter realised Burnside was referring to his being planted in the West by the Russians. Burnside went on, 'Your wife's activities, on the other hand, seem to me to be of genuine concern. It sounds from what you have said that she is actively engaged in an operation that is potentially very damaging.'

Dieter nodded. 'That is why I talked to Matilda. I have been very worried about it.'

'I know, and you are brave to come forward. It's much appreciated.'

Dieter was beginning to feel better, but even so he hesitated before asking, 'Can you tell me what it is that Irma is involved in? Is it something illegal?'

Peter Burnside sat back in his chair, looking as if he didn't know for certain what the answer to those questions was. He sighed, looked down at his hands resting in his lap. With a slightly puzzled face he said, 'As you know, your wife has been sending students from her school abroad. To the United States and now it seems, from what you have told me, to the UK. Possibly other places as well, we don't know. There's nothing wrong about that in principle; nothing illegal either, as far as I can tell. But the students she's sending all seem to be refugees, from what you've said – either orphans or long separated from their parents. That means that no one in Germany has any stake in what happens to them – or in finding out where they have been sent. And it looks as though some of them don't return.'

Dieter said, 'Yes. I told Matilda about the brochure of a place in England Irma was in touch with. But why are these children sent there? And to America?'

'I don't know but we need to find out. If you are right in thinking that Irma may be working with the Russians, then whatever is going on in Britain and America will not be good – either for us or for the children. You said that Irma's school took only the brightest of the refugee children, which may mean that they are being taught some sort of specialist skill. But all this is guesswork until we can find out more.'

'Do you think Irma knows what is happening to the children?'

Burnside shrugged slightly and sighed. 'I'm afraid she not only knows but she's playing an active part in it, probably by selecting the children.'

Dieter looked shocked, and Burnside added quickly, 'That's why I want to ask you to help us by finding out as much as you can about what she's doing.'

Dieter nodded.

'But you must be careful,' went on Peter Burnside. 'It could be very dangerous for you if you were caught. I think this is a serious business and they will do whatever they can to protect it.'

Dieter stood up. His face was flushed. The downtrodden, sad-looking, grey figure had turned into a warrior. 'The Russians,' he said, 'have played me for a fool. I will not stand by and let them destroy the lives of these poor children. You can count on me to do whatever I can to help.'

'Thank you.' Peter Burnside was amazed by the change in the man. 'If you have any information to pass on, ask Matilda to arrange a meeting with me. But please,' he repeated, 'be very careful.'

35

THE NEW STUDENTS were a strange bunch, thought Miss Girling, as she watched them filing into the new computer block. They must have arrived all at once in the evening – none of them had been there when she left for home the night before. What's more, they all looked foreign and they were all boys, quite different from the children who used to attend the school when she was a teacher – middle-class children from local families, never a brown or black face among them. This intake seemed to be all brown faces and she wondered where they had come from.

The other odd thing was that they were all amazingly quiet. In her day, a group of children going into lessons would have been chattering and laughing so loudly you couldn't hear yourself think. The problem was to quieten them down enough to start the lesson. She had never come across children so subdued. Perhaps they were tired after their journey from wherever it was, she thought to herself. As she stood and watched, the school cook came past on his way to the kitchens.

'Where are they from?' he asked Miss Girling.

'Heaven knows. I was wondering that myself,' she replied. 'They don't look English.'

'A spooky lot, I'd say. I hope they don't have a special diet. No one's given me any instructions.'

Spooky's a good word for the whole place nowadays, thought Miss Girling as she watched the headmaster's assistant, Cicero, following the children into the new classroom block. She went into the office where the accounts manager Miss Looms was working. Miss Looms, like Miss Girling, was a hangover from the glory days of the school, but her job was now severely curtailed from what it had been and she only came in two mornings a week to deal with the housekeeping accounts – food bills, utilities and simple upkeep of the building. Everything else seemed to be in the hands of the mysterious Cicero.

'I see the new pupils have arrived,' said Miss Girling. 'Where are they going to live? The old dormitories are not in a fit state.'

'No. They've got accommodation for them at one of the farms. They have converted some outbuildings into summer lets and the farmer was delighted to have more permanent lodgers – especially out of season. His wife's going to cook their evening meal.'

'Good luck to her. I've just been talking to Cook. He says no one's told him what they eat.'

Miss Looms shrugged her shoulders as if to shake off all responsibility.

Miss Girling waited two days, in case there were any more developments, then called the number the nice policewoman, or whatever she really was, had left with her. She got an answer machine and, flustered, hung up. But telling herself not to be silly, she rang back, this time leaving a message in as calm a tone as she could manage, saying simply that the new students had arrived.

What she hadn't said, since it took her another day or two to realise this, was that these new pupils seemed to spend all their time in the new IT block. As far as Miss Girling could tell, the classes they attended there were taught by Mr Sarnat or by another new arrival, a middle-aged man with a greying beard called what sounded like Gottingen. He was also foreign – probably a German, Miss Girling decided.

Miss Girling knew absolutely nothing about computer science, but she guessed that if something fishy was going on at the school, it must have something to do with what these new students were being taught. So she made a point of walking slowly past the computer block in the mornings when the students were in their lessons. She was vaguely hoping she might hear something or see something that might give her a clue about what was going on inside. But although the block had large windows, they were never open and no sound escaped.

However, on the third morning, becoming more daring, she looked into the window as she walked slowly past and noticed that Mr Gottingen was handing out some sort of paper document to each student. Maybe it was a test or instructions of some kind. If she could get hold of one of those, she thought, it might help someone more computer-literate than she was to understand what was going on. At the end of the lesson period, as the students were coming out for their morning break, she was back. She waited until the classroom had cleared and Mr Gottingen had gone to the staffroom, then she sidled in.

But Mr Gottingen must have taken everything away; the screens were all switched off and there was no paper lying around or anything at all to show what the students had been studying. She left the classroom empty-handed and nearly tripped over Cicero, who was standing just outside the door.

He stared at her unpleasantly. She told herself that it was not for him to question her whereabouts, but found herself nonetheless justifying her presence. 'I was just looking for Mr Gottingen,' she said. 'I have a message for him,' she went on nervously, realising her voice sounded shrill.

'Break time,' said Cicero shortly. He looked at her coldly, appraisingly. 'You should know that.'

'Yes, of course,' said Miss Girling. It seemed best to witter on; hopefully Cicero would decide she was simply doddery. 'How silly of me to forget. I'll go find him in the staffroom.' She felt her performance as a scatty old thing was quite convincing, until she saw the expression in Cicero's eyes.

If she couldn't actually get a copy of any handouts, then Miss Girling reckoned her best hope of finding out what was going on was with the students themselves. She was used to talking to students – goodness knows how many she had come to know during her years at Bartholomew Manor. But this lot were oddly unapproachable. They seemed to operate in an indivisible pack. Polite, yes; willing to reply to her questions, yes again – though only up to a point. The minute Miss Girling asked them anything more substantial than if they were enjoying their course, a shutter seemed to come down: their understanding of English suddenly grew worse, and her questions were answered with a show of bafflement and incomprehension.

Then on Friday, as she was about to leave the college to catch her bus, she found one of the students in a corner of the courtyard, quietly crying. She had noticed him before: he was smaller than the others, with dark cropped hair and big soulful eyes. Miss Girling stopped, out of natural curiosity and of kindness.

'Is there something the matter?' she asked gently.

The boy shook his head, vainly trying to fight back his tears.

Miss Girling said, 'What's your name?'

He replied in a whisper. 'Thomma.'

'Thomma? That's a lovely name,' said Miss Girling, though it sounded odd to her ears. 'I say, Thomma, come with me for a minute.'

The boy followed dutifully as Miss Girling led him into the main school building. She thought of heading for the staffroom but feared she might bump into the headmaster or, worse still, Cicero. Further down the corridor there was a small room used by the school nurse. She'd have left for the day, so Miss Girling went in there, Thomma trailing behind her.

It was a functional sort of room, with a bed, a big armchair, and a desk and office swivel chair. It smelled of antiseptic. Miss Girling waited for the boy to come in, then closed the door behind him. She settled Thomma in the armchair and sat down at right angles to him in the swivel chair. He really was a small lad, she thought; he looked lost in the armchair – his feet barely reached the floor.

'Now, Thomma,' she said, her tone sympathetic, 'please tell me what's the matter.'

'Nothing is wrong, miss,' said the boy shyly, not looking at her.

'Well, something must be wrong to make a big boy like you cry.' She waited but Thomma said nothing. 'Has someone been unkind?' she asked.

He didn't reply to this either.

'Is one of your teachers cross with you?' Again, he said nothing. In slight desperation, she thought of asking him if the school food was the problem, when she realised there was a much more obvious reason for his upset. 'You must be missing your parents,' she said firmly.

The boy reacted at last. 'They drowned in the ocean, on our way to Europe. I miss them.' He sounded wobbly.

'What country were you coming from?'

'Syria.' His voice sounded resigned, as if accustomed to telling this sad story.

'I see. And is that the reason you were crying?'

The boy hesitated. Miss Girling was becoming anxious in case anyone came in. She felt sure it wouldn't be good for Thomma or for her to be discovered there. But she told herself to be patient. Sure enough, he said confidingly, 'I am a Christian, Miss.'

'I see. Well, so am I,' said Miss Girling, wondering what this had to do with anything. She attended services in the village church most Sundays, despite an aversion to the modern Church of England's insistence on shaking hands with fellow congregants and the playing of folk songs on a guitar once a month.

But the boy was pleased, beaming at Miss Girling. Then he frowned, and said, 'The other boys are none of them Christian.'

Miss Girling sniffed. 'That shouldn't matter. I always say religion is a private matter.'

'They make fun of me when I say my prayers at bedtime. They shout out while I pray.'

'That's not very nice,' said Miss Girling, slightly shocked. She would have to have a word with Mr Sarnat, she told herself, before reminding herself that her priority was collecting information.

'And they will not let me go to church.'

'Really? Did they say why?' Perhaps transport was a problem, she thought.

'Mr Sarnat said I should be focused on my studies, even on Sundays.'

'You are all meant to work on Sundays, then?'

For the first time, Thomma raised his head and looked directly at her. 'Not really. It is our only free day and every other day we either have classes or lots of homework to do. Sunday is the day when we can sleep late, then the rest of the day is ours to do as we like. The others play football. I would like to play,' he added with a sheepish smile, 'but they say I'm not good enough.'

'I'm sorry,' she said consolingly. 'But then you'd rather go to church, wouldn't you?'

'Of course,' he said simply, and Miss Girling could see he meant it. An idea was forming in her head.

'There may be a way to get you there. To church, I mean,' she said.

Thomma looked at her brightly. 'Really?' he said hopefully.

Miss Girling was thinking. She didn't have a car, of course, but there were buses. A bus went past the end of the lane that led to the school. It was the bus she took every day and it passed near both the farm where the boy was sleeping and the church. She could come and collect him on Sundays and take him with her to church. Then when he got used to it, he would be able to manage on his own. She would just need to find out if the bus ran on Sundays, though she was pretty sure it did, and then work out which bus they would need to catch to get to church in time for the service.

She looked at the boy, almost pathetically innocent in his wish to go to church. She said, 'I may be able to take you with me to church, if you like.' Thomma beamed again. She went on, 'I could come and pick you up from the bus stop by the farm and bring you back but I'll have to find out the times of the bus. Do you have a phone so I can contact you?'

The boy shook his head. 'They took them away when we arrived.'

She wanted to ask why, but instead she said, 'Is there any phone you can use?'

The boy nodded. 'Yes. In the village near the farm, there is a phone box. We're not allowed to use it but some of the boys do after we leave school in the evening. I know how to use it because I went with one of the boys to ring his auntie – she lives in France. But he couldn't phone her because he didn't have money. They don't let us have money, though a few boys have got some hidden.'

'Here,' said Miss Girling, opening her bag and thrusting some coins into the boy's hand. 'This will be enough. Ring me if you don't hear from me before then. Though I will try and leave you a note here at the school with the time to meet me at the bus stop.'

As she spoke, she heard the sound of footsteps in the distance coming along the corridor. Panicking a little now, though she wasn't sure why, she grabbed a pad off the nurse's desk and tore off the top blank sheet, then scrabbling in her bag she fished out a pencil and wrote down her home telephone number. 'I've put my number down here.'

She started to put the pencil back when she saw the card the policewoman had given her, tucked in the pocket next to her purse. She took it out and wrote its number down as well on the slip of paper. 'And if for some reason you can't reach me and you need some help, ring this number. I'll write their name down, too.'

207

36

L IZ HAD BEEN LEFT feeling very puzzled after her meeting with Mischa. But more than that, she was worried. Whichever way she looked at what the Russian had said, she couldn't avoid the conviction that Bruno was at risk. Unless the Americans were simultaneously cultivating Boris in Moscow, Mischa's warning must refer to Bruno.

Liz didn't know any details of what moves Bruno was making in Moscow – how close he was to Boris or whether he was near to recruiting him – but it seemed pretty clear to her that Bruno was in danger and Geoffrey Fane needed to know as soon as possible. So when Sally Mortimer collected her to take her to the airport, she'd asked her to contact Geoffrey Fane and arrange a meeting with him first thing the following day. Sally had picked up on Liz's concern but was reassured to be told that it had nothing to do with the arrangements in Germany but was about something going on in Moscow. She certainly wouldn't have been reassured, reflected Liz, if she had known it was about the safety of her one-time boyfriend Bruno Mackay.

The next morning at nine o'clock Liz was in Geoffrey Fane's office in Vauxhall Cross, drinking coffee and sitting on one of the button-back leather chairs that Fane had somehow 'acquired' at the time of a Foreign Office refurbishment. She looked across at Fane, sitting opposite her in a similar chair; in the clear light coming in through the tall windows she could see that he looked surprisingly scruffy.

Fane was a man who prided himself on his appearance. Liz knew him well; she had worked closely with him for years and had made something of a study of him. He was a man of well-cut three-piece suits, crisp shirt cuffs showing at the wrist and striped, old-school regimental and club ties. His customary stance at meetings was to lean back languidly in his chair with his long legs stretched out in front of him and his perfectly polished brogues on show.

Now something was different. The clothes were the same but the posture was wrong and the suit, rather than enhancing his lean figure, seemed to be hanging off him. It was as though he had shrunk. Liz was concerned. In her own way she was fond of Fane, though her feelings were different from his for her. She would be sad if anything were to happen to him.

'Are you all right, Geoffrey?' she asked. 'You look tired.'

He looked at her sadly and sighed. 'I had HR up to see me yesterday.'

'Oh?' said Liz cautiously.

'Apparently, I could take my pension any time. First I knew of it. I said to them, "Is this your way of getting rid of me?"' Fane gave a small laugh, but he was watching Liz for her reaction.

She didn't have to feign her surprise. 'I would never have guessed, Geoffrey. Anyway, there can't be any question of your going. You're absolutely essential.'

Fane smiled sadly. 'It's kind of you to say so. But what if I wanted to go?'

'For heaven's sake. You can't want to go. Why would you?'

Fane sighed again, a long thoughtful exhalation. 'I'm starting to question myself, Elizabeth, in a way I never have before. The whole business with Jasminder Kapoor shook me, I have to admit. I keep thinking I could have handled things better.'

Liz said firmly, 'That's a perfectly natural response. Anyone who wasn't upset by what happened would be a monster. But you did nothing wrong. Nothing. In fact, I thought you handled the situation most sensitively.'

'Really? Then why did she do what she did?'

'Oh, Geoffrey,' said Liz, realising how much he was still upset. 'No one can take responsibility for other people's actions. She just did not have the strength or the confidence to handle the situation she found herself in. Don't forget, you didn't think she was the right person for the job in the first place, and she wasn't. If anyone's to blame it's me, for putting her name forward for the post.'

Fane sighed again, but did not disagree.

Liz said, 'You didn't put a foot wrong: you were firm but never unkind; you made it clear to her that you wanted the truth because we all *needed* the truth. And that is what you managed to get from her. You should have no doubts, and absolutely no guilt about the way you dealt with Jasminder Kapoor.'

'That's kind of you, Elizabeth. As you know,' he said, with something approaching his usual wolf-like grin, 'I don't customarily go in for so much self-analysis but it's just the combination of realising I've reached pensionable age with my lingering doubts over the way I behaved towards that poor woman that has upset my equilibrium.'

Liz was relieved to see that by now he was sitting up on his chair and the long legs were back, stretched out in front of him, crossed at the ankle in a familiar pose. 'So, let's hear what happened at your meeting with Mischa. What did he have to say?'

'Well, Geoffrey, that's why I asked to see you this morning. Because I'm worried about what he said – worried for Bruno, in particular.'

'Well, my dear girl, why didn't you say so at once, instead of going on about me?'

Liz ground her teeth but said nothing.

'Come on – out with it. What did he say?'

So she told him how Mischa's position seemed to have changed. Instead of reporting snippets of information that he picked up from his brother Boris when he was drunk, he now seemed to be delivering messages from him. Boris was not supposed to know anything about his contact with Liz and yet somehow Mischa knew that Liz had been identified from the photograph taken in the headmaster's study at Bartholomew Manor school. Even more importantly, Mischa issued a warning that no one should try to recruit his brother.

'He seemed to think that the Americans were alongside Boris, but he must have meant Bruno. It was definitely a warning. If I have been recognised from the photographs taken at the school, then perhaps Bruno has been identified too? If so, he is in real danger.'

'I think that's very unlikely,' said Fane. 'His cover is excellent and his disguise means he looks very different from the Bruno you know. So even though the Karpis couple recognised you from the photograph, I don't see how they could have connected the man who is living in Moscow with the Bruno who interrogated them in England with you.'

'Well, you say that, but Bruno is in contact with Mischa's brother, Boris. How careful has he been? Maybe Boris suspects that this Englishman who has suddenly appeared in his life is not what he says he is. Boris is an intelligence officer – he's trained to recognise another, and it's possible that Bruno's enthusiasm has got the better of his caution.' She paused and Fane said nothing. 'It is possible, isn't it, Geoffrey? We're talking about Bruno Mackay. He takes risks, doesn't he?'

'That's true – up to a point. But he is very experienced. He doesn't make stupid mistakes.'

'But supposing Boris had become suspicious. It would be natural to check out this new British acquaintance against whatever data bank they have and if the Karpises, who have recently returned from working in Britain, are around to be consulted, as they obviously are, then they would have been. A careful study of the man in Moscow could have seen through the disguise – you know it could, Geoffrey.'

Fane was looking less sure of himself. 'Tell me again exactly what Mischa said.'

'He said the Americans must not approach his brother. It was a warning. It sounded like a threat.'

'If Bruno has been identified, why did he refer to the Americans, not the British?'

'I don't know.' Liz was becoming exasperated. 'But it was clearly a warning. Maybe they don't know it is Bruno, but whether they do or not, they know there's an intelligence officer in contact with Boris and to my mind that makes Bruno's position very dangerous. If he is moving in to make a pitch at Boris I think he risks being arrested.'

Fane reached over to his phone. 'I'm getting Bruno's support team up here to tell us exactly what the state of play out there is.'

Liz listened while Fane spoke to someone called David and asked him to come up to his office immediately and to bring Charlotte. Fane put down the phone and sat gently tapping the desktop with the rubber end of a sharply pointed pencil. In a few minutes there was a knock on the door and a stocky, dark-haired man came in accompanied by a middle-aged woman with her glasses dangling on a cord round her neck. David and Charlotte were introduced and Fane asked Liz to tell them about her meeting with Mischa.

'So,' said Fane when Liz had finished, 'what is the current situation with Bruno and do you agree with Liz that he's in danger?'

Charlotte spoke first. 'Bruno has a lunch date with Boris in two days' time. It's at Boris's invitation and Boris's choice of restaurant. Bruno has asked permission to use this opportunity to make a first pitch at Boris. He intends to offer him the opportunity to write background papers on the economic and political situation in Russia for Bruno's investment company.'

'Of course,' chipped in David, 'there's no doubt that Boris will recognise that as the first step in a recruitment approach.'

'Yes,' said Fane. 'It's certainly not the first time that card has been played.'

There followed a heated discussion between Charlotte, who thought Boris was quite capable of looking after himself and should carry on, since the potential prize of an FSB officer in place in Moscow was worth the risk, and David, who was inclined to feel he might be walking into a trap. Throughout, Geoffrey Fane was attempting to unravel the mystery of why Mischa had issued the warning in the first place and what it all meant, questions Liz was happy to say she was unable to answer.

Eventually everything seemed to have been said and they all fell silent, looking towards Fane to make a decision, if one was to be made. He stood up and walked slowly over to the long windows looking out over the Thames towards Parliament. Liz held her breath. She was quite sure that Bruno should be got out as quickly as possible.

Finally, Fane turned around and said, 'It's too risky. He must not go to that lunch. Activate his escape plan. Can we get him out before the lunch date?'

'Should be OK,' replied David. 'We'll alert the Moscow Station right away. They know what to do. It's all in place.'

'Bruno will be very disappointed.'

'So will we all, Charlotte,' responded Fane. 'But we'd be more than disappointed if he got arrested and charged with espionage. Think how you'd feel then.'

37

IN HIS MOSCOW FLAT, Bruno was humming softly to himself as he got ready to go out. It was a habit he had developed when he was quite young. Faced with a difficult situation or a time of particular tension, he would quietly hum a tune. He was never aware of choosing which tune to hum – something just came into his head – but as the product of an English public school and therefore a regular attender at church services when he was young, he found that the tune was very often a hymn. Today it was a carol, 'In the Bleak Midwinter', that, when he thought about it, was particularly appropriate for Moscow in autumn.

He opened the wardrobe door and contemplated his rack of ties. What was appropriate for this lunch, a lunch that he hoped would mark the next stage in his cultivation of the FSB officer? Today he planned to offer Boris consultancy work for his mythical investment bank. Boris had invited him this time, which Bruno saw as a good sign. He must be keen to continue the relationship, which he surely must have recognised as connected in some way with intelligence gathering. So, what was the right tie? Something bright, confident and slightly flashy.

His hand was on a yellow and blue one when he suddenly changed his mind and decided not to wear a tie at all but to go in an open-necked shirt instead. That would look insouciant, he told himself. He was assessing the result in the mirror when his phone buzzed. It was a share update; he got them all the time. This one read: *BG +1.15%*.

Bruno stopped humming. A cold wave washed up from his stomach and his mouth went dry. This was his alarm call. His emergency escape plan had been triggered by London and 1.15 was the pickup time. Coupled with his shock, he felt intense disappointment. He was going to be denied his chance to have a go at suborning Boris Bebchuk, the man he had been patiently cultivating for weeks.

But there was no arguing. The whole thing had been rehearsed to a boring extent before he left home. Although it was real, it was no longer boring – rather alarming, in fact, if exciting too. Bruno loved a challenge and this was certainly going to be that. As he set about his preparations for departure he wondered what had happened to trigger this dramatic reaction from his colleagues in London, though he had little enough time to waste it speculating.

He went into the bathroom and crouched down beside the bath, sliding back a small part of the panel with a slight click, revealing a concealed safe. Bruno tapped in some numbers and the door swung open. He took out a packet of documents, locked the safe and replaced the panel. Putting the packet on the table, he opened it and extracted a Canadian passport in the name of Brian Anderson, Civil Engineer, born in Montreal. There was also a wad of bank notes made up of Canadian dollars, US dollars and Russian roubles, together with an assortment of credit cards, club membership cards, and all the assorted documentation that a Canadian engineer travelling abroad would be expected to possess. He laid it all out on the table, then he reached for his phone and dialled Michelle.

'Good morning, darling,' he said. 'It's such a lovely day and I know it's half day at the school. I was wondering if I might come with you to pick up Sergei. Perhaps we could stop at the park on the way home. I'm an expert at pushing a swing. That is, if you haven't made any other plans, of course,' he added, hoping she hadn't.

But she was clearly delighted. 'What a lovely idea! No. We had no plans. We were going to come straight home but that's a much better suggestion.'

'Great. That's a date then,' he said. 'I'll knock on your door in twenty minutes.' He felt rather ashamed of himself, but reflected that the French were on the same side, so even though she didn't know it, Michelle was serving her nation.

His next step was to change out of the clothes he had chosen so carefully for lunch with Boris into something more suitable for playing in the park – and for the journey he was about to undertake. Fifteen minutes later, he emerged from his flat wearing jeans, trainers and a leather jacket over a sweatshirt. The documents and cash were stuffed in his pockets. He was carrying a small bag containing his laptop and his British passport. He slammed the door shut with a slight sigh of regret. He had been so near, he reflected, to pulling off a massive coup, recruiting a FSB officer in place. But it was not to be, so, lighting a cigarette, he set off to collect Michelle.

At twelve minutes past one, Bruno drove Michelle's car into the park with Michelle and her son sitting in the back seat. He pulled up just behind a muddy BMW with two men inside. He put on the handbrake and turned off the engine. Then, leaving the key in the lock, he grabbed his bag off the seat beside him and got out, saying, 'Just got to do something. Back in a minute.'

Then he broke into a run towards the car in front, where he opened the rear door and climbed in. The BMW accelerated away and disappeared from view, leaving Michelle and her son open-mouthed.

Across the city in a restaurant near Lubyanka Square, Boris Bebchuk was sitting by himself at a table by the wall. The dining room was panelled in dark wood, a red carpet covered the floor and the heavy wood chairs were upholstered in red plush. The effect was formal, gloomy and old-fashioned. It was a place used mainly by government officials to entertain and impress foreign visitors. It also had special facilities, which was why Boris had chosen it for meeting Bruno. Many of the tables were fitted with concealed microphones, including the one at which Bebchuk was sitting, and there were concealed cameras scattered around that could photograph guests to order.

Bebchuk was sipping sparkling water and looking at his phone. A table for two near the door was occupied by a pair of young men. Neither was eating, and they didn't seem to have much to say to each other; they spent most of their time looking at their phones.

At one thirty, Bebchuk seemed to make a decision, for he stood up and walked towards the door of the restaurant, exchanging a few words with the two men as he passed. He left the restaurant and shortly afterwards they too got up and departed. The waiters exchanged knowing looks and reset the tables for the next customers. Clearly, something had gone wrong.

38

WHEN HER HUSBAND OWEN first took early retirement from his job at the Costco warehouse in
Halesworth, Agatha Jones had been worried how they
would make ends meet. They had moved from Southwold
to this village three years before, and were happy here, but
they still had a small mortgage on their cottage, and life
never seemed to get any cheaper, even for an elderly couple
with simple needs. She herself still worked part-time at a
bakery in Wangford, and she had wondered if she should
ask to do more hours.

But it turned out there was nothing to worry about.
Between Owen's Costco pension, the state pension and
Agatha's wages, they got by quite easily. They were even
thinking of taking one of those Saga cruises they'd read
about in the Saturday *Telegraph* last winter, though admit-
tedly it would only be a short one – perhaps to Scandina-
via or the Scottish islands.

So money was not a problem, but Owen's retirement
was still turning out to be a bit of a trial. The problem was
that he had never been a man for hobbies – unless you
counted reading the paper and watching the news as
'hobbies' – and even now that he had all the time in the

world, what he didn't seem to have was any interests. He didn't read books, he didn't like to garden, he didn't listen to music; the only thing he seemed to do was be under foot all day long. And it was driving Agatha mad.

Fortunately, she had her work, which got her out of the house, and her sister Maudie, who lived in Southwold still, was always happy to give her a cup of tea when she'd finished her hours at the bakery. The two of them had never been close, but anything was better than going home to find Owen dozing on the sofa with the television on.

Then there was her neighbour, Miss Girling. Funny how even now they'd got to know each other quite well, she was still 'Miss Girling' to Agatha. When they'd first arrived, Agatha had found her a bit offputting – it hadn't come as a surprise to learn she was some kind of schoolteacher. But once Owen had retired and Agatha had found an almost desperate need to get out of the house, she had made a concerted effort to get to know her neighbour better, and had partially succeeded. She wasn't altogether sure how much Miss Girling enjoyed her visits, at least at first, though it seemed a good sign that recently she'd begun to talk about the school where she worked – there had been a change of ownership, it seemed, and not one Miss Girling was happy with.

The students nowadays were all foreigners, and strange ones at that. What had been a school for boys and girls from local well-off families was now, according to Miss Girling, becoming a repository for immigrants. Agatha had enjoyed hearing about the children. You saw such terrible things in the news – all those people drowned trying to cross the sea in little boats, all that bombing and people getting their heads chopped off. It was a terrible world and she was pleased that at least some of the poor children had made it safely to Suffolk, even if the school was not as nice as it used to be.

She was looking forward to hearing more about the children today but unusually Miss Girling didn't seem to be at home. She'd gone round the previous evening, but to her surprise Miss Girling hadn't answered the door, even though she could see through the front door's frosted-glass window that a light was on in the kitchen at the back. When she'd telephoned this morning, the phone had rung and rung, and when she'd gone round again Miss Girling still hadn't answered the door.

This was most unlike her neighbour. Once in a blue moon Miss Girling went to see a school friend in London overnight, but Agatha couldn't otherwise think of an evening when she hadn't been there. She never went to the pub for a drink, she didn't seem to go on school trips overnight, she hadn't any family left, or at least she'd never mentioned any. So where could she be?

Agatha couldn't settle and at lunchtime she decided to try again, even though she knew that Miss Girling rarely if ever came home for lunch. Leaving the house, she walked to the little wicker gate that led to Miss Girling's front door, went down the path and pressed the bell, and heard its loud ring. Peering through the window in the door, she saw to her surprise that the same light was still on.

This seemed very odd. Agatha hesitated – she didn't know her neighbour that well, after all – but felt she must investigate. She walked around the side of the house nearest to her own. The blinds on both the kitchen window and the door were down, blocking any view into the room. This suggested that Miss Girling was away, but then why had she left a light on? Agatha was pondering this when she became aware of the faint sound of music. Putting her ear to the door she listened carefully. The music was coming from the kitchen – it sounded like pop music from a radio.

It was now that Agatha grew alarmed. It was one thing accidentally leaving a light on when you left a house, quite another to leave the radio playing. It didn't seem right – not like Miss Girling at all. As Agatha walked back to her house, there was a set expression on her face. The one her husband liked to call her 'I've made up my mind' look.

The police were sceptical and reluctant to act on Agatha's phone call, even when she described the oddness of the situation and her concern about Miss Girling. It was only when she threatened to make a formal complaint (something her husband had once told her to say) that a squad car was finally dispatched.

PC Willis turned up an hour later, looking grumpy. He followed Agatha to the next-door house, where he leaned on the doorbell for about a minute. Nothing happened except that a pair of wood pigeons who were canoodling on the roof rose up, flapping their wings in loud protest. Agatha showed the constable round to the back door where they could both clearly hear a radio playing. It was this that seemed to convince Willis that something was amiss.

The policeman pushed hard at the door, and it shook promisingly. 'Step back, madam,' he said, ushering Agatha out of the way. He was wearing heavy black leather boots, and he hopped forward on one leg and with the other kicked high up by the door handle. The wooden frame shuddered, the lock broke and the door crashed open, its edge splintering, and fell on to the kitchen floor with Willis on top of it, while Agatha peered in from behind him.

'Keep back!' the policeman shouted, from his position sprawled on the floor.

But it was too late; Agatha had a perfect view of the kitchen chair that had been kicked over and now lay on its side. Above it, a stout length of rope had been tied around a drying rack suspended from the ceiling; twelve inches below that, the cord's other end had been tied and looped into a noose around Miss Girling's throat.

39

THOMMA HAD NOT SEEN Miss Girling for two days. She had promised to take him to church, but there had been no sign of her on Friday when he tried to find her at school, and she had not left any note for him.

He wondered if he should try to phone her early the next morning – hopefully in time for them to go to church. After all, she had given him the note with her number, which he had hidden deep in the toe of one of his shoes. It was a good thing he had, because that evening there had been a bed check – they had them at random, with Mr Gottingen looking through their bunks and personal belongings, confiscating what he called contraband. Once he had found a mobile phone, which was strictly forbidden; another time he'd located a purse full of English coins. Confiscated again.

Thomma remembered how when the boat they'd crossed the sea in had landed with a scrape and a thump on the beach, he'd woken up with a start and immediately checked that his little stash of euros was still safe in his pocket. It was, but not for long – when they'd got to the farmhouse annexe where they slept, they had all been made to take showers, and when he'd come back and checked his trousers, his euros were gone. As he'd learned soon enough, it was useless to protest. Mr Sarnat would have said they didn't need money, since all their requirements were taken care of, and each boy was given an allowance in the form of chits, which they could exchange at the shop that was open in the main hall of the school twice a week. It had sweets and chocolate and magazines and toiletries but no stamps or writing paper.

That meant, of course, that no boy could do anything outside the college grounds or the residential block, since any activity like catching a bus or posting a letter or making a phone call required cash. Thank goodness, then, that whoever had taken his euros had not yet found the coins Miss Girling had given him. He had hidden them in a deep crack in an old beam in the wall behind his bed.

By bedtime on Saturday he had decided that it would be too difficult to try to get to the phone box to ring Miss Girling in the morning so instead he would go down to the bus stop at the end of the lane and wait for her to turn up. After all, she had said she would collect him and they would go together on the bus. Perhaps she had forgotten that she hadn't mentioned a time. After breakfast he made his way cautiously to the bus stop and waited. But though several buses came past, there was no sign of Miss Girling, and after two hours he gave up. He was very cold and very sad; she must have forgotten.

At lights-out time in the dormitory, most boys went to sleep right away. But there was a small group of older boys who chatted. That night Thomma was worried and uneasy and he stayed awake listening.

He heard a voice a few bunks away say, 'Did you hear that the old bag's died?'

Thomma tensed up. They called any of the older female staff 'old bags', and this included Miss Girling. Had something happened to her?

'Really? You sure?' Another voice whispered in the dark.

'I'm sure. I heard Cicero talking to Miss Looms in the office. They were yakking about sending flowers.'

'What did she die of?'

'She strung herself up.'

'What? You mean she killed herself?'

'That's what Miss Looms told Cicero. They found her hanging in her kitchen, and Miss Looms said the police had to cut her down. Why would she go and do that?'

'If I had a face like Miss Girling, I'd kill myself too.' Both laughed loudly for a minute. Then they started talking about football.

Thomma lay stunned. Miss Girling was dead. To him she'd seemed to be a kind of saviour in this miserable place where he wasn't even allowed to practise his religion. But now even this ray of light in his life had been extinguished. How could it have happened?

That boy had said she'd killed herself. Thomma didn't believe it. She went to church and was going to take him with her. Why would she kill herself? She must have had a heart attack or something. Then he realised this couldn't be – not if they'd had to cut the old lady down. Someone had harmed Miss Girling, he realised with a start. Miss Girling must have been *murdered*.

But why would anyone hurt her? Could it have anything to do with him? He tried to dismiss the thought – why would you kill someone for helping a boy go to church? Still, there was something very odd about her death – and about this place.

He shivered slightly, wondering what he should do. He felt a need to tell someone what was going on. He was worried about what they were being taught by Mr Gottingen. He had planned to tell Miss Girling about it when she took him to church. But now she was dead and he had no one to tell. He felt helpless and alone, and as the night slowly passed, increasingly afraid.

But then – he couldn't have said what time it was, only that it was still pitch black outside – he remembered the slip of paper Miss Girling had given him. She'd written her number on it but that wasn't going to be any use if she was dead. But there was another number on it. She'd said, *If for some reason you can't reach me and you need some help, ring this number.*

It was still dark when he slipped out of the dormitory, closing the door silently behind him. He was clutching the paper Miss Girling had given him and the coins he had hidden in the beam. He skirted the perimeter of the yard outside the accommodation building and slipped out on to the road through a gap between two farm buildings. The boys all knew this way in and out of the farm.

At night there was a security guard on duty, but everyone knew he usually spent the night in the office in the farmhouse, dozing and watching TV rather than policing the grounds or monitoring the CCTV cameras.

When the boy reached the main road, he turned right. The village was a mile or so away, and he knew that on its small green sat an old-fashioned red telephone box. He thought it was still working because the boy with the aunt in France had lifted the handset and heard the ringing tone. He hadn't been able to use it then because he had no money.

There was almost no traffic at this hour, just the occasional van or agricultural lorry, and Thomma was able to see their headlights from quite far away so he could get off the road into the trees and bushes before the vehicle reached him.

He had almost got to the village when behind him he heard a different engine sound. It was a car and quite a high-powered one by the sound of it. He'd reached a part of the road where there was a deep ditch between him and some heavy undergrowth and he was tempted to take a chance and stay on the road. It seemed unlikely that he had been spotted if the security guard was just watching TV in the warm office as usual.

But the car seemed to be going surprisingly slowly. This struck him as odd, so at the last possible moment he jumped down into the ditch, which was mercifully dry, and crouched down while the car passed by. As it moved away he cautiously lifted his head and looked as its back light faded into the distance. It was just starting to get light, a milky paleness suffusing the sky, and he could see quite clearly not only the car's make, but its colour. It was a bright blue Mini and the driver was looking from side to side. It must be Cicero – the blue Mini stood outside the school all day and every day and the only person who drove it was Cicero. Someone must have been monitoring the CCTV cameras after all and spotted him leaving. He couldn't go back now.

When the Mini had disappeared, Thomma waited for a moment, then climbed out of the ditch back on to the grassy verge. He was frightened but walked on, his eyes focused now on the traffic coming towards him for any sign of the Mini returning. In a few minutes he reached the village green and was about to cross the road to the red telephone box when he saw the Mini parked on the other side of the green. Walking away from it, towards the phone box, was Cicero.

Thomma drew back into the trees and watched. Cicero stopped beside the phone box, looking round in all directions as though he was waiting for someone. There were a few people about now; the village shop was just opening and a car stopped outside it. A few minutes later its driver emerged with a newspaper and a shopping bag. He didn't take any notice of Cicero, who went on standing outside the phone box for a few minutes, then walked across the road and into the shop. He came out a few minutes later empty-handed, walked back to the Mini and drove off in the direction of the school.

Thomma guessed he had been asking if anyone had seen a boy. He stayed in the safety of the trees, watching the comings and goings on the green and at the shop, trying to summon up the courage to emerge into the open and cross the road to the phone box.

He was glad he waited because in a couple of minutes he saw the Mini coming back along the road from the school. It was clear that Cicero was leaving nothing to chance. But having circled the green without stopping, he drove away again. Thomma was shaking, partly with cold and partly with nerves. He knew he had to make a break for it; he couldn't stay hidden in the trees all day. Finally, he ran across the road and into the telephone box where he quickly put in his money and dialled Miss Kingly's number, realising as he did so that it wasn't a local number – it looked quite different from Miss Girling's number written above it.

As he watched anxiously to see if the Mini was coming back, a man answered. 'Hello.'

'I want to speak to Miss Kingly, please,' said Thomma, reading the name Miss Girling had written down.

'She's not here at the moment but I can get a message to her. Can you tell me what it's about?'

'My name is Thomma,' the boy said hesitantly. 'Please tell her Miss Girling gave me her number. They said she killed herself but she can't have because she was going to take me to church. I have escaped from the school. They're looking for me and I'm scared. Please can she help me.'

'OK, Thomma,' said the voice reassuringly. 'I've got that. Who is looking for you?'

'Cicero. Cicero from the school.'

'I can tell you are in a phone box. Please tell me the number written on the phone.' Thomma read it out. 'That's good. Is there anywhere near the phone box safe for you to hide while I contact Miss Kingly? It will take me about fifteen minutes to do so, then I will ring the phone box and tell you what to do.'

'I can hide in the trees across the road but I don't know if I'll hear the phone ringing.'

'If you can't hear it, come back to the phone box in fifteen minutes and ring me again. Have you got a watch?'

'No,' said Thomma, 'but I can see the clock on the church tower. It says ten past six.'

'OK,' said the man. 'If you don't hear the phone ringing, call me again when it says half past six.'

'I have no more money.'

'Can you remember four numbers?'

'Yes.' That was something he was good at.

The voice spoke four numbers, enunciating each one slowly and clearly. He made Thomma repeat them back, then the voice said, 'Dial these and you won't need money. You'll get straight through to me.'

Thomma put the phone down and ran back across the road to the trees, the four numbers embedded in his memory. He crouched down in the bracken, his eyes firmly fixed on the church clock.

*

A hundred and twenty miles away the phone rang in Peggy Kinsolving's bedroom. She reached an arm out of the bedclothes and picked it up.

'Morning, Peggy,' said a cheerful voice. 'Duty officer here. Sorry to disturb your beauty sleep. I've got a bit of an odd one for you. Young man or boy, sounds Middle Eastern but speaks good English, says he got your number from – sounded like Miss Curling.'

'Girling,' interrupted Peggy.

'Ah good, you do know something about it then. He says she's dead – "They say she committed suicide but she can't have, because she was going to take me to church." That's what he said – maybe you can make sense of it. He also says he's escaped from the school, but someone called Cicero is looking for him and he's scared. He's been hiding in a wood across the road from the telephone box. I told him to get back in hiding and I'd ring the box at half past six and tell him what to do. I gave him the emergency number in case he didn't hear the phone ringing because he has no more money to ring again. Over to you. Hang on – just getting a fix on the phone box…It's in a village about nine miles from Southwold in Suffolk.'

Peggy looked at her bedside clock. It was six seventeen. Wide awake now, she was thinking fast. 'Get on to Suffolk Police HQ. Ask them to go and pick him up and take him somewhere safe and look after him. If they get any enquiries from the school – it's called Bartholomew Manor – tell them to stall them. Don't admit they've got the boy. Either I or Liz Carlyle will be coming up to talk to him asap. If they are reluctant to get involved, tell them to consult the Chief Constable. He's called Richard Pearson and he knows about the case.'

'OK, Peggy. Received and understood – will do.' He rang off.

At six thirty the duty officer's phone rang again. He had just finished talking to Richard Pearson, the Chief Constable who had authorised the pickup of Thomma from the village.

'It's Thomma here,' said the small voice on the phone plaintively. 'What shall I do?'

'Can you see the village shop from where you're hiding?'

'Yes.'

'Well, get back undercover and watch out for a police car. It will be a white car with *Police* written on the side. It will stop right by the shop and you should run as fast as you can and jump in. They will look after you until Miss Kingly can get up there to talk to you. Is that OK?'

'Thank you,' said Thomma and he put the phone down and ran back across the road to wait.

40

Dieter had lived a lie for so many years that it had
become his companion and his security blanket. The
truth of his background had long ago faded. If someone had
flourished a magic wand and said, 'You no longer have to
pretend. Now you can be Dieter Schmidt again,' he would
have been terrified. As far as he was concerned, Schmidt no
longer existed. For Dieter, his lie was his real life.

That his masters had never pressed Dieter Nimitz, their
creation, into service had previously never bothered him;
he had always been sure that one day they would appear
like a tailor with a long unpaid bill and expect him to pay
up. The payment could be anything, he had reckoned,
though since they had been the ones who'd pushed him to
take the job at the European Commission, he had always
assumed these long-time masters of his would want him
to supply information about the EU. How he would
respond when they did appear was something he had asked
himself from time to time, but the question was always left
hanging in the air; he didn't know the answer.

All these assumptions now seemed utterly miscon-
ceived. To have accepted the destruction of one's real identity to live as someone else was a betrayal of oneself. It had

seemed worth it while it had a purpose. To find out now that there was no purpose at all to a lifetime of deceit was too much to bear. Especially when it turned out that the role he had for so long thought was assigned to him had actually been given to his wife, Irma.

He wondered what would happen now that he had confided in Matilda and she in turned had talked to her husband, who was part of British intelligence. It seemed impossible that he would be allowed to stay in his Brussels post. The British intelligence people would feel obliged to discuss his case with their German counterparts, and one of these services would in turn speak with the security people at the Commission. The best outcome he could envisage for himself was early retirement, though probably without a pension, and the thought of returning to live in Hamburg with Irma seemed almost as bad a punishment as a prison sentence. Irma. The mere thought of her now filled Dieter with disgust. His disaffection with his wife had been tolerable only because he always had Brussels to look forward to. Without that, his life would be hell.

It was a tradition of the house in Blankensee that on Saturday evenings Dieter cooked supper, the only occasion on which he was allowed in Irma's kitchen. This afternoon he shopped locally, while Irma stayed at home doing her paperwork. He bought chicken and vegetables, ingredients for a stir-fry, something Irma didn't like very much, which in his new-found fury and despair made him all the more eager to prepare it. 'Too spicy,' she would complain when Dieter made a hot sauce to liven it up. This evening he found himself adding even more spice than usual.

He was wearing a long striped apron and using his favourite knife, a Japanese chef's enamel blade with a deer horn handle that had been given to him by a delegation visiting the Commission. *Chop chop chop* it went through the carrot he was cutting into batons, then *chop chop chop* through the three heads of garlic he would add to the stir-fry. The two chicken breasts were thick, and he hacked them into pieces, venting his frustration and anger on them.

'You're making a lot of noise.' Irma had come downstairs and into the kitchen without him hearing her. She was dressed as for work, in a grey jacket and skirt, a pair of carpet slippers the only concession to the weekend. With her short cropped hair and stocky figure, she was a dour sight.

He shrugged. 'Sometimes I think I've been silent for too long.'

'What do you mean?'

He turned towards her, holding the knife in one hand. Unaccountably, Irma laughed. 'What is so funny?' he demanded, incensed.

Irma put a hand over her mouth, though her shoulders still heaved. Struggling to stop laughing, she said, 'Forgive me, dear. It's just that you look ridiculous – the apron, I mean, and that idiotic Japanese knife you like so much.'

Dieter shook his head angrily. 'I am sure you find many things ridiculous about me. What I don't understand is why you have stood it all these years.'

'Stood what?' She was trying to sound baffled, but he could see it was an act.

'Being married to me. A man you have no respect for. Don't play with me, Irma; you know perfectly well there's no point in pretending any more. I know exactly who you are and what you've been up to. I've been a fool, but at least now I know the truth. I feel sorry for these children you are sending abroad. They're all refugees, aren't they? Just when they feel settled you send them off again to God knows what and where.'

Irma shrugged. 'They will be grateful to me and the Freitang *Gymnasium* one day. They are learning a lot – German children their age would kill for such an opportunity.'

'But do they know who they are doing this for?'

'What do you mean?' demanded Irma, widening her eyes in an effort at innocence. But she was also watching him carefully.

'You know perfectly well what I mean.' Dieter was not going to stop now.

'How do you know anything about this?' Irma's voice was curt now, and she took a step back, as if to gather some perspective on what Dieter was saying. On the rare occasions when Dieter got angry, Irma usually ignored it, treating him as a parent would a petulant child, waiting for the tantrum to pass. But not tonight. 'Is that what you've been doing in my study, poking around my papers?'

'That doesn't matter. I know.'

Irma considered this for a moment, stroking her chin with her hand. Finally she said, much more softly, 'I think it's best if we don't talk about this any more this evening. Let's have supper, and then we can listen to a concert on the radio afterwards – the Berlin Symphony Orchestra is playing Brahms tonight, and I know you love Brahms. We can talk about things tomorrow, when each of us is calmer. But do remember that we have been married a long time. I would not want some little misunderstanding to jeopardise all that we have together.'

She was smiling at him, with a saccharine expression he found repulsive. In the past he always accepted her efforts to calm any dispute, telling himself, *Irma knows best*. Had she not always been the strong one in the household? Had he not looked to her to bolster him up during moments of self-doubt, even though – quite unnecessarily he now knew – he'd never told her the truth about his past?

But something had changed, and now he couldn't just nod meekly and say, *Of course, darling*, and lapse back into being the servile husband he had been for so many years. It had all become too much. The burden of the past – his own, both the fabricated and real versions, and the past that the two of them shared – had all become overwhelming in the light of Peter Burnside's revelations.

For once, he would not let it go. Watching him, Irma seemed to sense this; her face began to alter from patronising to anxious. 'You're not going to do anything silly, are you, Dieter?' Her voice was trying to resume its usual commanding air.

'Silly?' he asked, his voice rising. 'Silly?' He was shouting now. He had had enough of her sneering. 'You mean silly as in – talk to someone else about all this?'

He was hoping Irma would be shocked, but her face was expressionless now. She said, sounding quite calm, 'I take it that means you already have.'

'And what if I have? What you are doing is wrong. It must be stopped.' He hesitated. 'It will be stopped.'

She nodded as if she were expecting this. 'Who was the lucky beneficiary of your revelations? I doubt it was the police, and I doubt you have contacts with the German secret services. That leaves work – someone in Brussels. Perhaps your friend Matilda? You've mentioned her often enough.'

Had he? He doubted it, though certainly he had dropped her name on occasion, to serve as cover were Irma ever to discover what good friends they really were.

'And her husband,' Irma went on. 'He's with the Embassy, if I remember. Some kind of attaché, I think you said. You smiled when you told me that; I think you thought he was a spy. In which case, who better to talk to about your perfidious wife?'

The uncanny accuracy of her deductions, the contempt with which she looked at him as she made them, stunned Dieter. But he fought back. 'The performance is over now. Over. Soon you will be talking to me through the bars of a prison visiting room.'

'Do you really think so?' she asked him, her tone sardonic. She seemed oddly undisturbed by what he was saying. 'You're such an idiot, Dieter. No wonder they never activated you but thought your most useful role would be as cover for me. Far from a prison cell, if what you tell me is true, I will be living in a nice flat in Moscow within weeks.'

'I don't think so,' he said, his voice rising. 'And even if they swap you, I wouldn't fancy your prospects in Russia. Not when your entire programme for subversion has been stopped in its tracks. You can't blame anyone but yourself for that.'

She looked him straight in the face, then she burst out laughing. He didn't understand this at all. He wouldn't have been surprised if she'd kept quite calm when he'd told her what he'd done, but why was she laughing at him? He felt his anger growing – why didn't she understand that he had blown her whole game out of the water, that he had finally taken his revenge? That he had won not only the battle but the war?

She was still guffawing, pausing only long enough to say, 'Oh, Dieter, you are an even bigger fool than I thought you were.'

'How dare you?' he shouted, and took an angry step towards her. 'I have uncovered a vile conspiracy. God knows what will happen to me, but your plans have been ruined. Do you hear me?' He only dimly realised how loudly he was yelling. '*Ruined!*'

'You sure of that?' she replied mildly, then she was giggling again. Soon her broad shoulders were heaving and she sat down at the little kitchen table, as if it was all too funny to go on standing up. 'Oh, Dieter, you've got it all wrong.' She gave a final chuckle and stood up. 'I think I'll just go to bed.'

'No you won't!' Dieter shouted, and he was glad to see surprise on Irma's face.

But she recovered almost at once, saying sarcastically, 'It is a little late to assert yourself, Dieter. As I said, I'm going to bed. Stay up if you like.' She added with a taunting laugh, 'And keep your apron on. It suits you.'

It was too much. Something gave way in Dieter, and he felt released from the ties that had bound him for years. He rushed at Irma, determined to slap her sneering face. He swept his arm towards its target, and he only realised halfway there that he was still holding the Japanese knife.

Flinching reflexively, Irma jerked her head back from his approaching hand, but in tilting it back she exposed her throat. The knife in Dieter's extended hand sliced through the protruding jugular as if it were soft butter.

Irma brought her hands up, eyes agog, and clutched her throat. But the wound was wide and deep – blood spurted through her fingers like water gushing from a broken pipe.

Dieter stood stock still while Irma tried helplessly to block the blood's flow. Her lips moved in an effort to speak, but only gurgling sounds came out. Dieter stared at her. He felt totally detached and made no move to help her.

Irma's eyes were terrified as she tried to sit down on the chair, her hands still pressed to her throat. But her legs seemed to give way and she collapsed on the floor. The blood was gushing from her neck now, and Dieter stepped back. It wouldn't do to get Irma's blood on his shoes, he thought, as he watched without concern as the blood streamed towards the stove and his wife stopped breathing.

41

It was just seven o'clock in the morning when Sally Mortimer walked through the door of the British Embassy in Berlin. With a *Guten Morgen* to the security guards she took the lift to the fourth floor where the MI6 Station's offices were located. Dumping her bag on top of the pile of newspapers that had already been placed on the small table outside the security door, she tapped the code into the pad and held the door open with her foot while she juggled her bag and the newspapers.

Once inside she dropped everything on her desk as the door closed again with a reassuring click. She was obviously the first one to arrive. She hadn't been sleeping well recently. The reason, she had decided, was that she was rather lonely. Not that there weren't plenty of opportunities to go out with people. The Embassy was full of them and one in particular, the ambassador's private secretary Giles Leith-Martin, was clearly very keen; he had asked her out several times. But, and it rather annoyed her to acknowledge it, she was missing Bruno Mackay. Their affair, if you could call it that, had barely got off the ground when he was spirited away on the mysterious operation for Geoffrey Fane.

Sally knew Bruno had a long-standing reputation in MI6 as a serial philanderer, though it had been noted that since he had come back from a posting in Libya, where it was rumoured something unpleasant had happened to him, he had seemed more serious. Sally had been hoping that he was seriously keen on her. But then he had been whisked away and all she had heard of him was a postcard she had received a few weeks after he had gone out of circulation. It was a picture of Chicago, sent in an envelope through the Embassy mail; it showed the Hancock Tower, all one hundred storeys soaring into the sky, and on the back in Bruno's handwriting: *Not as high as my feelings for you... X.*

She didn't for a moment believe that the card meant he was in Chicago or had been there on this trip, but it was something and it showed he had been thinking of her, at least when he wrote it – unless of course, as she suspected, he had written it before he left the country and had left it with somebody to post. Whatever the truth of it, she had propped the card up on the mantelpiece of her small flat in Berlin and she occasionally took it down and read it again.

While she was thinking about Bruno she was plugging in the large coffee machine that served the MI6 Station. The first thing everyone seemed to want when they arrived in the morning was coffee and it was the duty of the first in to get it brewing. As the smell began to permeate the room, she took her coat off and sat down at her desk, casually turning over the top newspaper so she could read the headlines. It was her job as the most junior intelligence officer in the Station to scour the papers every day for items relevant to their operations or articles that might be of interest to Head Office. Elsewhere in the Embassy the same process was going on, on behalf of the diplomats and the Foreign Office in London. The online press got the same attention. It was a job Sally rather enjoyed. It was good for her German and gave her status as the person who knew most about everything that was going on – including, of course, what was on at the cinema and whether the latest play had received good or bad reviews.

Settling down for a peaceful half hour or so, Sally turned over the first paper, the tabloid *Die Welt*, to read the headlines. It was immediately clear this was not going to be a normal morning:

Bloodbath in Blankensee

it shrieked. She read a few lines then grabbed another paper, the staid broadsheet *Frankfurter Allgemeine Zeitung*. It had the same story on the front page, though the wording of its headline was different:

Homicide/Suicide in Hamburg Suburb

The next one had:

School Head Murdered in Blankensee

And so it went on; each paper had its own version, all of the same story.

But what really gripped Sally's attention was the mention, repeated in different words in each paper, of the suspected involvement of the Russian intelligence service, the FSB. Irma and Dieter Nimitz were described as 'Soviet-era spies', who had been allowed to operate in a quiet suburb of Hamburg under the very eyes of the German security services. Two papers had picked up on the fact that Irma had been Head of a school for refugee children, but their assessment of the significance of that differed. One suspected a terrorist link, speculating that the Russians had been feeding radicalised children into Germany, but didn't speculate on why. The other hinted that the children were being trained as some sort of Fifth Column of spies.

As to who had killed Irma Nimitz and why, many options were offered to the readers, with promises of more sensational information to come. Sally switched on the television in the corner of the office and found that the news channels were also leading on the story.

By now Sally's colleagues were arriving. An urgent meeting was called and jobs were quickly allocated. Sally was to inform Peggy Kinsolving in MI5, who had asked for the surveillance that had first revealed Irma's connection to the FSB officer. Sally's boss, Charles Fairclough, the Head of Station, was going to the ambassador's morning meeting where he would have to answer questions about what the Station knew about the Nimitzes. A message was being drafted by someone else to inform Geoffrey Fane.

In the middle of all this, Sally's phone rang. It was Herr Lamme at the BfV. He was in a state of high excitement and Sally switched her phone to loudspeaker so her colleagues could hear the stream of furious German that was coming from him. He was accusing Sally and her colleagues of leaking the Russian connection to Irma Nimitz.

'How has it become public knowledge?' he was asking. 'We have been most carefully investigating Irma Nimitz under conditions of great secrecy. Only you, the British, knew of this possible connection. Now there is a major scandal. Questions are being asked of the Chancellor's office about what checks are being made on refugee children and how the schools they go to are controlled. The BfV is being accused of incompetence. They are saying spies have been operating under our noses and that the refugee policy has laid us open to infiltration. I have to go with the head of my Service to explain to ministers what we knew. We have a political crisis on our hands and I strongly suspect this information must have been leaked from your side.'

He stopped talking for a moment, having run out of breath, and Charles Fairclough seized the phone. He spoke soothingly to Lamme, assuring him that no one on the British side had leaked anything to the press and no one there had shared details of Irma Nimitz with the Americans. He phrased that part very carefully as he had no idea how much was being shared with the Americans in London; when he looked at Sally questioningly, she shrugged to indicate she didn't know either.

'It is probably just lucky speculation,' Fairclough said. 'One journalist feeding off another.' But Herr Lamme clearly didn't believe that and, to be honest, neither did Charles Fairclough.

Fairclough ploughed on nonetheless. 'Herr Lamme, we have no information here about what has happened in the Nimitz household except what we read in the newspapers, of course. Could you please tell me exactly what occurred?'

'All I can tell you at present is that at three thirty yesterday afternoon Dieter Nimitz threw himself under a train at Blankensee station. He was identified by the documents in his wallet. When police went to his house to inform his relatives, they found Irma dead on the floor of the kitchen with her throat cut; she had bled to death. It is clear that her husband killed her. His prints were on the knife they found in the kitchen beside her body. The pathologist reckons she died many hours before he did.'

By now Lamme was speaking more calmly and rationally but then his tone switched back to agitation. 'I am being called now to go to the ministerial meeting. I will tell the government that I have your assurance that the British have not passed information about German citizens to the press or to the Americans.'

'Yes,' said Charles, his fingers tightly crossed. 'Please do.' He put down the phone, let out a long heartfelt sigh of relief and left to go to the ambassador's morning meeting, while Sally poured herself a cup of coffee and picked up the phone to speak to Peggy Kinsolving in London.

42

ONE WEEK AFTER BRUNO had unceremoniously leapt from Michelle's car in the park in Moscow, leaving her and her son open-mouthed with astonishment, he was standing in the booking hall of Beijing railway station waiting for a car from the Embassy to pick him up.

He had not remained long in the muddy BMW that had collected him in the park. A quarter of an hour later, in a shady street in a Moscow housing estate, he had transferred to a high-powered silver Mercedes SUV containing two men and a woman. According to their passports, the men, Bill and Dave, were both Canadians and the woman was French, though in fact there was only one Canadian in the car and he had lived and worked in England for the last ten years. The Frenchwoman did indeed have a French mother but she also lived and worked in London. Bruno had his Canadian passport, having left his British passport and his other British identity documents with his initial rescuers in the BMW.

The Mercedes had driven steadily out of Moscow, heading eastwards in the direction of Kirov and Perm. The two men took it in turns to drive; Bruno's offer was firmly rejected. He was told to sit in the back and get some rest;

he was clearly the parcel for delivery and not expected to take part in the delivery process. The Frenchwoman, whom they called Maddy, seemed to be in charge of security and it was she who kept an eye on the traffic, looking out for familiar patterns of movement that might indicate they were being followed.

They had food for two days on board so they stopped only occasionally in small towns to fill up with petrol and buy coffee to keep them going. There were long stretches of boredom, especially during the night when there was very little traffic on the road, but also moments of tension and one of sheer panic. The last came on the outskirts of Kirov when they rounded a corner to be met by a battered-looking lorry heading fast towards them on their side of the road. By sheer bravado and fast thinking, Dave had avoided the lorry, whose driver must have been drunk or asleep, and they had driven on unharmed but shaky.

The moment of tension came when they were stopped at a checkpoint as they were leaving Perm. A large uniformed man with a gun over his shoulder and a cigarette in his mouth strolled out and asked for their documents. Just as beads of sweat were beginning to break out on Bruno's forehead, it turned out that Maddy was not only beautiful and French but also spoke excellent Russian, was very charming, and perhaps most importantly had a couple of packs of French cigarettes in her pocket that she decided she didn't really need. So the moment passed with best wishes and smiles all round.

Their destination was Yekaterinburg, where Bruno was to join a tourist train on the Trans-Siberian Railway. Bruno didn't know who had invented this long escape route. Maddy had hinted that much thinking had gone on in the Operational Security Department; the obvious route via the Finnish border had been too well publicised by the successful exfiltration of Oleg Gordievsky in the 1980s.

Though it proved a long slog, this method had worked, and they had arrived safely in Yekaterinburg quite late in the evening on the day before the train was due. Three interconnecting rooms had been booked in a hotel and Bruno had slept peacefully in the middle one with his minders in the rooms on each side. In the morning he had been delivered safely to the railway station. The waiting room had been full of tourists of various nationalities including, by luck or design he never knew, a group of Canadian engineers who had been working in a natural gas plant near Lake Baikal and were taking a scenic trip before flying home.

Bruno had been relieved to discover he had a two-berth compartment to himself and breathed a thank you to Geoffrey Fane who must have authorised the extra expense. For the first couple of days he'd spent most of his time in his compartment, glad to keep his distance from the Canadian engineers, who seemed a dreary bunch. Just short of the Mongolian border, Russian officials came aboard, and he'd been visited in his compartment by a passport officer who'd leafed slowly through his document's pages, looking at the many stamps it held from all over the globe with more longing than suspicion. After he'd handed the passport back and left, Bruno was starting to relax – only for another tap on the door. A small gnome in a cap and khaki uniform came in – the Customs representative, it seemed, for he peremptorily ordered Bruno to open his suitcase. No problem there, thought Bruno.

But he soon noticed that the gnome was glowering. What was wrong? Then Bruno remembered that he'd put a pint bottle of whisky that he'd brought from Moscow flush in the middle of the neatly pressed shirts and folded underwear and socks that the escape team had provided. He cursed himself for the oversight. Was he really going to be busted for a contraband bottle of booze? It seemed absurd, but also alarming. He envisaged himself taken off the train and put into a small windowless room, where he would face an interview that would be hard to survive unscathed. *What was the purpose of your trip last year to São Paulo? Tell us about your family, Mr Anderson? Do you have children? What do they do? You say you are married, Mr Anderson – what is the date of birth of your wife?*

A tiny trickle of sweat started to crawl along the back of his neck. Then inspiration came. Reaching down Bruno lifted the bottle of whisky, then looked away, blindly offering the bottle to the gnome. For a moment nothing happened. Then he felt the man take the bottle from his hand, and when Bruno turned round the deed was done – the whisky bottle tucked unobtrusively into the side pocket of the gnome's jacket. The little man stiffened his shoulders, nodded curtly, and left the compartment.

After this it had been plain sailing. As the train worked its way through Mongolia and then on to Beijing, Bruno had stayed in the safety of his compartment and tipped a conductor to bring him his meals on a tray, along with a bottle of expensive red Bordeaux. Now as he waited for a colleague from the Beijing Station to pick him up, he breathed another silent thank you to Geoffrey Fane for getting him safely out of Moscow. He still had no idea why he had been withdrawn so precipitously, but assuming he had been in serious danger he could only be grateful to have been rescued in such style.

43

Peggy,' said Liz, 'you've got to go.'

'They'll understand. They know operations come before everything. They can meet another day.'

'They won't meet again for another year. They're all busy people and there'll be an outsider there as well. The dates for these things are fixed well in advance. If you're not there this afternoon they'll think you're not interested. They'll also think that you imagine you are indispensable and don't understand the principles of delegation and teamwork.'

It was the morning of Thomma's escape from Bartholomew Manor and they were arranging who should go to Suffolk to interview him. In normal circumstances, it would have been Peggy, as it was she who had interviewed Miss Girling and given her the number that Thomma had rung for help. Liz had only met Miss Girling when she had shown Liz around the school. But Peggy was up for promotion and the board was meeting that afternoon. Liz had strongly recommended Peggy and was anxious that she should not miss her chance.

Silence fell. Peggy looked downcast.

'Come on, Peggy,' said Liz gently. 'It's my reputation on the line as well as yours. If you don't turn up, they'll think

I got it wrong. I've written you up in a big way, you know. I'll cope with Thomma. Your account of your interview with Miss Girling is very clear, and I'll read it again before I go. Also, I need to look again at your note about the call from the Berlin Station telling us about Irma and Dieter Nimitz's deaths. Let me have the file of photographs, and make sure it includes everyone involved, right from the start of all this. I have a feeling there are links here that we haven't yet made. And why don't you spend this morning at Grosvenor, briefing Miles Brookhaven on recent developments? Then go to the Promotion Board this afternoon and sock it to them.'

Peggy's face brightened and she smiled. 'All right. I'll go to the beastly board and do my best,' she said, standing up to go.

'Of course you will. And you'll wow them. You'll see. I just hope I'll do as well in Suffolk.'

As she emerged from Ipswich station Liz was not surprised to see a police car waiting for her. She was surprised, however, to see the Chief Constable sitting in the back seat.

'What are you doing here?' she asked. 'I was expecting Inspector Singh.'

'When I heard you were coming I thought I'd come myself,' Pearson replied with a smile. 'I hope that isn't a disappointment.'

'I'll get over it,' Liz said teasingly. 'And actually I'm delighted to see you, because I think this case is beginning to look more complicated than we initially thought.' She spent the hour of the drive explaining what had been going on in Germany and trying to make the connections with Suffolk. She found it helped her to go over it, but it clearly left Richard Pearson pretty confused, and neither of them knew quite what to expect from the young man they were on their way to interview.

The desk sergeant was expecting them, and it was obvious that someone had recently cleaned and tidied up the reception area of the small police station in the housing estate on the edge of Southwold. The floors were sparkling and there were flowers in a vase on the reception counter.

'Good morning, sergeant,' said Pearson. 'Where's the young man then?'

'I'll show you along, sir. Good morning, ma'am,' he said with a nod to Liz. 'He's in an interview room down the hall. One of our young family officers is looking after him.'

'Excellent,' replied Pearson. 'Let's go.'

The sergeant unlocked a door and led them down a corridor to a room that looked like the sitting room of a small house, containing a couple of armchairs, a sofa and a table at which a teenage boy and a young woman PC in uniform were sitting looking at a laptop and laughing. The boy was small and thin and Middle Eastern in appearance. He was dressed in jeans and a grey hoodie that was too big for him, and looked like countless boys seen every day on the streets of London and other English cities. But he had none of their bravado. As he looked up from the screen when Pearson and Liz came into the room, his face grew tense and he looked frightened.

'This is PC Norton,' said the desk sergeant, 'and young Thomma.'

'Good morning, sir, ma'am,' said the young woman, jumping to her feet. 'We were just playing a game on the computer.'

'Great,' said Pearson warmly. 'I expect you were better than Miss Norton at that,' he said, addressing Thomma.

Thomma seemed too frightened to reply, but PC Norton said with a smile, 'Yes, sir. He was beating me hands down.'

As the desk sergeant and PC Norton left the room, Liz said, 'Come and sit down over here, Thomma,' motioning to the sofa. She sat down next to the boy and Pearson took one of the armchairs opposite them.

Pearson said, 'First, the most important thing is: did they give you some breakfast and, as it's nearly lunchtime, are you hungry now?'

The boy smiled hesitantly and replied, 'No, thank you, sir. I had bread rolls and jam for breakfast and I have just had a sandwich and a coke for lunch.'

'That's good,' said Liz. 'Now perhaps you could tell us why you ran away from the school.'

The boy thought for a moment. 'I was scared.'

'What frightened you?'

'It was when I heard the other boys talking. About Miss Girling.'

'What were they saying about Miss Girling?'

'They said she was dead. She was going to take me to church with her. But she didn't leave a note, so I thought she had forgotten.' The boy bit his lip and frowned, then said, almost angrily, 'I know she is dead, but the other boys said she killed herself. I don't believe that. Something bad happened to her.'

'Why do you say that?'

'Because she wanted me to phone her if I didn't hear from her. Why would she say that if she was going to kill herself?' He explained how she had first found him when he'd been upset because the other boys laughed at him for being Christian; how she had comforted him, then offered to take him to the local church service.

'Who would have harmed her, do you think?' asked Liz.

'Cicero,' he said without hesitation. 'He came looking for me when I left this morning. I think he would have harmed me, too.'

Pearson interjected, 'You mustn't worry about that. We're not going to let anyone come anywhere near you.'

Thomma nodded. He no longer seemed the fragile boy of a few minutes before. Seeing his confidence rise, Liz asked, 'Can you tell us a bit more about the school at Bartholomew Manor? What were you studying there?'

'Computers, miss.'

'Yes. But was it just computing in general?'

'Oh no, we've all had the basic training before. This is specialised.'

'Let's start at the beginning. Where did you originally come from and how did you get here?'

'And,' added Pearson, 'how do you come to speak such excellent English?'

So Thomma told a story which he had probably recounted many times before – how he had been born and brought up in Aleppo in Syria. His father had been an English professor at the university and had taught his children to speak English. They were Christians. When the fighting started, his father had decided they must leave but he couldn't find a country that would take them. So the family, his parents and his two sisters and Thomma, travelled to the coast. His father paid people smugglers to ferry them to Italy. They paid a lot of money, said Thomma, to get a better boat than the unsafe inflatables. But when the boat came it was old and rickety and had no life rafts. When they were in sight of the Italian coast a storm blew up and the boat capsized. In the chaos that followed he lost sight of the rest of his family. He swam for as long as he could and was eventually washed up on the shore all alone.

He had managed to evade the government officials who would have put him in a refugee camp and joined a group who were walking across Europe. It took him about two months to reach Germany, where they were very kind and found him temporary foster parents. He had to take some tests to decide which school he should go to, and he got very high marks. So he was put in a school outside Hamburg that specialised in maths and computing. During his third year he had been chosen to join a group of boys going to England for specialised training.

'What is the school in Hamburg called?' asked Liz.

'The Freitang.'

'And the name of the head teacher?'

'Frau Nimitz.'

Liz took a folder of photographs out of her briefcase and selected one. 'Is this the Head?'

Thomma nodded. 'Yes. That's Frau Nimitz.'

'Tell us about your journey here, Thomma,' asked Richard Pearson. 'Did you come by plane?'

'Oh no. It was like when we came from Syria only this time the boat was better. I don't know why we came that way. All the boys were asking why we had to travel at night and land on a beach in the dark.'

'What did the people in charge say?'

'They said it was cheaper and there was not much money for educating immigrant children. That did not make us feel good.' He went on to describe the regime at the school, which sounded more like a prison camp than an educational establishment.

'Tell us about the lessons. What were you being taught?'

'We were not really taught, sir. Mr Sarnat – he's the Head – believes you learn by doing. That's what he likes to say.'

'I see. Tell me what you were doing then.'

'We were divided into groups, four of us in each one. I was assigned to Computer Defences.'

'What did that mean exactly?' asked Liz.

'We were developing programs that companies could use to protect themselves against hackers.'

'Did you try and use the software against attackers?'

'There aren't any attackers at present.'

'Then how did you know the software would work?'

Thomma looked surprised. 'We didn't,' he said innocently. 'Instead, we tried to get into other sites. That way we could see where their weaknesses were, and find ways to make those sites stronger.'

It was a touchingly naïve assessment of what was going on. To Liz, it was perfectly clear that Thomma and his fellow students were being taught how to hack, not how to prevent it. She said, 'Did you practise on real companies then?'

'Not real ones,' said Thomma. 'That's next week.'

'Oh,' said Liz casually. 'What are they?'

'We are going to test something called jaysee browncow.'

'What is that?' asked Liz, puzzled.

'It's a meat company and it runs refrigerated lorries. They have a computer program that tells the lorries where to go. If someone hacked the program they could send the lorries somewhere else and steal the meat.'

'J.C. Brown and Co,' murmured Pearson. 'Big meat suppliers.'

Liz pressed on. 'You said you were divided into groups. What were the other ones working on?'

'Social media mainly.'

'Like Facebook?'

'Yes. One group, I know, was working on updating the profiles of social network users. On Facebook, and Snapchat and Instagram, and Twitter – and many others too.'

'Really? Did they have permission from the users to do this?' It sounded very odd.

A smile was struggling to break out on Thomma's face. Finally he giggled.

'What's funny, Thomma?'

'You asked if the users would mind. But you see, none of these users are real!'

'Really? How do you know that?'

Thomma explained that when one of the other boys made a mistake with dates, their teacher Mr Gottingen said it didn't matter; no one was going to complain because no one owned these profiles. Thomma also heard Mr Gottingen talk to Mr Sarnat about their work – he said the 'Legends' group was doing very well. Gradually, Thomma said, the other boys had realised they were working on the profiles of people who didn't exist.

Liz was beginning to understand. Legends were the fake histories or cover stories assigned to Illegals – the spurious 'facts' of a CV that transformed a Russian agent into a thirty-four-year-old Norwegian businessman called Erik Nilson, educated in Oslo, married with two children, multilingual with a passion for painting. All the detail needed to bamboozle everyone from immigration authorities to his new neighbours in a Surrey suburb that he was who he said he was, and not the Russian Illegal he actually was. And Thomma's fellow students were supplying the details for these phony personae.

'That was one social media group,' said Thomma. 'There was another one too. They spent their time looking for *real* people on social media sites. I'm not sure why.'

'Who were they looking for?'

'They didn't have actual names. They looked for interests and languages. American or English people who spoke Russian or Chinese. People who had travelled there. And people who had worked there.'

'How did they find them?'

'LinkedIn,' said Thomma. 'That was the best site for finding them.'

Of course it was, thought Liz. It provided a useful first step to finding which young employee in a Western embassy *didn't* have a Facebook profile or belong to LinkedIn. That would be equally revealing –a telltale sign that they might be engaged in clandestine work.

From what Thomma had to say, it seemed clear that these teams at Bartholomew Manor were at work on much more than how to protect against hacking. Sixteen pupils working full time could get an awful lot done. But then why had they not been more effectively disguised? If even Miss Girling had had her doubts, surely other people would soon ask questions? It seemed very strange.

Liz looked at Thomma. The boy was clearly tired. It might be better to continue talking to him tomorrow. But there was one further question she wanted to ask.

'Thomma,' she said kindly, 'you've told us a lot and been very helpful. We may want to speak to you again, but in the meantime, we'll sort out somewhere for you to stay tonight. Don't worry – it will be completely safe. There will be a policeman to protect you.' The boy looked reassured. 'But before we stop, just tell me something. Are all the other boys on the IT course from the same school in Hamburg?'

'Yes.'

'And the teachers – are they from Hamburg too?'

Thomma shook his head. 'No.' Then he hesitated. 'Well, there is one. He's a sort of assistant teacher. I knew him in Hamburg – he's called Aziz. He's a few years older than me. He went on a course in America and he stayed on there to teach. He must have been very good. I was quite friendly with him at school because he came from Syria too. I was surprised to see him here at Bartholomew Manor.'

'Have you chatted to him at all? Did he tell you why he was here?'

'No. He pretended not to know me, probably because I am a student and now he is a teaching assistant. And I was scared to approach him because he's working for Mr Sarnat.'

Liz flicked through her folder of photographs again and picked one out. It had been sent over weeks ago by the FBI, when they had first investigated the death of the man in Burlington, Vermont. It was a young man, slightly older than Thomma but not unlike him in appearance.

Thomma nodded. 'Yes. That's him. Aziz.'

Liz realised the network was now fully connected. Moscow with Blankensee, Blankensee with Suffolk, Suffolk with Vermont and Vermont back to Moscow. They were the nodes of a circular network, but it seemed that only one node, Suffolk, was live.

Thomma looked drained now, and Liz turned to Pearson. 'Shall we wrap it up for today?'

Pearson nodded. 'We're most grateful to you, young man. You did the right thing getting out of that school when you did. The ones running it are not good people. We're going to look after you now and keep you safe, and after a few days we'll be talking to you about what you would like to do next. I'll send in Miss Norton to look after you now while we sort out a nice place for you to stay. I think it must be time for something else to eat. What would you like? There's a Lebanese in town if you want something that reminds you of home.'

Thomma shook his head. 'I'd like a burger,' he announced with an enormous smile that said he was already becoming westernised. 'With chips, please.'

44

Eddie Singleton was guiding his milk float cautiously up the drive to Bartholomew Manor. It was just getting light and the morning was faintly frosty. There was a faint red glow in the sky to his left and thin fronds of mist were hanging in the trees that bordered the drive. The red, brown and yellow fallen leaves lying on the verges sparkled in his headlights, each with its fringe of white hoar frost.

He drove carefully because of the potholes in the drive. He knew most of them of old but they were increasing – no one seemed to be doing any maintenance these days. Eddie had been delivering milk to the school for years. Four crates twice a week; that used to be the order. Now it was just one – hardly worth the effort, especially now the drive was getting into such a bad state.

He'd heard that the kids were all foreigners now – maybe that explained why they didn't need so much milk. Lots else had changed. He used to drive right up to the kitchen door and carry the crates in for them. It would be all bright and warm and smell of bread and bacon. The cook's assistant used always to give him a warm sausage roll or a bacon sandwich. Now the kitchen was empty when he arrived and he just dumped the crate at the door. The kids lived over at the farm and probably had their breakfast there but he didn't deliver to the farm so he didn't know.

He took the final turn by the big elm tree cautiously. There was a bit of a slope there and he expected it to be quite icy. A dazzling beam of light struck his eyes, blinding him. He slammed on the brakes and the milk float jolted to a stop, then began to slide slowly towards the big tree, all the crates rattling in the back.

'Steady,' said a deep voice. A tall figure loomed up beside Eddie, who could just make out that it was a policeman.

'What did you do that for?' said Eddie shakily. 'You could've killed me if I'd hit that tree.' Another policeman, this one holding a firearm, materialised beside the first and Eddie could now see that there was a group of police cars parked beside the kitchen door.

'Is there a problem?' Eddie asked nervously.

'Not for you, mate,' said the first police officer. 'Just leave the milk right there and skedaddle.'

An hour earlier, while it was still dark, Liz had arrived at Bartholomew Manor in the third of the convoy of five black police cars. The convoy had assembled at the small police house in Southwold while Liz was snatching a few hours' sleep on a narrow bed in the medical room.

Just before they'd left, Pearson had taken a call from the police pathologist. He'd listened intently, said a quiet thank-you and turned to Liz. 'We're not the only ones who've been up all night. I've been pushing for the post-mortem on Miss Girling, and it's just come in. Apparently, she was dead *before* she supposedly hanged herself in her kitchen.'

'How did she die?'

'She was strangled. Whoever killed her fractured some bones that couldn't have been broken by hanging.'

The convoy had driven through the crisp and misty Suffolk countryside, which was just a dark blur of trees and hedges and shadows where nothing was awake except themselves. They had driven slowly up the bumpy drive and drawn up at the side of the house by the service entrance, blocking the top of the drive so no car could leave. There were eight police officers, four of them armed, and also Chief Constable Pearson and Liz. The operational command officer was Inspector Singh. He split the team up, sending two officers to the back of the house with instructions to detain anyone found in the classrooms or the grounds. 'Have a good look round that new computer room we've heard about,' he added. Two men were sent to keep an eye on the farm where the students were sleeping. 'No one is to leave until I give the order.' Two other men were to stay with the cars and prevent anyone coming in or going out via the drive and the final two men were to accompany Inspector Singh into the house via the front door. Liz had firmly refused the invitation to 'stay in the car, ma'am, until we are sure it's safe', and followed the police to the front door of the house, walking a little way behind, with the Chief Constable. She wondered how they intended to get in as she remembered the front door of the manor was a huge old oak affair, but she didn't think it wise to ask.

They climbed silently up the big stone steps in single file, the armed officer at the front. The steps sparkled with frost in the light of the police torches. The lead officer reached the front door and Liz held her breath, wondering what would happen next. But the door swung open to his touch and they were all able to walk in unhindered. Liz pointed to the left where she remembered the headmaster's study and the offices were.

Inside, the rooms looked as if a hurricane had struck them. In the headmaster's office, the drawers in the filing cabinets were pulled out and papers and files were strewn messily all over the carpet, along with half the contents of the bookcase behind Sarnat's desk. The video camera that had caught Liz on tape had been ripped out, its brackets swinging loosely from the wall.

In the office where the secretaries had worked it was the same story – drawers pulled out, papers on the floor. It was as though a gang of hooligans had rushed through, creating as much havoc as they could as they went. Liz felt sure this wasn't the work of the students, but why it had been done, she couldn't guess. Maybe they had intended to burn the papers but hadn't had time.

As they searched through the rooms on the other side of the hall they discovered a uniformed security guard, sitting in a cubicle next to the nurse's room. He was wearing headphones plugged into a laptop and from the drowsy look on his face it was clear he had been asleep and had not heard them arrive. When he finally spotted an armed officer, he then looked very awake. Opposite where he sat there was a bank of screens; they were all blank.

'What's happened to the CCTV system?' asked Liz.

'Don't know, miss,' he said, confused. 'Looks like someone's turned it off. It was working when I came on duty.'

'What time was that?'

'Ten o'clock, miss.'

'Did you go to sleep straightaway?' asked Liz. The guard grinned weakly but said nothing.

'Is anyone else in the building?' demanded Pearson.

'I don't know,' said the guard again. 'I haven't seen a soul since I came on last night. I thought I heard a car earlier on, but it was going out, not in, so I wasn't bothered.'

'Who's usually here at night?'

'Mr Sarnat and Cicero. And the new chap – Gottin-something.'

'Where do they sleep?'

'Upstairs. I always hear them when they go to bed, but last night there wasn't a peep.'

'What you mean is, you didn't hear anything because you were asleep,' responded Pearson.

While this conversation was going on, Inspector Singh had dispatched the police officers to the upstairs floors and now they returned. 'Upstairs is empty, sir. No one's there. But one room's locked.'

'Can I have a look?' Liz asked, turning to Pearson.

'Of course. I'll come with you. Show us please, constable. You know the layout now.'

They went up the elegant curved oak staircase with its carved banisters to the floor above. The bedrooms were large but sparsely furnished. The beds had not been slept in. It wasn't difficult to determine who slept in which room – on his chest of drawers, Sarnat had a large framed photograph of himself, standing in snow outside a ski chalet; on Gottingen's bedside table were two postcards addressed to him, apparently from a girlfriend in Germany.

In the third bedroom, among some correspondence, was a bill for a new tyre from the local Mini dealership. This must be Cicero's room, though it was bare of any personal touches: no other letters or cards, no photographs or pictures. In the wardrobe a solitary jacket hung from a hanger, pristine in a dry cleaner's plastic cover. Above the clothes rail there was a high shelf, which Liz reached to explore. At first she felt nothing but dust, then her fingers touched something rough. She stood on tiptoe, reached in further and tugged, and a large coil of rope came sliding out, unravelling snake-like as it landed on the carpet.

'What on earth is that doing there?' asked Pearson.

'I don't know.'

The constable who was watching what was going on coughed. 'Excuse me, sir,' he said. 'I'm PC Willis. It was me that found that woman who used to work here. The one that hanged herself in her kitchen – Miss Girling. It's just the same rope.'

'Are you sure?' asked Liz. 'All rope is much the same, isn't it?'

'No, ma'am. You see this is thicker than what you usually find. It's more what you'd use as a tow-rope for a car or a boat. I remember thinking the old lady hadn't taken any chances: you could have hung an ox from what she used.'

Liz turned to Pearson. 'It makes sense, given what the pathologist's told you. But why didn't he get rid of it?'

'He probably didn't see the need. Thought he'd got away with it; thought no one would ever think it wasn't suicide. Also, from the state of Sarnat's office, it looks as if these three left in a hurry. If he was panicked about getting out of here, he probably forgot all about the rope.'

'But why the sudden hurry anyway? It's as if something – or someone – tipped them off that we were coming.'

'Or else they just took fright when they couldn't find Thomma?'

Liz pondered this. 'Maybe. But Thomma had been gone for hours before these guys left – if the guard's right that it was late last night. If they were that scared of what Thomma might say, they would have left immediately.'

Inspector Singh's radio buzzed. 'Go ahead, Walker,' Singh said. He listened for a minute, then turned to Liz and Pearson. 'Walker says the students are awake now. They say the last time they saw any member of staff was yesterday evening. Someone called Cicero came round to check on them.'

'Right,' interjected Pearson. 'Tell Walker to keep them there for the time being. Tell them there are no lessons today. We'll go over and speak to them once we're done here.'

Liz turned to PC Willis. 'Where's this locked room you mentioned?'

Willis led them to the other end of the corridor and pointed; Pearson tried the handle and rattled the door. Like all the doors in the manor it was solid, heavy wood. Pearson shook his head. 'We'll need one of the locks team to get us in there.'

Willis asked, 'Shall I have a go at breaking it down?'

'Not yet. The security guard must know where the master keys are. Try him first.'

As Willis thudded off down the stairs, Inspector Singh's radio came to life again. It was the team from the back of the house.

'We have apprehended a male at the rear of the house. Claims he is a teacher and lives in the house. What do you want us to do with him?'

'Bring him in,' replied Singh. 'Upstairs.'

Liz heard the sound of a door slam from the ground floor and heavy footsteps on the stairs. The steps grew closer and looking over the banisters she saw a slim young man in a black tracksuit climbing the stairs, followed by a large flak-jacketed policeman with a semi-automatic at the ready.

As the pair reached the landing, the young man stopped abruptly at the sight of the group standing there.

'Who are you?' asked Inspector Singh.

'I think I know,' said Liz. His photograph was back at the police station in her briefcase, along with a report sent by FBI agent Fitzpatrick several weeks earlier. And when they had questioned Thomma in Southwold the previous day, he had told them this man was here. He resembled Thomma but was slightly taller and physically more mature. 'You're Aziz, aren't you?' said Liz.

The man nodded, glancing nervously at his armed companion. 'Is something wrong?' he asked.

'What are you doing here?' asked Inspector Singh.

Aziz pointed at the locked door. 'That's my room,' he said simply.

'Why's it locked?'

He shrugged. 'I like to get up early and go out for a run. I always lock my room.'

That would explain why the front door had been open, thought Liz. 'What do you do here?'

'I'm a teacher.'

Liz continued, 'Originally from Syria, but then from Hamburg, and most recently from Vermont. Is that right?'

Aziz's eyes widened. 'How do you know so much about me?'

Liz ignored the question. 'Where are the others? Sarnat, Cicero and Gottingen?'

Aziz hesitated, but only briefly. 'They've gone; I heard them go. It was late last night.'

'Where did they go?' Pearson asked.

Aziz shrugged.

Liz said sharply, 'Why didn't you go with them?'

Aziz stared at her; he looked confused. 'Why would I?'

269

'They brought you over here from Vermont. Surely you've been working closely with them.'

'That's not true,' said Aziz, sounding stung. For all his seeming mildness, he spoke more sharply now. 'I came because the Americans wouldn't renew my visa. Things have changed over there. They no longer let people like me stay.'

'And you just happened to end up here at Bartholomew Manor?'

'No. Mr Sarnat called me. He said they knew from Mr Petersen that I had done good work in Burlington and I could help teach their students. He said the students were from the school I went to in Germany, so I would fit in. That I could be very useful, working on counter-cyber strategies. To help companies protect themselves. The university in Vermont helped me get permission to come here.' His voice faltered slightly.

'But that wasn't really what they wanted you to do, was it?'

He was looking increasingly vulnerable. Liz went on, 'You were brought here under false pretences, weren't you? Just as you were in Vermont. These people don't want you to help anybody; they want your expertise to make trouble, to subvert, to destroy.'

There was a long silence. Aziz looked close to tears. Finally, he said quietly, 'I know. But I promise to God, I did not know that until I came here. I thought it was... legitimate. What could I do?' he asked Liz, and his voice was imploring. 'The Americans didn't want me; I couldn't go back to Germany. My home' – and Liz realised he meant Syria – 'is not a home any more. So I believed Mr Sarnat, and I came over. But soon I realised what was going on. At least I think I did.'

'I think you were right,' said Liz gently. 'It does sound as though none of this is your fault. But did you know the others were going to leave?'

'No,' he said emphatically. 'But I knew something was up. They had a bonfire in the grounds at the back; they were burning papers, I think. I thought that was strange, so I went downstairs. That's when I heard them talking and realised something was going on.'

'Did you hear where they were going?'

'No.' He hesitated. 'But it couldn't have been far from here.'

'Why?'

'Because I heard Mr Sarnat say they would take Cicero's car. Cicero said it only had a quarter of a tank of petrol in it, but Mr Sarnat said that would be more than enough. He even laughed.'

Liz looked at Pearson. 'It can't be Stansted then. Or Norwich airport. And if they were staying in the UK, they wouldn't stay close by. Which must mean the coast. They're going out by sea.'

'Singh, we need to alert Border Force. Better get on to the Coastguard too,' Pearson said. 'This young man can give you their description. Though even with just a quarter of a tank of petrol, there's still a hell of a lot of coastline to cover and they've been gone several hours already.' As he stopped speaking, his mobile phone began to ring.

45

GEOFF GUMM WAS USED to waking early, usually when the seagulls started screaming as the first hints of light filtered through the darkness in the east. This morning, though, he woke even earlier than usual and it was still pitch dark. He lay in bed for a while, then, realising he would never get back to sleep, he rolled over, swung his legs out from under the blankets and stood up. He went downstairs in his pyjamas and put the kettle on. Then, shivering in the cold, he went back upstairs and dressed in thick trousers and a warm fisherman's sweater. Downstairs again he brewed coffee in a jug. Out of the window he could see the first faint hints of daylight in the eastern sky and that there had been a very early frost. The leaves of a sage bush in the herb bed were etched with white. As he stood warming his hands on his mug and watching the light gradually increase, his sheepdog Judy gave a low bark. He took no notice but a few seconds later she barked again and, thinking she needed to go out, he opened the kitchen door. She rushed out and he followed her and stood just outside the door, taking deep breaths of the ice-cold sea air.

It was the hazy time between night and sunrise. He watched Judy rush down to the track and into the tall, gently waving grass. It was then he saw the car parked on the verge of the track a hundred yards away. That it was there didn't surprise him; early bird fishermen keen on surf casting for bass often left their cars on the lane near his cottage. There were three men in the car, as far as he could make out, and he wondered why they weren't up and out by now, putting up their rods and lines, ready for the early morning advent of the bass. And how on earth did they get all their fishing gear into a Mini?

He whistled for Judy, who did a long tour of the front garden then came into the kitchen again, where he fed her, finished his coffee and got ready to go down to his workshop. He was looking forward to getting a good morning's work done with such an early start. As he came out Judy rushed ahead, but she didn't bark, and he could see that the men were no longer in the car.

He left his garden and made his way through the feathered grass and the powdery sand along the path between the dunes until he saw the sea spreading out in front of him like a blanket under a low layer of cloudy sea fret. He was about to turn towards his workshop when something caught his eye in the other direction. Turning, he saw three figures huddled together at the base of a dune. There was no sign of any fishing equipment. Gumm stared at them, but from that distance, and with fret, he couldn't make much out. Part of him wanted to go closer, but he sensed that could be dangerous, though he didn't quite know why.

He went on to his workshop, unlocking the door he padlocked every evening – otherwise he'd find a tramp there in the morning, keeping warm. As he started to close the door behind him he heard a mild hum, out to sea, and made out a fishing boat about a quarter of a mile out, illuminated by the first ray from the rising sun. The boat was motionless and must be anchored there; the noise was coming from a large inflatable dinghy with an onboard motor, moving swiftly towards the beach.

Gumm watched as the dinghy grew close, its motor cutting out only as it reached the shallows. The figures hunched on the beach had stood up and now they ran across the strip of shore. When the dinghy hit the pebbles with a thud, the men were already up to their knees in the water. He watched the three of them clamber into the dinghy, the last one pushing the little boat off and turning it to face the sea. It took off at high speed, heading directly back towards the fishing boat.

Geoff Gumm wondered what was going on. Why the hurry? These couldn't be illegal immigrants – they were leaving, not arriving. But there was something odd happening. He remembered the last time Inspector Singh had come down to see him, when he'd brought his boss, the Chief Constable. They'd said to contact them if he saw anything strange. Well, this was strange. He had Singh's number pinned on his noticeboard, so he picked up his phone, walked over to it and dialled the number. Engaged. He tried again a few minutes later. Still engaged. Geoff was getting worried now. He could see through the window of his workshop that the dinghy had reached the fishing boat and was being hauled on board. He remembered the Chief Constable had talked about possibly wanting to buy a boat and he'd left his card. It must be somewhere on the table. Throwing a Chinese takeaway menu and a *Norfolk Today* magazine on to the floor and pushing some bills and invoices out of the way, he uncovered it: Chief Constable Richard Pearson. He hesitated for a moment, then reached for his phone. wondering if it was too early to disturb such a high-powered person, but then he remembered what they had said: *If you see anything unusual again, ring any time. Day or night.*

46

'WE SHOULD BE HEARING from them soon.' Pearson drummed two fingers on the tabletop and frowned. 'I'm surprised it's taking that long. There's not a lot of traffic off this part of the coast. I know they're short of boats and crew but I would have expected a quicker response than this. We flagged it up as urgent.'

He and Liz were in a spare office back at the Southwold station. Liz had a view of the street. The window was covered with burglar-proof mesh that made a tractor, crawling along the road, oscillate surreally as Liz gazed out.

They had left two armed officers at Bartholomew Manor on the off chance that Sarnat, Cicero or Gottingen might return, though Liz thought that given what they'd heard from Geoff Gumm it was unlikely. While Pearson spoke to his HQ and ordered them to contact Border Force, Liz had accompanied Aziz to the farm annexe. She announced to the students that he was in charge and they were all to remain where they were for the day. Their initial puzzlement had turned to glee at the prospect of a lesson-free day. Leaving two policemen on guard she was driven over to join the Chief Constable in Southwold.

Gumm had been extremely precise in his description of the boat that had picked up the escaping trio and clear about the direction it had taken as it left the coast. At first it seemed simple enough, and at nine thirty Border Force had contacted Suffolk Police HQ to report that their own craft had set off an hour before from Great Yarmouth. On its way south, it communicated with a large tanker, which reported seeing a fishing boat matching the description Gumm had given – and also supplied its name. *Fortunes High* had been spotted about five miles offshore, moving north towards Lowestoft. The tanker estimated it was travelling at no more than 10 knots.

'That's slow, isn't it?' asked Liz when Pearson told her this.

'Yes, that's *very* slow, especially for a getaway. You'd expect something a lot faster. Unless something's wrong with the boat, or they are trying to rendezvous with another vessel.'

By eleven o'clock he was looking both worried and frustrated. They both knew there was nothing they could do but wait. Liz had contacted Peggy in Thames House to set in hand enquiries about the ownership, nationality, etc. of the *Fortunes High*. She had also received some information in answer to enquiries she had made previously about the ownership of Bartholomew Manor. 'It's not clear who actually owns the place. There's a shell company, then another, then another. For a while I thought it might be the Chinese behind it. But it's pretty obvious now, given everything that's happened in Germany and what we've learned from Moscow, that it's been the Russians all along – though I don't suppose they'll be coming forward to claim it. The whole thing will keep the lawyers busy for months to come.'

Pearson smiled and said, 'The property issues can wait. What I don't know is what will happen to the students there.'

'Who knows? I don't think there's much chance that the Freitang will want them back. If it still even exists, given that the Head is dead and turned out to be a Russian agent. The whole thing is a huge scandal in Germany and we're left with all these kids. I don't suppose they'll get much choice in the matter, poor things. It's tragic when you think what they've already been through to get to Europe in the first place and now they're stuck in limbo. It all depends what status they had in Germany, I suppose.'

'What about Thomma? Can you put in a word for him? He seems a nice boy.'

'I'll do my best. As for Aziz, he must have had a work permit to come to the school. He said the university in Vermont helped him. He flew from Boston to London last month and he has an EU passport. Hopefully he can transfer to a proper kind of job over here. IT skills get looked on favourably by Immigration.'

Time passed slowly, as it always did during the waiting phase of an operation. At one o'clock Liz was about to suggest they go out and grab a sandwich, when Pearson's mobile rang. It was the Ops Room at Police HQ. Liz watched as he listened, struggling to keep his voice from rising. Gradually his features settled, his expression hardened, and she saw it was not good news.

'They did *what*?' he said, sounding incredulous. He looked at Liz and shook his head, half in sorrow, half in disbelief. He said more calmly now, 'I hope you expressed our disappointment.' The voice at the other end said something and Pearson smiled grimly. 'Good. That sounds like suitably undiplomatic language. Tell them we want a full report on how they failed to apprehend three important international criminals.' And he ended the call. He turned to look at Liz. 'You're not going to believe this.'

'I can tell it's not great.'

'The Coastguard has been keeping an eye out for our escapees – Border Force have only one vessel on this stretch of coast. They spotted our friends anchored as if they were waiting to meet another ship, off a stretch known as Braddle Beach. They alerted Border Force in Ipswich and they relayed the message to their patrol boat. Then they got confused somehow – or else the boat didn't hear the message very clearly. They headed straight for a point called *Battle* Beach – it's named for the pillboxes they built along its bluff during the war. The problem is that Battle Beach is ten miles south of Great Yarmouth and Braddle Beach is twenty miles north. By the time they discovered their mistake and retraced their steps, *Fortunes High* was nowhere to be seen.'

'They could be anywhere by now.'

'Exactly,' said Pearson grimly. 'So far they haven't done anything one would expect – slow boat, hanging around: you'd almost think they wanted to be caught. But there's no sign of them now, and they could have easily made it to Holland or Belgium. Our chaps are getting in touch with the Dutch and the Belgians. If they've stayed along our coast, we'll get them, but I can't believe they'd be that stupid. They're probably drinking champagne aboard a Russian cruise ship by now.' He sighed. 'What a cock-up.'

'It's not your fault.'

'I can't help but feel responsible. It happened on my turf.'

'I know, but it's not your screw-up.'

There was no point in them hanging on any longer in the little Southwold police station. There was nothing more they could do. Assorted social workers and local departmental officials had been dispatched to the farm to look after the welfare of the students and to try to determine their status. It was going to be a difficult task as only Aziz had any documents.

'What are your plans now?' asked Pearson.

'Well, I've got to be in the office tomorrow fairly early. I'll need to sort things out at our end and talk to Six and find out what's going on in Germany. Could one of your drivers take me down to Ipswich and I'll catch a train?'

'Yes, of course. But do you have to get back tonight?' She looked at him inquiringly. He went on, 'I have to be in London myself first thing tomorrow – a meeting at the Met. I'm being driven down and could easily take you too. Why don't you stay here and we could have dinner somewhere and drink to our disappointment that those bastards escaped? I could put you up in my spare room and we'll drop you off at your flat in the morning.'

Liz hesitated before saying, 'Thanks. That sounds like an excellent idea. Much better than going back to an empty, foodless flat.'

It seemed to take Pearson a moment to realise she was saying yes, then he beamed. Liz found herself drawn to his mix of professionalism and straightforward charm. He was unlike any man she'd known well before. And certainly not remotely like Martin Seurat.

But there was nothing wrong with that. She would always have her own memories; she didn't need someone to remind her of them.

They stopped at the police station at Bury St Edmunds so Pearson could catch up with the details of what was going on and Liz could brief Peggy and ask her to arrange a meeting with Geoffrey Fane the following morning.

'It might be a good idea to invite Miles Brookhaven too,' Liz added.

They drove to the Crown, an old inn in the village about five miles west of Bury St Edmunds where Pearson lived. They'd agreed on an early supper as neither of them had eaten anything except sandwiches and pizzas for more than twenty-four hours and they were starving. The Chief Constable was clearly a well-known and well-liked customer and the welcome was as warm as the low-beamed room with its log fire burning in the big fireplace. They ate tender slices of pink lamb while talking companionably; it was all so peaceful and relaxing after the frenzied last couple of days that Liz almost fell asleep. Finally Pearson said, 'Come on. I think we need to get some rest,' and after friendly goodbyes all round they drove the short distance to Pearson's house, which Liz was surprised to see was a thatched cottage.

'Your room's along here,' and he led Liz down the cottage's one corridor and opened a door. 'Oh no,' he said, almost reeling back.

'What's the matter?' Liz was peering over his shoulder as he flicked on the light.

'I asked the cleaner to clean out this room. And it's not been done.'

Liz saw why he was dismayed. Half the world's fishing gear seemed to be contained in the little room.

Pearson said, 'I'm so sorry. Why don't you relax in the sitting room and I'll sort it out?'

Liz looked dubiously at the enormous amount of gear – poles and nets and boxes of lures – that lay on the bed, on the floor and perched precariously against the wall.

'It will take you for ever,' she said. 'And where are you going to put it all?'

'Well…' Pearson looked embarrassed. 'You can have my bed, and I'll sleep on the sofa.'

Liz gave him a long, contemplative look. There was something touching about a chief constable acting so awkwardly.

'You could,' she said slowly. 'You certainly could.'

47

Six o'clock the following morning saw them up and drinking coffee while they waited for the Chief Constable's car to arrive. The *Today* programme was burbling away in the background but neither of them was really listening. When they caught each other's eye, they smiled.

'Do you know,' said Liz, 'I've never been to bed with a chief constable before.'

'And I hope there's only one chief constable you'll go to bed with again.'

The traffic was heavy but the driver was efficient at weaving his way through. Pearson was reading *The Times* while Liz sat comfortably beside him, trying to keep awake.

Her mind was on Martin Seurat, dead now for almost two years. Richard Pearson was the first man who had struck any spark in her since then and she wondered if she was feeling a twinge of regret – or even guilt – about this new man in her life. It must be even harder for Richard, she thought; his wife had died after years of happy marriage. She knew he had had relationships with other women since his wife's death – he'd told her so – but nothing had proved serious. Which left unspoken what he thought would happen with Liz.

Now he reached over and touched her hand lightly. She smiled.

'I was just thinking about Martin. I don't think he would want his memory to hang over us now.'

'Funny you should say that,' he said. 'I was just thinking the same thing about Lucy.'

By the time they reached central London they were travelling at little more than walking pace. The driver was an expert navigator, however, and managed to have Liz outside her Pimlico flat by eight thirty, which gave her time to change before going in to the office.

Pearson said, 'After the Chief Constables' meeting I have a call scheduled with my Police and Crime Commissioner – he's asked for a briefing on what's been going on at Bartholomew Manor. I won't go into too many details, but we'll have to say something to the press pretty soon, since quite a few people will have noticed there's been extensive police activity at the school.'

'OK, but can you keep it fairly general for the moment? I'll be discussing the angles with my colleagues first thing – could you join us after lunch? We can talk then about what we need to do next and lines to take with the press.'

'Of course. I'd be glad to.'

Peggy was at her desk in the open plan when Liz looked in and waved for her to join her in her office.

'Well, what happened?' Peggy looked at her questioningly. 'You know,' said Liz. 'The important stuff.'

'Do you mean my meeting with Miles?'

'No. I mean your interview with the promotion board. How did it go?'

Peggy started to speak, then stopped. 'Go on,' said Liz. 'Spill the beans.'

'Well, not bad, I think,' Peggy said slowly. 'But I won't know until later today. Officially, that is.'

'And unofficially?'

'I saw DG in the lift. He wasn't on my board but he seemed to know all about it.'

'And . . . ?'

Peggy was starting to smile. 'He said he'd heard I'd given a "cracker of an interview".' Peggy's face lit up with a big grin.

'Yippee,' said Liz. 'I knew it.' She was delighted, though a little sad too, since it made it much more likely that Peggy would be moved out of her section. Her promotion meant that she had been flagged for greater things, and inevitably the Service would want to put her in different sorts of postings to broaden her experience.

The Geoffrey Fane who appeared in Liz's office an hour later seemed a new man – or, rather, the self-confident Fane of old. He appeared to have recovered from the dreadful realisation that he had reached the age when he could retire. He'd had a haircut and it seemed he had paid a visit to his tailor; he was wearing an elegantly cut new suit of pinstriped grey. He sat down in the sole spare chair boasted by Liz's small office and crossed one leg leisurely over the other, revealing bright yellow socks above his polished black brogues.

'Smart socks, Geoffrey,' said Liz.

'Gift from a friend,' he said breezily. He smiled in an avuncular way at Peggy, who was perched on the corner of Liz's desk, as if to say that someday she might grow up to have friends too. Peggy and Liz glanced at each other. They were both thinking the same thing – *Geoffrey's got a girlfriend.*

'I've booked a meeting room,' Peggy said, and they decamped from Liz's tiny office to a roomier space along the corridor.

As they sat down at one end of the conference table, Fane said, 'I was hoping to bring Bruno along.'

'I didn't know he was back. Congratulations on getting him out so smoothly.'

'Thank you – it all went tickety-boo, if I say so myself. But he isn't back yet. He said he had some personal business to attend to in Berlin. God knows what that could be; he hasn't any German relations that I know of.' He caught the slightest grin on Peggy's face and the smile Liz was trying to repress. 'Why are you two smirking? Is there something I should know about Bruno and Berlin?'

'Not at all, Geoffrey,' said Liz. 'We're just delighted that Bruno is safely out of Russia.'

Fane clearly didn't believe her explanation and knowing him she was sure he would not rest until he had found out exactly what – or who – had taken Bruno to Berlin. 'Anyway, he's safe and sound – or as much as Bruno will ever be. But we can talk about Russia later.' He looked at Liz. 'You said there had been new developments on your side?'

Liz nodded and gave a quick summary of events in Suffolk in the last few days. She described their further investigation into Bartholomew Manor – Miss Girling's suspicious death, the call from Thomma and her interview with him, and the raid on the college.

'So, this Miss Girling was an old teacher who'd been at the school for years and had been kept on by the new regime.'

'I think they were using her as a sort of respectable front if people applied to the school and wanted to look round,' said Peggy.

'Yes. Her job was to put off nice middle-class parents – though I don't think she knew that's what she was there for.'

'And then they murdered her?' asked Fane, puzzled.

'That's what the pathologist said. She was strangled before she was hanged with a rope. And we found the identical kind of rope in the wardrobe of the bedroom that the headmaster's assistant Cicero had used. It's not proof enough for a court, but it certainly wasn't suicide and I'm pretty confident it was Cicero who killed her. He was a really sinister character. He followed me after I'd visited the school and I'm pretty sure he broke into my flat to scare me off.'

'My dear Elizabeth. I hope you've had the locks changed. But why kill a harmless old lady?'

'They must have been worried that she was spying on them and learning too much. What do you think, Peggy? You interviewed her.'

'Yes. She certainly wasn't a natural spy. I just hope it wasn't what I said that caused her to act suspiciously.'

'I think it was more likely that she had been taking a close interest in the boy Thomma. From what he said, she had promised to take him to church with her and they wouldn't have liked that. That's the obvious explanation, I think.'

'I sense a "but", don't I?' asked Fane.

'Well, only because we'll never know for sure. The three main characters have disappeared.'

'That sounds like a regular balls-up. What happened? From what I've heard they should have been sitting ducks.'

'I know,' said Liz, annoyed at the suggestion in Fane's tone that this was somehow her fault. 'You can have apologies from Border Force, the Coastguard and the Suffolk

Constabulary if that's what you want. But it isn't going to help. Those three got away. They could be anywhere.'

'Europe?' asked Fane almost hopefully.

'Anywhere on the continent. Or Moscow, more likely. Once they got away they won't have hung about.'

Peggy added, 'Despite that, we've found out quite a lot about these operations. They all seem linked. The children were initially selected in Hamburg, then the Head of the Freitang school there, Irma Nimitz, sent them off – to the UK, but also to America to Vermont University. One of the older ones who'd stayed in Vermont came on to Bartholomew Manor when the US operation was aborted. The FBI have confirmed it's the same guy.'

'I hope you've got him under lock and key.'

'Something like that,' said Liz, since it seemed pointless to explain that Aziz, like all the students at the college, was just an innocent dupe of those behind the operation. 'But the real issue is what the Russians were hoping to get out of these linked operations. Because it is very clear that the Russians are behind all this, using their long-time recruit Irma Nimitz, the Head of the school in Hamburg.'

'I should think it's perfectly obvious.' Fane leaned back in his chair with a sigh, looking superior. 'They were training these refugees in cyber subversion, of course. I don't claim myself to understand how it all works but take it from me, that's what it was all about.'

'Yes, Geoffrey. I'm sure you're right. We've been in touch with GCHQ and someone from the National Cyber Security Centre is going down to talk to the students and find out exactly what they were doing. I couldn't get a lot of sense out of the boy Thomma when I interviewed him because he only really knew about the part he was involved in, and I'm not an expert in this sort of stuff either.'

'You need to be careful. There's a lot of trouble in Germany over the Hamburg end of this,' said Fane. 'Questions in their Parliament. A huge fuss in the press about the immigration policy. Why was the school not better monitored? How could a Russian spy have been appointed as Head? Why did the BfV not know about the Nimitzes? How did he get a job in the European Commission and was he working for the Russians there? The head of the BfV may have to resign, and the interior minister too.' He sighed. 'It's almost worse that the Nimitz couple were uncovered. Might have been better if no one had ever known they were "Cold War spies", as the media put it.'

'Exactly,' said Liz. 'The three men from Bartholomew Manor would have been exposed as well if there hadn't been a cock-up with the coastal services. They were hanging around at the college for more than twelve hours after young Thomma escaped. Why?'

'The escape plan wasn't in place, I imagine,' said Fane briskly, staring at Liz. He was silent for a moment, then he said, 'I'm not sure what you're getting at, Elizabeth.'

'I'm not entirely sure myself,' said Liz. She wanted to think this through but needed to do so on her own. 'Shall we break for lunch now? Geoffrey, I would be happy to treat you to the best from our canteen.'

Fane shook his head, suppressing a shudder at the thought. He looked at his watch. 'That's very good of you, Elizabeth, but actually I have a lunch appointment. Shall we reconvene here at two thirty?'

'Yes, and I've invited the Chief Constable of Suffolk to join us; he's in London for a meeting this morning.'

48

LIZ FOUND HERSELF ALONE – Fane had sauntered off to his rendezvous, and though Peggy had apparently gone back to her desk, there was no sign of her when Liz went to look for her. She had arranged to meet Pearson in the front of Thames House at two fifteen, but it was only half past twelve now, so she decided to leave the building for a stroll. She wanted to sort out exactly what this complicated series of events had been about.

On the Embankment, the sun was making a rare autumnal appearance, flooding the river's surface with a low, misty light. She hesitated between directions, then decided to walk west towards the Tate. There she found tour buses jamming the inner kerb, and tourists taking selfies on the front steps. Weaving a way through them, looking for something peaceful to help her clear her mind, she ignored the notices for the special exhibitions and went into the Modern galleries, where she found old favourites and a new one – the latter wearing a dark suit and staring at a large Francis Bacon triptych.

She said from eighteen inches behind his broad shoulders, 'What do you think of that then, governor?'

He didn't move an inch, but said slowly, 'Not sure. I know he's a great painter and all that, and there's undoubtedly enormous power to the picture, but I have to say it's not exactly cheering.'

Liz laughed as Pearson turned around with a broad smile on his face. 'Great minds think alike, I see,' he said. 'I thought you'd be up to your neck in meetings and that I should kill a bit of time. Seems you had the same idea.'

'The meetings are over for the time being and everyone's sloped off to lunch. I actually came in here to think and then I spotted you. But I can't think in front of a Francis Bacon. Why don't we walk over and look at the Turners?'

They spent twenty peaceful minutes in the Clore Gallery without much conversation. Outside again, they walked back slowly west towards Thames House, passing a group of schoolchildren eating hot dogs bought from a cart.

'I'm starving,' said Liz.

'Want one?' asked Pearson, and he walked over and bought two. They ate them sitting on a bench facing the Thames.

'I wonder if I could persuade you to come back to Suffolk this weekend,' said Pearson. 'It would be an enormous help if you would come with me to a meeting with my Police and Crime Commissioner on Saturday morning. He's very supportive but he's feeling a bit out of his depth in this Bartholomew Manor business. Not surprisingly, to be fair. It's not the sort of thing rural forces normally get involved in. I think he'd find it very reassuring to meet you.'

'Well, yes, I could,' said Liz. 'I could come up on the train first thing. What time is the meeting?'

'Ten thirty. I could meet you at Ipswich station at about ten. The meeting's at our main headquarters, not far from there. Then,' he went on, 'I was going to try out a boat that Geoff Gumm is lending me. Do you fancy a bit of sailing? The weather is forecast to be quite good.'

Liz hesitated but only for a moment. 'Why not?' she said. 'I won't be a lot of use but you can tell me which ropes to pull. And it would be great to blow away a few cobwebs.'

As they approached Thames House Liz was saying, 'You'll have to go through the visitors' entrance, but I've told them you're coming,' just as a voice called from the steps.

'Liz!' It was Peggy, standing at the top of the steps, wearing her winter coat and beaming.

'Hello,' said Liz, catching sight of another figure walking away towards Horseferry Road. Even from the back he seemed familiar, but she didn't have time to think who it was because Peggy had run down the steps towards her.

'I got it!' Peggy exclaimed. 'I got the promotion.' Throwing her usual reserve aside, she gave Liz an enormous hug.

Laughing, Liz extricated herself and gestured towards Pearson. 'You've met the Chief Constable, I think.'

'Oh yes,' said Peggy, slightly abashed.

She shook hands with Pearson, who was smiling at Peggy's obvious joy. 'Congratulations,' he said politely. 'I'm sure it's very well deserved.'

'I don't know about that,' Peggy said modestly, but then she beamed again at Liz. 'Thank you so much for recommending me, I'm really thrilled.'

'We must celebrate. Can we have a drink together this evening?'

Peggy suddenly looked embarrassed. 'Could it be another day, Liz? You see, Miles has just asked me out to dinner.' She blushed and Liz realised why she had recognised the back of the youthful man heading off towards Horseferry Road. It was Miles Brookhaven.

*

Fane was only slightly late and had clearly lunched well. He had the flushed face and the faint smell of good food and wine that spoke of a couple of hours spent in his club. Liz introduced him to Pearson, and Fane gave the newcomer a quick once-over with suspicious eyes. Liz was amused to see that even with his new lady friend, if indeed she existed, Fane was still alert for any competition for the position of top dog in the room. But something about Pearson's quiet confidence seemed to soothe Fane's proprietary vigilance when it came to Liz.

'Chief Constable,' she said, addressing Pearson and feeling slightly absurd using his title, 'thank you for joining us. We will want to discuss the fallout from events in Suffolk shortly, but I'd like first to finish up where we left off this morning. Geoffrey,' she said, turning to Fane, 'we were discussing why the various Russian operations have been so easily discovered.'

'Easily? Did I say that?' mused Fane.

'Not exactly, but let's take a minute to think about what we know. The scandal in Germany that you were describing this morning came about because of a leak; otherwise the death of Irma and Dieter Nimitz would have passed as a violent domestic quarrel – nasty but not remarkable. But *someone* told the media that they were Cold War spies. Who knew that? We did, but we didn't leak it; Herr Lamme swears it wasn't from his people. The only others who knew the story were … the Russians.'

'But why would they want to do that?' asked Peggy. 'Surely they'd want to protect their operation and the fact that they'd planted these two Illegals?'

'Not necessarily. Think about what's happened because of the leak. It's caused havoc in Germany and may even bring down the government. It has the German security services tied up in knots, wondering if anyone and everyone is secretly working for the Russians. And it hasn't actually hurt the FSB at all. It's magnified their reputation for disruption while maximising that disruption in their traditional enemy – Germany.'

Fane chipped in. 'What about in America?'

Peggy said, 'That operation was stillborn because Petersen died. They couldn't put anyone else in to take his place; Petersen had been there several years. And young Aziz wasn't a trained agent; he couldn't take on the operation. He was just there to do what Petersen told him to do – but Petersen went and died.'

'And what about here in Suffolk?'

This time it was Liz who replied. 'Ah, that's where they were really clever. They set up their operation in an existing college, got their recruits – these young men from the Hamburg school – chosen for them by Irma Nimitz, and went to work, preparing to do as much cyber damage as they could. We'll have to wait till the cyber security team have done their enquiries to see exactly what was going on. I expect some of it would have been plain destructive hacking – what our young friend Thomma was being trained to do. Some of it would, I'm sure, have been a lot more sophisticated and damaging.'

'But we found them easily enough,' said Fane.

'Well … think about it. The actual operations were intelligent, well thought out and well run – they could have gone on longer and done a lot of damage. We were lucky because we got on to it through Dieter, who via the Burnside couple in Brussels provided us with the name of Bartholomew Manor School. Even if we hadn't had that tip-off, I'm sure it would have still come to our attention before long. How could you ever expect to hide the fact that sixteen young immigrants were smuggled into the UK to work on high-level software projects? The answer is – you couldn't. That's true, Chief Constable, isn't it? Even in rural Suffolk?' She looked at Pearson.

'Particularly in rural Suffolk, I'd say,' he replied. 'Odd happenings stand out a lot in the country where mostly life goes on to a pattern.'

'The Russians must have known that. They may have been surprised when I showed up at the college so quickly – even before the students had arrived. But once they learned who I was, they didn't abort the project. I do wonder though whether Cicero and Sarnat knew the whole thing was meant to be discovered eventually. If so, why did they kill Miss Girling when they suspected her of snooping, and why did they pursue Thomma when he escaped?'

'That would also explain why Sarnat and Cicero and the other teacher tried to cover their tracks by destroying documents,' said Pearson. 'That would make no sense if the whole thing was always intended to be discovered.'

Liz nodded. 'Once they had killed Miss Girling they had to get away. None of them would have fancied a life in prison, and the FSB was never going to tell them they were supposed to stay and face the music as sacrificial lambs. Look at the escape plan: they left hours after Thomma escaped; they were picked up at the same place as the students had arrived, a pretty basic no-no; their getaway ship had roughly the speed of a tricycle. That's not what I'd call a brilliant fallback plan if things went wrong, and it was only through sheer luck that they got away.'

'So they were *meant* to be caught?' asked Fane sceptically.

'Not necessarily, though they would have been if there hadn't been such a stupid cock-up between Border Force and the Coastguard.'

'And if they had been caught, how would that help the FSB?' Fane asked, but intrigued now.

'Because then the whole affair would have blown up – just like it did in Germany. The press would have been on to it in a shot. I can see the headline now: *Private School a Secret Nest for Spies.* The broadsheets would have run with it for days. *Major Security Lapses, The Enemies Within.* Etc etc. I don't know if this government would have fallen, but it would have taken a hell of a knock. And so would we – MI5 and your Service, Geoffrey. We would have looked like fools. An internal inquiry would have been the least of it. Heads would have rolled.'

Fane smiled wryly, perhaps recalling his visit from HR suggesting he could take his pension any time. 'As it is, aren't people going to be asking questions?'

Pearson replied, 'They already are. The local papers have been ringing us about the events at the college. But I think it can be handled.'

'Really? And what do you propose, Chief Constable?' Fane asked a touch condescendingly.

Pearson was unruffled. 'Well, I can't guarantee anything. But we've devised a cover story that I'm pretty confident will fly. Child refugees arrive here thinking they are in the hands of kind people who are helping them to resume their disrupted education. At first, things go swimmingly. But unbeknownst to these young immigrants, their supposed patrons are crooks – no better than traffickers – who have brought them here specifically to defraud the authorities and philanthropic individuals for whatever they're worth. Once suspicions are aroused, the trio do a runner and the kids are left behind, innocent victims yet again. That is near enough to the truth to satisfy my conscience, and my police commissioner agrees.'

He stopped and Liz said nothing, her eyes on Fane. But he nodded grudgingly. 'I can see that working.' Then as if unwilling to concede too much, he added, 'Mind you, don't overdo it.'

Pearson smiled. 'We won't.'

Fane turned back to Liz. 'So, what you're saying, if I understand it correctly, is that in fact it's a good thing these men got away.'

Liz thought for a moment. 'Yes. No scandal, no press, no publicity. It's not as if we did anything brilliant. We were just lucky all the way through, particularly in failing to catch the Bartholomew three.'

Fane had his elbows on the table and steepled his fingers together in a pyramid. 'The Russians couldn't really lose on this one. If we hadn't discovered what they were up to, then they'd have continued on their merry way and done a lot of damage.' Liz nodded. 'If, conversely, we did uncover their operations, there would be a maelstrom of bad publicity about the ineptitude of Western intelligence agencies, the vulnerability of our institutions – from an American university to the European Commission and our fee-paying shills. None of which would do anything but help the reputation of the Russians – it's not as if the world expects better behaviour from the FSB. Bloody hell, I wish I could see something retrievable in this situation.'

'Cheer up, Geoffrey,' said Liz. 'Look on the bright side. If we manage to avoid a political storm like the Germans have got, then we will have succeeded. We've discovered what was going on; we've stopped it and hopefully there will be no fallout. What more do you want?'

The room was silent as everyone tried to decide whether they were looking at a success or a failure.

There was a sharp knock on the door and a familiar face looked in.

'My God!' exclaimed Fane. 'From Russia with love.'

49

Bruno Mackay pushed open the door with one hand and came in, carrying a leather holdall in the other. Liz looked at him in astonishment. The man who walked into the room had the face and voice of Bruno Mackay but everything else about him was different. The straight blonde hair was now a wavy mahogany; the Savile Row suit had morphed into jeans and a leather jacket, and the striped Jermyn Street shirt and silk tie into something plain, dark-coloured and open-necked. This was Alan Urquhart, the investment banker, straight from Moscow via Beijing and Berlin.

'Good heavens, Bruno,' said Liz. 'I'd never have recognised you.'

'That's rather the idea,' he replied dropping his bag on the floor and reaching across the table to shake hands with Pearson and introduce himself.

'I'm relieved to see you back,' said Fane. 'I hope the journey went well.'

'It was quite an experience. Especially the drive out of Moscow. That team you sent to rescue me was quite something. But I'm still in the dark about why you pulled me out.'

Richard Pearson stood up. 'If you'll excuse me, I think I'll leave you all to it now. We've covered everything that affects me; I'm sure if anything else comes up you'll let me know. Liz has agreed to come to Suffolk tomorrow to meet my commissioner, which will be a reassurance for him and a great help to me. But I'd like to thank you all for your help. And congratulations on your safe return,' he said to Bruno, then left the meeting.

There was a general reshuffling. Peggy waved a hand at the small table in the corner where tea and coffee were set out. 'Help yourself, Bruno,' she said.

Geoffrey Fane and Bruno both stood up and moved across to the table, talking quietly. Then, to her great surprise, Liz saw Fane shake Bruno's hand and pat him on the back.

Fane turned around. 'Bruno has just told me something that has come as a complete surprise. You won't often hear me say that,' he said with a rare touch of self-mockery. 'Go on, tell them, Bruno.'

For the first time in a long acquaintance with Bruno, Liz could see he was embarrassed. 'Er,' he started, then hesitated. He took a deep breath, then said, 'I've just told Geoffrey that I've got engaged. I'm going to get married.'

Peggy and Liz were transfixed. This was the great Lothario of MI6 speaking. The most famous bachelor in the intelligence community.

Peggy recovered first. 'Do we know her?'

'Yes. You do and she's a great admirer of yours and Liz. It's Sally Mortimer. That's why I stopped in Berlin. I wanted to grab her before one of those Germans took her out of my grasp.'

'From what I saw of them, there's not much fear of that,' said Peggy. 'I'm so pleased, Bruno. She's great. But I hope you aren't going to whisk her away from Berlin. She's doing so well there.'

'We certainly can't allow that,' chipped in Fane severely. 'I'm always being told that a woman's career comes first.'

'Congratulations, Bruno.' Liz was beaming. 'This is news I never thought I'd hear. I wish we could whistle up a bottle of champagne. There's another cause for celebration today. Have you heard that Peggy's been promoted?'

More handshakes and smiles all round until Liz said, 'Sorry to break up this *bonhomie*, but I think we'd better finish our analysis of what's been going on and decide what if anything more we need to do.

'I'm glad you're back, Bruno,' she went on, 'because we need to try to understand the Moscow angle on what's been happening here and in Germany and in the States. You'll all remember that we originally learned about the FSB's Illegals operations in the West from our source Mischa, and his information came from his brother the FSB officer, who we now know is Boris Bebchuk.

'It was as a result of his information that we were able to uncover the two Illegals operating here, the Karpis couple, who were sent back to Moscow last year. Mischa also told us that there was another Illegal at work in America but that he was ill and not operating. The FBI persevered with that lead and eventually identified the man who had been working at Vermont University in the IT Department. He was dying but their interest was aroused when a mysterious visitor appeared who seemed to have been sent to clear up after he died. Everything else that has followed sprang from that.'

'Yes,' broke in Bruno, 'and on our side, we and the Agency decided we would make a recruitment pitch to Mischa's brother, who seemed to be the source of all this information.' He looked at Fane. 'So I went off to Moscow. I thought I was doing rather well there. Our Station in Moscow, working with the Americans, had found the brother, Boris Bebchuk. I got alongside him, cast the fly and he was nibbling at it. Another cast and I was confident I'd have him hooked, when you pulled me out. What happened?'

'You should be glad we did get you out while we could,' said Fane sharply.

'We had a pretty clear warning,' said Liz, 'that the FSB were on to you. There was every possibility that if you'd shown up for that lunch with Boris, you would have been taken in for questioning.'

'You mean my cover was blown?'

Fane said, 'Almost certainly. Apparently, after you failed to turn up, security people went round to your flat and took it to pieces.'

Bruno looked startled. He turned to Liz, 'But how did you learn that the FSB were on to me?'

'About ten days ago, Mischa called me to another meeting in Berlin. He gave me a message – it was a warning, really – that no one should make a pitch at Boris. He clearly knew that someone was sniffing around his brother; he seemed to think it was the Americans, but that may just have been a blind. We know all his information has come from Boris, so it was clearly a message from Boris. He must have sussed you.'

'Boris sussed me?' said Bruno glumly. Then he went on, 'But if he had spotted me, why did he tell Mischa and why did Mischa tell you? Boris doesn't know Mischa is leaking stuff to us – or does he?' he asked after a moment's thought.

'Well,' said Liz, 'that's what's been bothering me. This is what I think. It's only a theory, and as we can't check it with Boris and Mischa, I can't prove it. But for what it's worth here's my view:

'At the beginning Boris was a loyal FSB officer who had the unfortunate habit of confiding in his brother when he drank too much. Mischa didn't share his loyalty, and in return for payments from the Americans and later from us too, he relayed the information about FSB operations that he learned from Boris.

'But when we rounded up the Illegals operating here last year, Boris, along with his bosses, started to wonder how we had got on to them. Boris knew what his bosses in the FSB didn't know, that he had been talking freely to his brother Mischa. It wouldn't have been a huge leap for him to wonder if Mischa could have been talking to someone in the West. It wouldn't surprise me if Mischa wasn't starting to flash his cash around a bit, what with the retainer from the Americans and then what we started paying him. Boris would have wondered where the money was coming from – their army isn't exactly Goldman Sachs – and put two and two together.

'I think Boris might have confronted Mischa, who perhaps admitted what he'd done. Boris certainly wasn't going to shop his brother – he would have been shopping himself, after all. So he decided to get in on the act as well. Between them they resolved to keep feeding us information – and split the proceeds.'

'Right,' said Bruno thoughtfully. 'So then what happened, according to this theory?'

'You showed up. Boris, knowing what he did by then about Mischa's activities, must have been suspicious from the first. As I said, he may have thought you were American, and I know he has a low opinion of our transatlantic friends, so he started to worry that his FSB bosses might have spotted you as well. To cover himself, he reported his contact with you and his suspicions.'

'Bastard,' said Bruno. 'After all the vodka I fed him – *and* I threw a great party.' His face grew pensive. 'But why didn't he just let me get caught? Why send a warning through Mischa?'

'Because once he had reported you, you were being watched. If he'd let you go on to make a pitch at him, he would have had to report it for fear they would discover it independently. You would have been picked up and he would immediately have come under suspicion. It doesn't do an FSB officer any good to be the subject of an approach by a foreign intelligence service. The obvious question is "Why you? What have you been doing to attract the enemy?" And of course, we would have dropped Mischa like a hot potato, so the cash would have dried up. Bad news all round.' Liz continued, 'But this way he and Mischa hoped we'd be convinced they were both on our side, while simultaneously they hoped the FSB would think Boris was completely loyal to them. For that to work, they had to warn you off making an overt approach.'

Bruno whistled lightly. 'A bit risky for them, I'd have thought. But I'm glad you got me out of it.'

Fane said, 'If you're right about this, Elizabeth, they didn't cater for Bruno's sudden disappearance. There are bound to be questions about why he's vanished.'

'There's not much we can do about that. We'll have to wait and see whether Mischa resurfaces. Then we can decide what, if anything, we should do.'

'But even if Mischa resurfaces, can we trust anything he told us?'

Liz looked at Fane and shrugged. 'Who knows? We'd just have to judge that at the time. After all, isn't that what they pay us for?'

There seemed nothing left to discuss. Everyone started gathering their things when Fane said, 'It seems to me that we have much to celebrate. I'd like to invite you all to take a glass of champagne with me. I know just the place.'

'Good gracious, Geoffrey,' said Liz. 'That's the nicest thing you've ever said.'

50

'COMING ABOUT,' SHOUTED PEARSON into the wind, and Liz had learned enough to duck as the boom slowly swung her way. The main sail shivered as they turned directly into the wind, then as air filled the vast cotton pocket and the sail ballooned firmly, the boat gathered speed, heading towards shore.

It was called *The Rubicon*, and Geoff Gumm had built it himself. Constructed of larch and oak, it had elegant lines and was twenty-five feet long, drawing four foot, with a remodelled cockpit and bulkhead. The current owner was moving to California and the price was greatly reduced because he was desperate to sell. Gumm had urged them to take her out for a trial, saying it would be its last sail for the season before he put it up for the winter in the nearby boatyard.

Liz had come up on the train that morning for the meeting with Pearson and his commissioner. Pearson's driver had collected her from Ipswich and driven her to Suffolk Police headquarters at nearby Martlesham. There she had explained MI5's role in the investigation of Bartholomew Manor, omitting any reference to Mischa and his brother and Bruno's activities in Moscow. The commissioner had seemed satisfied and grateful that she had come and hadn't pressed for more information.

After this, Pearson had sent his driver home, and Liz and he had driven in Pearson's own car to the boatyard a mile south of Geoff Gumm's working shack. On the way, Pearson described what had been happening at the college. 'I've spoken to the police officers at Bartholomew Manor this morning,' he said as they left Martlesham and drove north on the A12. 'Everything's OK for now. Aziz has got the students working on projects, and they all went to the college yesterday and worked in the IT building. Aziz has moved over to the annexe at the farm, so he's acting as head teacher and warden. He's also made Thomma his assistant. Both of them sound happy from the sound of it.'

'That's a relief.'

'I've talked to the Home Office, and they'll send somebody up this week to begin interviewing the students. I'm not sure what's going to happen, but at least they understand that these kids are victims, not criminals.'

'Good,' said Liz, confident that with Pearson involved, none of these refugee teenagers would be forgotten. They'd suffered enough and shouldn't suffer any more at the hands of an indifferent bureaucracy.

After meeting Geoff Gumm, they had taken *The Rubicon* a couple of miles out to sea, where a stiff breeze helped Pearson put the little boat through her paces. It was surprisingly warm for autumn, and the water sparkled in the sunlight from a largely unclouded sky. Eventually they turned back, the sail fixed on a steady course towards harbour. The wine was opened, the deli-bought panino produced, still warm from their foil wrapping. There was nothing left to do but enjoy the moment.

Perhaps this was the problem. Liz said tentatively, 'It may sound odd, but I think I'm going to have to learn how to relax all over again.'

Pearson smiled, handed her a glass of wine, then sat next to her on the seat in the cockpit of the boat. 'Cheers,' he said, and they clinked glasses. 'You're not alone in that, you know.'

'What do you mean?'

'Well, I'm the same,' he said, looking out at the gentle swell. 'I've tried to do all the sensible things – sailing where I couldn't get a mobile signal and be contacted by the office; helping out my brother-in-law when the mackerel were running; even doing DIY. But all the time I'd be thinking of work – the latest case, the most recent staff problem, what I had to do as soon as I stood on dry land again. To tell you the truth, I'm still trying hard not to do it.'

Liz asked, 'Has it always been like that?'

'No. How about you?'

'Not at all. I used to enjoy all sorts of things. Then—' and she stopped, not wanting to mention Martin again. It seemed wrong to let her memory of him intrude on this moment.

But Pearson got her drift. 'Same here. It was only after I lost my wife that it became a problem. Before that, I could switch off *bang* – just like that. I looked forward to holidays then,' he said, as if recalling a lost Golden Age. 'But after Lucy died, I was so shattered that I found only work could distract me. It wasn't that work gave me *pleasure*, but it did take my mind off how bad I felt the rest of the time. Does that make sense?'

'Of course it does. It's exactly how I felt. I wouldn't say I forgot about Martin when I was at work, but somehow the job made life bearable. Whereas whatever I did outside work, I just felt unbearably sad.'

Pearson reached for the bottle of burgundy and topped up their glasses. 'It's funny, when people talk about addictions, they don't usually think of work.'

'I don't know about that – why else do they talk about workaholics?'

'That's true. But for both of us, it seems that work isn't an addiction; it is more a necessary escape.' He reached forward and twitched the sheet for the main sail and the boat slowly adjusted.

'Don't get me wrong,' he said, leaning back on the bench. 'I love my job; it's obvious to me that you love yours, too. But it's just that because of our … situations, we don't like doing anything else that gives us too much time to think. And I feel guilty about *enjoying* anything.'

'Me too.' She stared down at her glass. 'Yet I've started to realise I'd like to feel I was living life again.'

Pearson nodded but said nothing; he seemed deep in thought. Then he turned to Liz, and said, 'I will if you will.'

'Will what?' she asked, curious.

'Try living again. It's about time. Only I can't do it on my own.' He paused. 'Maybe you can't either.'

'No, I can't.' She looked towards the shore, which they were approaching alarmingly fast. 'Though you may want to alter direction a bit, before we run aground.'

Pearson looked up, then quickly reached for the rudder behind him and steered *The Rubicon* safely away from the shoals.

Liz said with a small laugh. 'First obstacle successfully tackled by the two of us.'

'There may be more to come,' said Pearson.

'I'm sure there will be,' said Liz confidently. 'It would be nice to tackle those together, too.'

A NOTE ON THE TYPE

The text of this book is set in Adobe Caslon, named
after the English punch-cutter and type-founder
William Caslon I (1692–1766). Caslon's rather
old-fashioned types were modelled on seventeenth-
century Dutch designs, but found wide acceptance
throughout the English-speaking world for much
of the eighteenth century until replaced by newer
types towards the end of the century. Used in 1776
to print the Declaration of Independence, they were
revived in the nineteenth century and have been
popular ever since, particularly amongst fine
printers. There are several digital versions, of which
Carol Twombly's Adobe Caslon is one.

ALSO AVAILABLE BY STELLA RIMINGTON

THE GENEVA TRAP

A Russian agent. A deadly secret. The embers of the Cold War are about to about to reignite...

It all began by accident. Geneva, 2012. When a Russian spy approaches MI6 with vital information about an imminent cyber attack, he refuses to talk to anyone but Liz Carlyle of MI5. But who is he, and what is his connection to Liz? At a US Air Force base in Nevada, officers watch in horror as one of their unmanned drones plummets out of the sky, and panic spreads through the British and American Intelligence services, Is this a Russian plot to disable the West's defences? Or is the threat coming from elsewhere?

As Liz and her team hunt for a mole inside the MOD, the trail leads them from Geneva, to Marseilles and into a labyrinth of international intrigue, in a race against time to stop the Cold War heating up once again...

'She bids to join the ranks of such secret agent authors as Somerset Maugham, Graham Greene and John le Carré'
WALL STREET JOURNAL

ORDER YOUR COPY:

BY PHONE: +44 (0) 1256 302 699; **BY EMAIL:** DIRECT@MACMILLAN.CO.UK
DELIVERY IS USUALLY 3–5 WORKING DAYS. FREE POSTAGE AND PACKAGING FOR ORDERS OVER £20.
ONLINE: WWW.BLOOMSBURY.COM/BOOKSHOP
PRICES AND AVAILABILITY SUBJECT TO CHANGE WITHOUT NOTICE.

WWW.BLOOMSBURY.COM/AUTHOR/STELLA-RIMINGTON

BLOOMSBURY

CLOSE CALL

The most dangerous threats are those closest to home

In a Middle Eastern souk, CIA agent Miles Brook haven was attacked. At the time he was infiltrating rebel groups in the area. No one was certain if his cover had been blown or if the act was just an arbitrary attack on Westerners. Months later, the incident remains a mystery.

Now Liz Carlyle and MI5 have been charged with the task of watching the international under-the-counter arms trade: a trade that has been booming in the wake of the Arab Spring. As the clock counts down, Liz finds herself on a manhunt through Paris and Berlin, and into her own long-forgotten past. A past buried so deep that she never thought it would resurface…

'This is something rare: the spy novel that prizes authenticity over fabrication that is true to the character and spirit of intelligence work'
MAIL ON SUNDAY

ORDER YOUR COPY:

BY PHONE: +44 (0) 1256 302 699; **BY EMAIL:** DIRECT@MACMILLAN.CO.UK
DELIVERY IS USUALLY 3–5 WORKING DAYS. FREE POSTAGE AND PACKAGING FOR ORDERS OVER £20.
ONLINE: WWW.BLOOMSBURY.COM/BOOKSHOP
PRICES AND AVAILABILITY SUBJECT TO CHANGE WITHOUT NOTICE.

WWW.BLOOMSBURY.COM/AUTHOR/STELLA-RIMINGTON

BLOOMSBURY